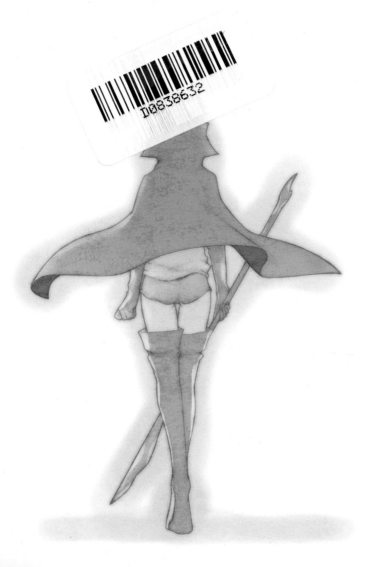

FUJINO OMORI

ILLUSTRATION BY
SUZUHITO YASUDA

IS It WRONG to TRY to PiCK UP GiRLS iN A DUNGEON?

VOLUME 5

FUJINO OMORI
ILLUSTRATION BY SUZUHITO YASUDA

YEN ON

NEW YORK

IS IT WRONG TO TRY TO PICK UP GIRLS
IN A DUNGEON?, Volume 5
FUJINO OMORI

Translation by Andrew Gaippe

DUNGEON NI DEAI WO MOTOMERU
NO WA MACHIGATTEIRUDAROUKA vol. 5
Copyright © 2014 Fujino Omori
Illustrations copyright © 2014 Suzuhito Yasuda
All rights reserved.
Original Japanese edition published in 2014
by SB Creative Corp.
This English edition is published by arrangement
with SB Creative Corp., Tokyo, in care of
Tuttle-Mori Agency, Inc., Tokyo.

English translation © 2016 Hachette Book Group, Inc.

Yen On
Hachette Book Group
1290 Avenue of the Americas
New York, NY 10104
www.hachettebookgroup.com
www.yenpress.com

Yen On is an imprint of Hachette Book Group, Inc.
The Yen On name and logo are trademarks of Hachette Book Group, Inc.

The publisher is not responsible for websites (or their
content) that are not owned by the publisher.

First Yen On edition: April 2016

Library of Congress Cataloging-in-Publication Data

Names: Ōmori, Fujino, author. | Yasuda, Suzuhito, illustrator.
Title: Is it wrong to try to pick up girls in a dungeon? / Fujino Omori ;
    illustrated by Suzuhito Yasuda.
Other titles: Danjon ni deai o motomeru nowa machigatte iru darōka. English.
Description: New York : Yen ON, 2015– | Series: Is it wrong to pick up girls in
    a dungeon? ; 5
Identifiers: LCCN 2015029144| ISBN 9780316340144 (v. 2 : pbk.) |
    ISBN 9780316340151 (v. 3 : pbk.) | ISBN 9780316340168 (v. 4 : pbk.) |
    ISBN 9780316339155 (v. 1 : pbk.) | ISBN 9780316314794 (v. 5 : pbk.)
Subjects: | CYAC: Fantasy. | BISAC: FICTION / Fantasy / General. |
    FICTION / Science Fiction / Adventure.
Classification: LCC PZ7.1.O54 Du 2015 | DDC [Fic]—dc23 LC record available at
    http://lccn.loc.gov/2015029144

10 9 8 7 6 5 4 3 2

RRD-C

Printed in the United States of America

VOLUME 5

FUJINO OMORI
ILLUSTRATION BY SUZUHITO YASUDA

PROLOGUE · THE FIRST OMEN

The sun lit up the sky.

It rose above the eastern wall of the city, illuminating all of Orario in the process. The massive white tower in the middle of the city, the solemn Pantheon where adventurers gather, the wide Coliseum—all of them were bathed in soft morning light. The city's citizens were already going about their day. Humans and demi-humans filled the streets, the sounds of their voices and footsteps making Orario come to life.

"Sorry t' drag ya out this early in the mornin', Phai-Phai. Don't want ya thinkin' I'm forcin' ya."

"It's nothing. I'm always alone, so it's nice to eat breakfast with someone every now and then."

Two goddesses sat around a table of food in a building located between Northwest Main and West Main streets. Noise from the people outside came in waves as they passed by.

One goddess, the vermilion-haired Loki, squinted her already narrow eyes as the crimson-haired goddess with a bandage around her eye, Hephaistos, smiled back at her.

"Just wanted t' say thanks again for lending my kids some of your smiths for their expedition. They're a big help."

Hephaistos graciously accepted Loki's words of gratitude and asked a question of her own. "Think nothing of it. First access to drop items from the Lower Fortress is all the thanks we need. What about your children? Do you think they'll make some progress with this expedition?"

The wooden building where they were eating was a perfect square. The two deities sat on the second floor with no one around except for one animal-person staffer. The restaurant all to themselves, Loki and Hephaistos reached for the cutlery sitting on top of the white cloth covering the table between them.

"They had quite a bit of trouble last time, but I got a hunch that this time's the charm. Even left chanting 'Gonna make it!' And now Aiz's Level Six. Everyone's lookin' the part."

Chomp. Loki's jaws clamped down hard on a piece of meat at the end of her fork. Directly across from her, Hephaistos elegantly manipulated her utensils and took small bites as she watched Loki gulping down the water in her glass.

"...By the way, Phai-Phai. Got any info on Itty-Bitty's kid? Anything at all?"

"Oh? Hee-hee, what's this? You're curious about Hestia?"

"Curious ain't the right word...She's just so full of herself. Swingin' those ridiculous knockers of hers around for the whole world ta see, gettin' all cocky. It's really pissin' me off..."

Hephaistos couldn't help but crack a smile as Loki continued her litany of complaints.

"One of my children has joined a party with Hestia's boy. I believe they're going to the middle levels today."

"Eh? So you've been two-timin' with me and Itty-Bitty? Sending smiths all over the place, aren't ya."

"He's signed a direct contract with the 'Little Rookie.' My child appears to be quite taken with Hestia's boy." Hephaistos brought another piece of food to her lips, still smiling as she spoke.

Loki, however, was not the least bit amused. Her face turned sour.

"Ya're horrible, Phai-Phai. Cheatin' on me with Itty-Bitty."

"Be glad no one was around to hear that. They might get the wrong idea."

Their friendly banter went on for a few more moments, when suddenly—

The building shook enough to make their bodies lurch. They froze in place.

"...Yet another quake."

"Kinda boring, if y'ask me...Been happenin' a lot recently, though, these earthquakes."

The water left in the glasses next to their plates rippled.

This particular quake was small enough to only be noticed by those sitting still. Most likely, the people outside it hadn't felt a thing.

Loki and Hephaistos sat silently as the rumbling continued.

"If these were just the normal earthquakes, we'd shut 'em up in no time...But there's this dangerous thingy right below our feet... What'cha think, Phai-Phai?"

"The Guild is constantly sending up prayers, so I think it's just a coincidence...But yes, it feels like something is about to happen."

The two deities looked out the window. The people below were going about their business as usual. If anything, the city streets looked busier than when they arrived.

"Huh?" uttered Loki as her eyes happened to catch something interesting in the backdrop.

Members of a certain *Familia* were gathering at a corner down the road.

"..."

The god Takemikazuchi cast his gaze to the ground at his feet.

He narrowed his eyebrows in thought as he felt vibrations shake the soles of his shoes.

"Lord Takemikazuchi, we shall return."

The deity lifted his eyes from the ground in response to a spirited, high-pitched voice.

A beautiful young girl stood before him. Long, shiny black hair framed a face with bluish-purple eyes. Her back was perfectly straight in a sign of respect.

What little skin was showing from beneath thick lavender battle clothes was a smooth, almost milky white. Her face had such perfect symmetry that she could have been mistaken for a goddess herself.

A loving smile grew on Takemikazuchi's face as he looked at the girl, a member of his own "family."

"Yes, but don't push yourself too hard, Mikoto. I always say this, but never forget how you felt on your first day as an adventurer."

"Yes, sir!"

After the girl named Mikoto gave a curt nod, he looked around to face the other members of the unit. "The same goes for all of you," he said.

The small battle party consisted only of humans.

Including Mikoto, the group of six made up the entirety of *Takemikazuchi Familia*.

Takemikazuchi Familia was just one of many Dungeon-crawling *Familias* in Orario. Just as the name states, they made a living collecting drop items and magic stones from the Dungeon and selling them for profit.

Rumors of a promising rookie had been spreading through the ranks of lower-level adventurers. Now that Mikoto had leveled up, *Takemikazuchi Familia* had become relatively strong for a lower-ranking *Familia*.

"We should be on our way, Lord Takemikazuchi," came the voice of the male leader of the group.

"Indeed. Best of luck to you all," he answered as he saw them off.

Mikoto gave another bow before turning to join the others.

"And don't come back without everyone..."

Takemikazuchi watched their forms disappear into the distance and looked down at his feet again.

A few moments passed before he lightly sighed as he scratched his head.

"...I should get to work, too."

Turning on his heel, the deity rolled his shoulders and cracked his neck. He wanted to help his family in any way he could, so today he would once again be making fried potato puffs. "Still losing in sales to Hestia's place up north..." he mumbled to himself as he turned back to his *Familia*'s home, just a few paces away, to get ready.

"Hey-hey, Takemikazuchi—!"

Takemikazuchi froze with his outstretched hand just above the door handle.

The bright, cheerful voice coming from behind him sent shivers down his spine. His eyes shook as they darted from side to side.

Takemikazuchi knew who it was all too well. He practically flung his body around to face the owner of the voice.

"Hermes…!"

"Yes, it is I, Hermes! Been about a week, hasn't it, Takemikazuchi?"

Just as he expected, a rather slender god was coming toward him.

This new deity was of medium height, his skinny arms and legs sticking out of his traveler's clothes as he approached. Being a god, Hermes's features lined up so well that no one would be able to find a flaw. He reached up and pulled off his winged, broad-brimmed hat to reveal flowing locks of orange hair.

His effeminate looks and overwhelming charm were the complete opposite of Takemikazuchi's masculine refinement.

Smiling from ear to ear, Hermes started twirling his hat on his finger as he walked all the way up to the other god.

"What, what are you doing here…!"

"Aw, don't look at me with that angry face. And I came all this way just to talk to you too, Takemikazuchi!"

"Don't say such things, even as a joke! Aren't you the one who leads all those other idiots in making my life miserable?!"

"Ha-ha-ha, sorry, sorry! I just can't help teasing you when I see you, Takemikazuchi!"

Hermes's insolent tone did nothing to brighten Takemikazuchi's mood. The god's face was turning bitterer by the second.

Every god has one or two quirks about them, but Hermes took the cake when it came to wild behavior.

In fact, Hermes routinely left his *Familia*'s home, the one place he had any influence in Orario, to travel around the world. Takemikazuchi wasn't sure if Hermes was just a born traveler or if he just couldn't stand being in the same place for a long time, but he did know that the deity had never stayed in the same place for more than half a year. It went without saying that *Hermes Familia* was an autonomous group run by its members—who were completely left to their own devices.

"I just came back into town and happened to pass by, so I thought

I'd stop in and congratulate you…Congrats on little Mikoto's leveling up, Takemikazuchi. Your *Familia* has gotten quite a bit stronger. We'll have to do business in the future."

Whether in the heavens or on the earth, Hermes had always been extremely good at positioning himself to succeed.

Such diligence is the key to not making enemies, Takemikazuchi thought to himself.

Hermes extended his hand, but Takemikazuchi didn't reciprocate the offer right away.

"Hermes…why are you back so soon?"

After participating in the last Denatus, Hermes had packed his bags and headed out for parts unknown. Usually once he left the city, he wouldn't be back for a month at the very least.

But this trip lasted only ten days. It was by far his shortest.

Takemikazuchi didn't try to hide the suspicion on his face. Hermes paused for a moment before smiling once again.

"Heh-heh, what with all the interesting rookies taking the stage, you can't blame me for being curious about them. So I took care of some things and came back a little early.

"Especially…" Hermes continued.

"Hestia's 'Little Rookie.' With him being the new record holder, I'm sure I'm not the only one interested in the boy."

Hermes's narrow eyes opened just a little bit wider as he flashed even more teeth in a confident smile.

Takemikazuchi frowned as the charming god revealed his true intentions.

"Takemikazuchi, you see Hestia quite a bit, yes? Do you happen to know anything about one Bell Cranell?"

"Nothing. Even if I did, I wouldn't tell you."

"Ha-ha, you're so cold."

Hermes squeezed his shoulder blades together, thrusting his head forward as if he were trying to peer into Takemikazuchi's face. At long last, he took a few steps back with that charismatic smile still plastered on his lips.

A sudden gust of wind came out of the west, their hair dancing in the sudden breeze.

Hermes broke off eye contact from the other god's sidelong glance and looked up toward the sky as if guided by the wind.

"Ah, I can't wait to meet him."

I can see ash-colored rocks everywhere I look. The walls, floor, and ceiling are all made of solid stone. The air is dank, almost musty.

It looks like any cave deep in the heart of the mountain. If I didn't know any better, I'd say that's exactly where we are. Standing here at the top of the thirteenth floor, the so-called "front line" of the middle levels of the Dungeon, that's the only way to describe this place.

"So this is the middle levels..."

"Lilly's heard about it before, but it's much dimmer in here than farther up."

Welf, his hand on the handle of the broadsword strapped to his back, and Lilly, her eyes quickly scanning the room, voiced their first impressions.

A seemingly endless descending stone tunnel was waiting for us after we left the upper levels. It had to be the pathway that connected to the first "room" on this level. But still, this is the first time I've ever seen a straight path that doesn't have a visible exit.

Also, there are large well-like holes in a few places beside the walls—pit traps connecting to the lower levels—in here, too. The landscape, the poor visibility...it's nothing like the upper levels.

"Level thirteen is known for its long hallways going from room to room. We can't safely engage monsters in this area, so Lilly suggests we find the first room as quickly as possible."

Welf and I nod to each other as Lilly explains the situation.

From what I can see, I'm pretty sure that this hallway is wider than the ones upstairs, but we'd still have a hard time if a monster showed up.

It's too cramped in here to fight effectively as a team, especially if we're surrounded by a group of them. Trapped among monsters in the middle of the hallway—with no escape route and no backup... just the thought of it gives me chills.

Engaging monsters in a room with plenty of space to systematically take them down one by one, on the other hand…Numbers and strategy are very valuable in a fight, and that's exactly what a party gives us.

"Let's advance while there aren't any monsters around. Mr. Welf, this is a one-way path, so please move ahead as quickly as possible."

"All right."

Lilly must've spent a lot of time studying the information available at the Guild. It's like she has a map of level thirteen in her head or something. She's not just a porter, she's a *supporter* in every meaning of the word. As I think about how lucky I am to have her in the party, I look ahead at Welf.

The three of us advance through the middle levels in a straight line while making sure to keep some space between us.

"…But still, these things are awesome!"

"The salamander wool?"

"Yeah, can't complain about a thing."

Welf starts up a conversation just as the eerie silence of the Dungeon was starting to get to me. Lilly quickly joins in.

Conversations like this are rather pointless, but they help ease the tension. I think that's a hidden benefit of working with a battle party. The loneliness and isolation of being solo really adds up after a while.

"Lilly never dreamed of the day that she would be able to wear this fancy fabric. Thank you so much, Mr. Bell. Lilly'll take good care of it."

"Ah-ha-ha-ha…I did get a discount."

I turn my head around to see Lilly happily grinning at me. All I can do is force a smile and take a look at how each of us is wearing salamander wool.

It's a glossy red fabric that's so light and thin that it almost flutters with each movement. Most people would think it were weightless if they saw someone wearing it on the street. My inner shirt and pants, Welf's long jacket, and Lilly's new robe are all made from the same material.

"Fairy Protection"—cloth that fairies have literally woven their magic into. Basically, it's an item that has some kind of magic effect because of them.

"Even with a discount, just one set of fairy-made material costs an arm and a leg! How much was it for three?"

"Well—um…To put it simply, they were five zeros on the end…"

"Mr. Welf, make sure that you pay back every val Mr. Bell spent on you, got that?"

"You're quite the calculating prum when it comes to money, you know that?"

Eina had insisted that we all equip salamander wool before venturing into the middle levels, and I followed through on my promise. The others took a little convincing, but now all of us are wearing it.

Welf and I are wearing ours under our armor while Lilly is draped in one big robe that covers her entire body. I suppose it could be thought of as fancy fabric, since it practically sparkles vibrant red in the low light.

"To think that a High Smith couldn't make anti-flame equipment on par with this wimpy jacket…I don't got a chance. Those fairies are something else."

I can feel a bit of resentment toward fairies in his voice as he straightens the sleeve on his jacket.

Just like animal people, fairies—salamanders, sylphs, undines, gnomes, and so on—are classified by their element and place of origin, which also means that "Fairy Protection" items also vary depending on what kind of fairy created it.

Salamander wool, made by the fire-wielding salamanders, is very good at protecting against fire and heat. I'd call it an "anti-flame material." It's said to be very good against cold as well.

Fabric made by the water-dwelling undine not only protects the wearer from water-based attacks but can keep him or her cool in areas with intense heat.

I've even heard people say that items blessed with a fairy's spiritual protection are like a gift from "another god." While this fabric may not be as strong or sturdy as the kinds that we humans make, the strong elemental forces that dwell within the material more than make up for it. Just as Welf said, even the High Smiths' work can't hold a candle to the things fairies can do.

"But Lilly's glad we have them. Lilly feels less anxious about going into deeper levels."

"...Hellhounds, right?"

That's the name of one of the monsters on this floor. They're the main reason that Eina was so insistent that we have salamander wool.

These doglike monsters are also known as Baskervilles. Compared with other monsters in the middle levels, they're not all that physically powerful. The real danger is the flaming projectiles they shoot out of their mouths.

The flames are hot enough to get even some of the better types of armor to crack. It's been said that the inferno unleashed by a pack of hellhounds can be strong enough to reduce an unlucky battle party to ash on the spot.

Whenever reports of a battle party being wiped out on the thirteenth or fourteenth level come to the surface, it's more than likely hellhounds are to blame. There is a good chance that even adventurers who have leveled up will be reduced to cinders if they take a direct hit.

"Mr. Welf, Lilly believes you already understand this, but—"

"Yeah, I'm gonna stop you right there. If a hellhound shows up, charge forward and take it down, right? I have no interest in bein' cooked alive."

This is just my opinion, but I think that this is an adventure's rite of passage in the middle levels.

All the monsters in the upper levels could only attack from short range and charge with claws, clubs, and whatnot. But the monsters here have learned how to attack from a distance. Maybe saying that they've learned how to use something like magic would be easier to understand?

The upper levels and middle levels are very different.

Lyu's words echo inside my mind; they seem to be etched inside my memory.

In any case, hellhounds are very dangerous monsters that we have to be aware of while we're in the middle levels.

"…!" After walking down the rocky path for a few minutes, all of us stop talking and freeze in place at almost the same moment.

My updated status also strengthened my hearing enough to hear a *tup…tup…*sound. Something's coming this way. The three of us get into position, all of our eyes locked on the darkness before us as the sound gets louder.

"…Right off the bat."

Welf's voice echoes through the musty air.

Two dark shadows appear in the dim light. Coming from the other end of the path, the monsters finally come into view.

Their muscular bodies are completely black. Eyes glowing a deep red, they practically embody the meaning of the word "monster."

Four-legged frames far too brawny to be a dog's. Hellhounds.

Their faces, too vicious to be mistaken for wolves, distort as the two of them howl in our direction.

"So, how's this distance? Should we get closer?"

"My adviser warned me not to underestimate the hellhound's range…"

"Well then—charge!"

Welf hoists his broadsword over his shoulder as he gives us the signal to attack. I quickly get into position behind his right shoulder.

The two hellhounds roar in unison before charging at us with all speed.

A distance of about fifty meders is gone in the blink of an eye.

"OooooooOONN!"

One of them howls and jumps straight at Welf.

Despite being the size of a small cow, the beast carves through the air. I jump in front of it before it can reach its target and raise a shield.

I've got a small, buckler-style shield in my left hand and the fifty-celch-long shortsword in my right.

Welf prepared them for me during the week that we spent practicing our battle formation on the eleventh and twelfth floors. Since I'm in the middle, I need to be able to both attack and defend.

I catch a glimpse of its razor-sharp teeth as it comes at me with its jaws wide open—before I shove the buckler straight into its mouth.

"Gah…!"

It's heavy.

But I can take it.

Even with its sharp fangs around my shield and taking the full force of its jumping attack, I manage to keep my feet and stop its momentum.

The hound is stuck in the air, legs flailing.

Welf charges in as if he'd been waiting for that moment and slices the beast's defenseless body in two with one swift, arcing strike of his broadsword.

"aGA?!"

The two halves of its body fall to the ground.

A strong defense paired with a powerful counterattack, perfect coordination between middle support and the front line.

I pull my blood-splattered shield out of the fallen beast's mouth.

"Uuuuuuu…"

The remaining hellhound growls at us from a distance as it raises its hindquarters and lowers its head to the ground. All of us realize immediately that it is getting ready to spit fire.

It bears its fangs at us. I can see sparks flying around in its mouth, in the spaces between its razor-sharp teeth.

"—A little slow!"

"GYAN?!"

However, the hellhound takes a golden arrow to its right eye just as it was about to launch its fiery attack.

It came from Lilly's hand bow gun. It might not be the most powerful weapon, but it packs more than enough punch to stop an enemy in its tracks with good accuracy.

Welf dashes by me with the red swish of his jacket, straight up to the injured beast. He brings his broadsword down over the beast's head in one continuous motion.

The last hound lets out a yelp before falling, its cheeks still bright red from the flames.

"Not a bad start, eh?"

"We'd be in a lot of trouble if we couldn't work together at this point. This amount of coordination should be expected."

"Yes, but that worked pretty well."

The battle over, we return to our usual selves.

Sure, there were a few moments that made me a little nervous, but I feel very relieved that we were able to slay two hellhounds that easily. As long as we're careful, we should be strong enough to take any monsters on level thirteen. Just knowing that much is worth a lot.

We also learned that the hounds need time to build up their fireball attack...I've got a good feeling about this.

Anxiousness starts leaving my body as Lilly sets to work retrieving the magic stones.

"Oh? We've got more company."

"!" I snap back into battle mode at the sound of Welf's voice.

The next monsters to emerge from farther down the path are three surprisingly large rabbits.

Floppy ears, white and yellow fur, and a fluffy tail. They're hopping along on their hind legs, a long sharp horn sticking out of their heads. I think they're about Lilly's height.

These monsters are basically needle rabbits that learned how to walk on two legs.

"Is that...Mr. Bell?!"

"Of course not?! What are you saying?!" I snap back at a wide-eyed Lilly.

The rabbit monster, Al-Miraj. First appearing on level thirteen, these things may look cute but are actually extremely aggressive.

"So we're fighting Bell, huh?...That's a tough joke."

"Is—is that a joke?!"

Welf tries his best to make a serious face but I can see him holding back tears of laughter.

The small pack of Al-Miraj in front of us each go to one of the small rocks on the ground and smash them open with a hard stomp. All of them pick up a piece of the rubble, the latest natural weapon provided by the Dungeon.

It looks like a small tomahawk that each of them can carry in one hand. Does that mean that all these rocks on the ground are actually landform weapons?

Three monsters all equipped with weapons. Suddenly all of the horned rabbits look in our direction, their pale red eyes softly glowing.

"Three on three."

"Lilly is just saying, but it needs to be three on one, three times, yes? We'll be overwhelmed if each of us tries to take one on alone. If Mr. Welf makes one mistake, Lilly will be very vulnerable."

Al-Miraj are actually some of the weakest monsters in the middle levels. As long as you're aware that they are more agile than silverbacks, then even the upper ranks of Level 1 adventurers can hold their own against one.

However, there's a reason that these rabbits are classified as Level 2 monsters: They're surprisingly dangerous in groups.

Each one of the Al-Miraj lets out a series of high-pitched squeaks as they advance on our position.

"The one on the right first!"

"G-got it!"

"But, you know, this is the first time I've ever felt bad about slayin' a monster…These things are too damn cute."

"*Kyauu! Ki, kiii!*"

A three-man battle party versus a group of three monsters.

Six shadows charge forward and clash in the dim light.

"Hermes is back?"

Hestia handed a customer a fried potato puff as she turned to face Takemikazuchi.

"Isn't it still too early? He was even at the last Denatus."

"That's what I'd like to find out. He wouldn't come back so soon without a reason."

"Thank you very much!" said Hestia to the customer and gave a short bow. Takemikazuchi stood next to her, resting his elbows on the counter and wearing a scowl.

They were at a food stall on North Main Street. Hestia's friend had shown up unannounced during business hours and said, "We need to talk." Hestia couldn't say no to him, so she listened to what he had to say while working behind the counter.

"My, my…Aren't you doing good business over here?"

"Heh-heh, of course. I'm here, aren't I?"

"Curses! I had no idea that a mascot had this much impact…"

There was a constant stream of customers at the food stall, enough to make lines at the cash register. Takemikazuchi, who was not used to this much activity, looked around with a look of defeat on his face. Hestia put her hands behind her back and puffed out her chest.

Since the two of them were wearing aprons, both of them blended in very well despite being deities.

"So, what did Hermes do? You said he came to your place, Také?"

"He did…Have you seen him since his return, Hestia?"

"Nope, I haven't. I didn't know he was back until you told me."

Hestia's body practically moved on its own as she bagged freshly fried potato puffs that a female animal person had just prepared and handed them to a series of customers. Every single one of them smiled as they took their potato puffs, patting Hestia on the head before leaving the stall.

"He said that he was interested in that boy of yours, Bell Cranell… or something like that. I can't help but feel that he's planning something."

"Um…Aren't you overthinking this a little bit? I don't think Hermes is the kind of god who would start something."

The god Hermes was not one to instigate a fight.

Whether he was very good at maneuvering through various situations or just very shrewd, Hermes was a well-connected god who often played peacekeeper when other gods or goddesses were fighting among one another.

The Hermes that Hestia knew was open-minded and assiduous.

"He's not the only one to try to make a move on Bell recently...Just this past week, there's been so many that it's getting annoying?"

"You carry his burden well, Hestia. As for Hermes, I can't stand him. There is not a word out of his mouth that I'll actually believe."

"Ha-ha-ha. Hermes does give you a hard time, doesn't he, Také."

Hestia's and Hermes's domains in Tenkai were right next to each other. They were neighbors, in a sense. They had been on good terms long enough that they knew a lot about each other.

Hestia smiled and laughed with a half-elf girl who was even shorter than she before sending her back to her mother.

"It's not that I don't understand what you're saying, Hestia...I've just got a feeling that this time is different."

"...Any reason why?"

"Call it divine intuition."

Hestia thought for a moment as she stared back into Takemikazuchi's violet eyes and scratched her chin.

If he was depending on his intuition, he had no proof.

"—Takemikazuchi, are you sure you should be wasting time in a place like this..."

"Ah, my apologies, Manager. There was something I had to do... No, I'm sure our sales will increase soon, yes. I'll work very hard."

"You can say anything you want, but you could learn a thing or two from Hestia..."

"I will, sorry for the inconvenience. I will double my efforts— you'll see what I can really do tomorrow!"

Hestia was lost in her own thoughts as the food-stall manager appeared and Takemikazuchi bowed in apology over and over. She happened to catch a glimpse of this and wondered what this world was coming to, a god having to bow and scrape to one of the children. She completely ignored the fact that she herself had multiple part-time jobs and had done the very same thing on countless occasions.

"I'll take my leave, Hestia. It might be meaningless to tell you to be careful, but still, keep an eye on Hermes."

"Sure, thanks, Také."

Takemikazuchi made his way past the manager and turned around to wave one last time before returning to his own shop. Thankful for her friend's concern, Hestia smiled and watched him leave.

"Hermes, huh…"

She stuck her head out of the side of the food stall and looked toward the blue sky.

She thought about her neighbor, especially about that charming smile of his.

It happened to remind her of one other deity.

"…There's no way, right?"

Her soft voice was carried away by a whimsical gust of wind.

The sun shone down through a blue sky filled with white puffy clouds.

West Main Street was filled with crowds of people and countless horse-drawn carts bathed in the soft sunlight of early afternoon. A certain deity and one of his followers made their way through the middle of all of it.

"So then, Asfi, what did you find out?"

"According to the public information available at the Guild, he has completed level eleven and spent the last ten days on level twelve."

The deity having a conversation surrounded by the hustle and bustle of the citizens of Orario just happened to be Hermes. Asfi, the human woman he was talking to, followed close behind as he made his way through the crowd.

The woman wore a white cloak and rather unusual sandals on her thin feet, each of which had a pair of golden wings curving around the sides.

"Also, someone at Babel Tower had something interesting to say… He apparently bought enough salamander wool to equip a small battle party earlier this morning."

"Oh, don't tell me he's gone to the middle levels?"

"Most likely," responded Asfi. Hermes's lips curved up in a smirk.

"And only ten days after leveling up. Just how a record-holder should be. Very fast indeed."

"In addition, I have discovered he possesses extremely powerful Magic. He used what must have been a very long spell to cast magic so powerful that it wiped out an infant dragon on level eleven. There were many witnesses."

The woman giving this information to her god would have looked right at home in the company of other deities as well. She had a perfectly symmetrical face, her eyes brimming with knowledge, and brilliant silver glasses framing her feminine features. Her hair was a stunning aqua blue with a few lighter shades mixed in. It was as if strands of water were flowing from her head.

Ignoring the eyes of the animal people and dwarves that passed by, Asfi continued her report.

"…That's not the only reason."

"Go on."

"Many adventurers believe that the only reason he defeated a Minotaur is that he was lucky enough to land this Magic attack. That he is a weakling who only finished off a Minotaur that had escaped from *Loki Familia*. Some go as far as to call him the 'Phony Rookie.'"

"Ha-ha-ha-ha! Phony Rookie! Got a nice ring to it!"

Hermes's mouth opened wide as he laughed.

Many people were startled by his roar of laughter and stared as he passed by. But Hermes was enjoying himself too much to care, his shoulders jumping up and down in glee.

"But he *only* managed to hit it with his Magic, he *only* delivered the last blow to a monster with its foot in the grave…A god's Blessing won't be fooled by cheap descriptions…But yes, I understand what you're trying to say."

Hermes narrowed his already thin eyes as soon as his own laughter died down.

"I believe these opinions can all be explained by one thing: the fact that he leveled up so quickly…"

"Ah, yes. Adventurers are always so hard on one another."

"I have confirmed that Bell Cranell is not very well-liked by other adventurers."

At that point the noise on the street became too loud for their conversation to continue.

A group of bards composed of many races had set up their instruments in front of a shop nearby and were giving a live performance for the townspeople under the blue sky. They sang of the many places they had visited, the things they had seen with their own eyes, and expressed everything with upbeat tones and sometimes dark chords as their story unfolded. A large ring of people formed around the bards on the street. Even people on the upper floors of the surrounding shops and houses opened their windows and leaned outside to hear them.

Hermes stopped to listen to their songs as well. He clapped just as loud as the rest when they had finished and gave them some gold coins.

The traveling bards couldn't believe their luck. This smiling god had not only enjoyed their performance, but given them money as well. Their gratitude was immeasurable. The people on the street who witnessed what just took place looked at Hermes with adoring eyes.

Asfi asked her god a question as soon as they started walking again. "Do you plan on doing anything to the Little Rookie?"

Hermes could feel her eyes boring into the back of his head as they continued forward, but he listened as she continued.

"Ordering me to collect information without giving a reason, you must be very interested in him…"

"What's this, Asfi? Are you jealous because I haven't been around?"

"Hardly!"

Asfi dropped her formal tone in an instant of anger, quickly turning her head away and massaging her forehead.

Hearing her god's teasing tone had brought out all the frustration that had built up while working for him over the years. Her composure was gone.

A face that had exuded an aura of knowledge now only showed the resentment of someone who had been led on wild-goose chases by a particular deity for far too long.

"I'm saying I've had enough of your errands. I've done so much so that you can just go anytime! Think of what I've been through!"

"I'm grateful to the others, and especially to you, Asfi. Without you, things would fall apart pretty quick. I'm counting on you quite a bit. Trusted by your friends and your god—ha-ha! That's quite the position!"

"…I hate this."

She sounded like she was about to cry for a brief moment. Hermes just smiled at his follower and playfully patted her on the head. Asfi's silver glasses were jarred loose from the impacts and fell to the tip of her nose as she looked at the ground.

"…Have you made contact with Hestia yet?"

Asfi sighed as she pulled herself together and asked a completely different question.

Realizing that her rambling god had no intention of revealing his plans to her, she decided to try a different route.

In response to her question, Hermes forced a smile and said, "No, not yet.

"I must talk with a certain someone before I can do that."

Before a stern-looking Asfi could respond with another question, Hermes came to a stop in front of a certain bar.

It was a rather large bar and café built on West Main Street. A large sign above its front door read THE BENEVOLENT MISTRESS, written in Koine, the universal language.

The café terrace was filled with customers at this time of day. Hermes and Asfi walked right by it and through the entrance.

"Welcome, meow!…Mew? Lord Hermes?"

"Oh! Chloe, it's been too long! Sorry, but could you call Mia for me?"

Hermes smiled brightly at the cat person who greeted him at the door.

The catgirl stared at Hermes and Asfi for a long moment before saying, "Sure, meow. Just a moment, meow!" She wasn't about to refuse the request of a god.

Chloe disappeared into the back of the bar and not two seconds later—

The floor creaked as the massive body of a dwarf woman appeared behind the bar.

"The hell's a god want in the middle of the lunch rush?"

"Don't look at me with those sour eyes, Mia. You're ruining your pretty face."

"Any more jokes and I'll take off yer head. I'm busy, y'hear? Ya got somethin' to say, then out with it."

Mia was not the least bit intimidated by the god in front of her. In fact, the owner of the bar was scaring Asfi enough to shake in her sandals behind Hermes.

The deity, on the other hand, was not the least bit afraid, and walked right up to the counter, resting his elbows on the edge.

"Well then, I'll get right to it—could you make an appointment with Lady Freya for me?"

Hermes lowered his voice as he leaned over the counter between them, his face right in front of Mia's.

The dwarf held her ground, locked eyes with Hermes, and cocked an eyebrow.

The deity's orange gaze and her piercing stare bored into each other. Until finally, "Humph."

"I'm not a messenger for fool gods. You've got feet—if you wanna talk to the Lady so bad, use 'em." Mia practically spit the words out of her mouth, flatly rejecting Hermes's request. "Hmph," she angrily sighed out of her nose and disappeared back into the kitchen. Hermes watched her robust body vanish behind the door before turning to Asfi, forcing a smile as if to say, *That didn't work.*

Not my problem, she seemed to reply with her disinterested look.

"…Lord Hermes?"

Hermes looked over his shoulder in response to hearing his name, his expression changing in the blink of an eye. "Hm? Oh! If it isn't Syr! It's been so long! How've you been?"

Syr, dressed in her waitress uniform, had just come into the main part of the bar after returning from her break.

"Yes, a very long time indeed, Lord Hermes. I'm glad to see that you are well."

"Ahh, you always were the one with the best manners. What do you say, Syr, want to get out of here and have some fun? A date with you would go a long way to healing the heart that Mia just ripped to shreds. You'd do that for me, right—Hey! Ow-ow-ow! Let go of my ear, Asfi, you'll tear it off!"

Syr politely smiled at the god's attempt to use what just happened as a pretext for something completely different. "I'm going to have to decline," she responded as Asfi punished Hermes while silently glaring at him.

Syr guided them to a seat at the bar, Hermes grudgingly massaging his ear along the way.

"Please have a seat here…"

Syr gestured to a seat at a table, but Hermes walked right past it toward the counter.

The chair that Hermes plopped himself down on was normally the seat that Syr reserved for Bell, his usual spot.

The girl was speechless as Asfi took her position behind Hermes. The deity looked up at Syr and smiled.

"Hey, Syr, can I ask you something?"

"Yes…What is it?"

"If you happen to know anything about Bell Cranell, would you tell me?"

The girl's shoulders twitched.

All the waitresses within earshot made eye contact, silently communicating with one another in the noisy bar and café. Syr looked down at Hermes's ever-charming smile and constructed a friendly face to hide her true feelings.

"Why would you ask me a question like that?"

"Well, I heard that he is rather fond of this bar."

Hermes took a quick glance behind him at Asfi before looking back up at Syr.

"You see, I'm very interested in the Little Rookie. What? Don't tell me you think I'm going to do something strange to him. So how about it?"

Syr politely smiled again at Hermes's verbal advances.

"There's nothing that I want to tell you at this time, Lord Hermes."

She didn't even blink as she spoke. It looked as though the waitresses had decided to protect the boy.

Hermes shrugged his shoulders like he was joking around. "You don't trust me?"

The young waitress's smile expanded as wide as it could go. "No, not the least bit."

"—CHIGUSA!" a man fearfully called out to his ally.

His shrieks of terror echoed through the rocky cave as a human girl fell to the ground with a stone tomahawk coming out of her shoulder.

Thud! Dry gravel shifted as she landed hard.

A stream of fresh blood was illuminated by the flickering light of torches around her.

The monsters around them let out a series of high-pitched squeaks and squeals, celebrating their kill.

"Someone from the middle, advance! Cover Chigusa's spot!"

"H-help her! That wound is deep!"

A group of adventurers and a swarm of monsters were engaged in combat on the thirteenth floor of the Dungeon.

The adventurers' armor and weapons were all decorated with the same crest, a sword sticking out of the earth. *Takemikazuchi Familia*'s crest.

The party of six adventurers—currently five standing in a ring—were in a defensive struggle against the onslaught of a group of seven Al-Miraj.

However, there had been a weak spot in their ranks.

The rabbit monsters' quick movements had momentarily confused the battle party and one of the beasts seized the opportunity to take down one of their frontline members with a tomahawk throw.

The surprise attack had come from an Al-Miraj that stayed behind the other monsters running circles around the adventurers. It was a potentially lethal blow from a monster that had mastered the use of the landform weapon.

"*Kyiiah!*"

"Gah?!"

The Al-Miraj suddenly changed their strategy. They could all see the gigantic opening in the trembling *Takemikazuchi Familia*'s formation and quickly moved to exploit it.

The monsters in the upper levels didn't have the ability to read the situation. While there wasn't much change in physical strength, the difference in intelligence between the monsters of the upper and middle levels was worlds apart.

Clashes of steel and stone rang out through the cavern and were quickly followed by human screams of pain and agony.

The Al-Miraj had surrounded the party in a netlike formation—no matter where the humans looked, they could see the ring of monsters getting closer and closer.

"Yah!"

"*Kyuiii!*"

The battle party was losing ground in the face of the monsters' onslaught.

One girl lashed out against the attack, her shiny black ponytail fluttering behind her.

Stepping in front of her fallen comrade to protect her, the girl swung her blade so fast that her allies saw only afterimages as it sliced through the nearest Al-Miraj.

"Captain Ouka, lead the retreat! I'll cover you!"

"Thanks, counting on you!"

Mikoto's violet-and-purple armor glinted as she stood tall and urged her allies to make an escape.

The man in charge of the group gave the order and Mikoto took her place in front of the monsters to cover their retreat.

Her weapon of choice was a curved katana blade more than ninety celch long.

Mikoto faced down the monsters' pursuit with both hands firmly clasped on the hilt of her blade.

"...Haaaaanh!"

Yelling at the top of her lungs, she charged the first Al-Miraj with lightning speed. She easily dodged its attack as her counterattack hit flesh. The rabbit monsters outnumbered her, but none of them could get past her.

Her graceful, refined movements were completely different from those of the other adventurers and monsters around her. Mikoto's Level 2 skills made her more than a match for anything on the thirteenth floor of the Dungeon.

Even the Al-Miraj, known as one of the most agile monsters in the middle levels, couldn't keep up with her movements.

Any one of them that was careless enough to attack her head-on was cut to shreds.

"—oooooghhh!"

"!"

The tables turned yet again when a savage roar strong enough to send vibrations through the cavern came from farther down the tunnel.

Mikoto and the remaining Al-Miraj turned to face it.

Two gigantic bodies the size of boulders rolling toward them greeted their eyes.

"Hard Armoreds!"

Hard Armoreds were armadillo-like monsters that had the best defense in the upper levels. The small shield strapped to Mikoto's back was made from the plating that covered their bodies.

Mikoto was lost for words. She knew that her badly injured and vulnerable friends were still right behind her. They would not be able to escape without her help.

A Hard Armored in its rolled-up state was practically invulnerable to physical attacks. Most blades would just bounce off its spinning body, not even slowing it down.

Her allies would have no time to brace for their assault should either one get by her.

—*No choice!*

Mikoto stopped backpedaling and let the rest of the party gain some distance.

The surviving Al-Miraj took cover against the walls of the cavern as the Hard Armoreds picked up speed. The average adventurer would have turned tail and run, but Mikoto drew her shield and dug in her heels. Determination swelled within her, her eyebrows arched over her eyes in readiness.

Leaning forward and dropping her hips, Mikoto sprang toward the oncoming monsters.

"—*Grgh*—!!"

She braced the shield against her left shoulder and dove toward the closer of the two. The impact shook her to the bone.

Dadadadada! The space between each of the Hard Armored's plates slammed into Mikoto's shield at high speed, sending even more shock waves into her torso. Each hit was so loud she wanted to cover her ears.

She kept her eyes locked on the monster's rotation, her feminine frame shaking to endure the sheer force of its attack. But her shield held strong and her stance did not break, heels still firmly braced against the ground.

—*NOW!*

She summoned up every ounce of strength she had left.

The Hard Armored that she had stopped struggled to regain its balance and started to roll to the side. However, the other one was still rolling full speed and coming up fast. Mikoto moved to engage.

The two monsters slammed into each other with incredible force. The impact sent all three combatants flying, the Hard Armoreds toward the walls and Mikoto straight back.

This proved to be a blessing in disguise. Both monsters hit the walls with such force that their limp bodies fell to the ground. Their bodies unrolled, and Mikoto could see a blank look in their eyes that was synonymous with head trauma.

"Mikoto, that's enough! Catch up to us!"

"On my way!"

Her party had built a considerable lead and called out to her.

Body beaten to a pulp and armor heavily damaged, she rolled over, stood up, and turning her back on the remaining Al-Miraj, took off with all the speed she could coax out of her legs.

"Are you hurt?!"

"I can still fight! What of Chigusa?"

One of her party members cast fire Magic at the Al-Miraj behind her to slow them down, as Mikoto caught up with the rest of her allies. She wasted no time in asking about her injured friend.

She ran past the end of the line and all the way up to the front of the group.

"Not good. The potions we have may be able to save her, but first we need a safe place to heal. It's too dangerous here."

If a simple potion were enough to treat her, there would be no problem. However, Chigusa's wound was far too deep for items to be of much use.

There was no way to predict when monsters might come bursting out of the walls. The chances of being surrounded while healing if they chose a bad location were extremely high.

Of course Chigusa would be unable to fight, but the person healing her would need to be protected as well. They needed a place where they could survive for a short time at only a fraction of their battle strength.

"That means…"

"Yes, we'll pull back to level twelve…Sorry to ask so much of you."

"Please don't say such things! We are a battle party!"

Mikoto was quick to brush off Captain Ouka's apology. Defending allies was common sense to her.

The echo of boots on gravel echoed through the cave. Not far behind the members of *Takemikazuchi Familia* were the shrieks and howls of the monsters in hot pursuit.

The entire left side of Mikoto's body—the side that had taken the brunt of the Hard Armored's rolling attack—throbbed in pain.

Doing her best to hide this from the others, she looked toward Chigusa.

Her arms were draped around the shoulders of two other party members, the tips of her feet dragging on the ground as they ran. The stone tomahawk was still buried in her shoulder blade, her armor and clothing dyed a deep bloodred. The shallow rise and fall of her chest was the only proof that she was still alive.

Mikoto grimaced at the state of her poor ally. She could barely breathe when their eyes met.

The normally shy girl's cloudy eyes were partially hidden by her bangs, but the expression on her face said only one thing: *Sorry.*

Mikoto shook her head.

"…Not good."

"What is it?"

"More monsters. Now there are hellhounds chasing us…!"

"…!"

The rear watchman's warning made everyone break out in a cold sweat.

Mikoto took a glance behind her only to see the group of Al-Miraj bounding toward them accompanied by four dark, dog-shaped shadows with glowing red eyes.

It was not difficult for the adventurers to visualize their own bodies burned to smoldering cinders, just looking at the monsters' hot breath.

The true extent of the Dungeon's darkness and despair flashed before Mikoto's eyes.

"Move!"

All of them pushed their bodies even harder at Ouka's command. Everyone knew Death had them cornered. Even Mikoto was running with everything she had.

At last the cavern came to an end and they emerged into a room. This room wasn't square, but a massive dome.

The ceiling was unbelievably high. There was a stone hanging precariously from its highest point in the center. It looked as though the slightest vibration could send it crashing to the floor below. The walls were extremely rough and full of holes. All the scraps of rock on the ground could mean only one thing: a swarm of monsters had just been born.

The sounds of the fierce battle echoed through this wide space that any party could use to its advantage.

Are they...a Familia *new to this area?*

A small battle party was trying to fend off a group of monsters on one side of the room.

A group of three, two human men and a prum girl by the looks of them. Mikoto had never seen a battle party like that in all of her trips to the thirteenth floor.

She reasoned that today must be one of their first trips to the middle levels.

"...We're going over there."

"?!"

Mikoto's body lurched as if Ouka's words had been a slap in the face.

No one in the group had to ask. They knew what he was planning to do.

A "pass parade."

It was a strategy used inside the Dungeon. Simply put, it was a way for one battle party to escape from a monster by passing it off to another battle party that happened to be nearby.

There was an unwritten rule that battle parties made as little contact with one another as possible in the Dungeon, but everyone accepted that there were times when sacrifices were necessary to protect something important. Accidents happened every day in the Dungeon, and using another party was one way to get your own out of a sticky situation.

"Please reconsider, Captain Ouka?! If we do that, then those people..."

Executing a pass parade now would mean the small party of adventurers would become that "sacrifice."

She could tell that that party was struggling as it was. They were trying to fend off a large pack of Al-Miraj just as Mikoto had done only moments ago.

They would be overwhelmed if any more monsters joined the fray. Should the pack chasing *Takemikazuchi Familia* get too close…

"Your lives are far more important to me than some random people."

"…!"

"If it leaves a bad taste in your mouth, you can scold me to your heart's content when we get out of this."

Ouka's decision was final. Mikoto's face looked like that of a child who'd realized her parents had disappeared.

She looked back at her allies.

They were in dire straits. Most were covered in blood, their breathing shallow and staggered as they sprinted for their lives.

Their *Familia*'s emblem glinted dark red beneath a splattering of fresh blood.

Mikoto was on the verge of tears for the first time since this ordeal started.

…I'm so sorry!

It was too late to change their route now. They were close enough to see the whites of the other adventurers' eyes.

She caught the gaze of a white-haired boy as he sliced through one of the rabbits and tried her best to communicate a heartfelt apology.

Bell could hear, could feel all of the Al-Miraj coming at them from all angles.

The continuous onslaught of monsters didn't allow for a moment of hesitation.

"Not even enough time to breathe, eh?"

"Then don't talk!"

Welf swung his large blade, sweat flying everywhere, as Lilly delivered the final blow to a monster with a well-placed arrow.

Bell was fighting very well despite being completely surrounded.

With the exception of Agility, Welf's Status was greater than or equal to the Al-Miraj. He fought on the front lines with Lilly's support. It was Bell's job to make sure that they didn't get flanked by taking out as many of the monsters as he could.

Most of the rabbits fell to a single slice from Bell's blades. It didn't take the monsters long to figure out that it was useless to take him head-on. His speed and power were just a little bit higher than the average Level 2 adventurer.

"Welf, get down!"

"Gotcha!"

Seeing that Welf was about to be hit from two sides, Bell jumped to his aid.

Bell flew over the back of his kneeling friend, slicing one Al-Miraj in half with the blade in his right hand and slamming the side of his buckler into the head of another.

That was too close…!

The boy might have been holding his own, but his mind was racing.

Fatigue was beginning to catch up with him. His limbs had never felt this heavy at any time in the upper levels.

Of course the most powerful member of an unbalanced party had to carry the largest workload in combat, but the increase in number and intelligence of the monsters in the middle levels served to make that burden even harder to bear.

Bell was starting to realize just how little endurance he had. Another second and he would have been too late to save Welf. That thought sent a drip of cold sweat down his face. He was going to need a rest, and soon.

…?

Bell saw something strange out of the corner of his eye as he watched Welf deliver the final blow to the dazed Al-Miraj.

It was a party of five—no, six adventurers. The members of a different *Familia* came closer and closer by the second.

Bell raised his eyebrows in confusion. Battle parties preferred to avoid as much contact as possible in the Dungeon to avoid problems on the surface. He could understand if they were heading directly toward the exit, but their current path would bring them *very close*.

Almost as though they were targeting him.

"—"

The heavily damaged battle party was coming toward them on purpose.

They passed within a stone's throw of Bell on their way by. He happened to catch the eyes of the girl with a glossy black ponytail.

Blue velvet eyes on the verge of tears locked with ruby-red ones for a brief moment.

"—?! Oh no! They led more to us!"

Meanwhile.

Lilly was the only one able to respond to the other battle party's actions and tried to warn her allies.

She had experienced this very same tactic during her time as a thief. She knew this practice all too well.

"Huh…?"

"We've been used as a decoy! More monsters are coming!"

Lilly practically screamed at Bell's dumbstruck face.

A moment later, just as she predicted, another swarm of monsters appeared in the room.

There was almost double the number of Al-Miraj they had been fighting, as well as a few hellhounds coming at them. The color instantly drained from Bell's and Welf's faces.

Bell spun around just in time to see the last member of the other *Familia* disappear through the room's exit.

"Retreat! Mr. Welf, the tunnel to your right! Move!!"

"What the—You've got to be kidding?!"

Bell's battle party scrambled in confusion.

Fear was beginning to rear its ugly head. Welf wildly swung his broadsword in front of him. The blade didn't cut through the Al-Miraj blocking his path, but it was strong enough to force the monster out of his way. The tunnel entrance now clear, he followed Lilly's orders and dove straight in.

Bell and Lilly weren't far behind.

We can't get away…!

The tunnel path slowly widened before them as Lilly came to a sudden realization. Bell would have to hold them off.

These monsters were faster. While Bell might be able to get away, it was a given that a supporter with a weak Status had no chance in one of the middle levels' connecting tunnels.

The pack of monsters formed a line, bared fangs flashing in the dark. None of them could tell how many monsters were there—the beasts were kicking up enough dust to hide their numbers. It was a sight that would make any normal person collapse on the spot.

Bell chanced another look over his shoulder as he ran next to Lilly. It was as though a nightmare had come to life.

"Mr. Bell?!"

"Hey, Bell!"

"I'll catch up!"

The decision was made in a flash.

Ignoring Lilly's and Welf's objections, Bell turned his back to them. Basically, he spun 180 degrees.

He planted his feet and squared his shoulders in the face of the oncoming wave of monsters.

He raised his shielded left arm straight out and took a deep breath.

"Firebolt!"

He unleashed three rounds of his Magic straight down the narrow tunnel.

The rocky pathway was filled with three pillars of flaming electricity in the blink of an eye. The whole path was illuminated in violet flames, incinerating everything in their path.

A blast of hot air expanded from the sea of flames. Using this kind of Magic in such a small space was technically illegal in the Dungeon due to the high possibility of other adventurers taking damage, but these were desperate times.

Bell lowered his arm, his body illuminated by the flames.

Shadows danced on his face for a moment before—his eyes shook with fear.

Four shadows emerged from the wall of flame.

It didn't finish them?!

The hellhounds survived.

Every other monster in the swarm was burning. Their seared

carcasses littered the floor of the tunnel. Perhaps because hellhounds had the ability to spit fire themselves, they also had an unusually high resistance to fire magic.

Their crimson eyes cloudy, bodies decorated with fresh wounds, the group of demonic dogs hacked the ash out of their lungs and released a ferocious howl in unison.

"OWoooooooooooooOOOOOOOOOO!!"

"!"

They launched themselves at Bell in a vicious rage. He was quick to dispose of the first one with a swipe of his shortsword and knocked the second one into the air with his shield.

But the remaining two ran right past him.

"Lilly, Welf—!"

Completely ignoring the white-haired boy, the two beasts had their eyes set on the other two adventurers farther down the tunnel.

Lilly and Welf took emergency action as Bell's warning came echoing off the walls.

Lilly did a half turn. Her best chance to survive the initial assault was to use the broadsword attached to her backpack as a shield.

Welf took a defensive stance and raised his own sword high above his head.

"—Garrrrrrrrrrrrrrr!!"

"Aggh?!"

"Come get some!"

Impact.

The sword on Lilly's backpack successfully repelled the hellhound's tackle, but she wasn't strong enough to stay on her feet, so she fell to the floor.

Welf's powerful swing missed its intended target.

The other hound had Lilly pinned down, standing on top of her backpack and snapping its jaws just above her head. Bell flew in from out of nowhere and kicked the dog to the side after disposing of the one that came after him.

The kicked dog hit the ground hard, its body broken at the same moment that the hellhound that dodged Welf's attack collapsed.

"Are you guys okay?!"

"Y-yes..."

"Somehow...Damn."

Lilly dusted herself off as she stood up. Welf smirked a thin, pained smirk as he grabbed his arm. The hound's claws must've hit their mark; long streaks of fresh blood ran down his forearm.

The pain of knowing he hadn't been able to protect his allies pierced Bell from within. However, what he saw behind Lilly and Welf made his blood run cold.

"T-there's more!"

The boy could see the shadows of several monsters making their way up the tunnel from the other side.

At the same time, Lilly saw even more shadows coming from behind Bell and said in a very raspy voice:

"Pincer attack..."

"Well, isn't that depressing..."

A pack of Al-Miraj had made its way through the burned hallway, all the way up to their current position.

The three adventurers were quick to take a triangular formation, their backs turned toward one another. Bell scrunched up his face as he looked past the remains of the hellhounds and to their next opponents.

"Why is it that monsters spawn so fast in the middle levels? I need a break."

"Because it's the middle levels, right?"

"Ha, ha-ha..."

Lilly pulled a few potions from her backpack and passed them around as the boys tried their best to lighten the mood.

The liquid could restore their physical strength, but there was nothing they could do about the mental fatigue taking over their minds.

It was hard for any of them to concentrate.

"Mr. Bell, Mr. Welf, Lilly recommends we retreat. We need to rest and regroup. There will be no end to the monsters at this rate."

"Sounds great to me, but what are we gonna do about this?"

"Focus on one side and…break through?"

"Yes, Lilly believes that is best."

Lilly nodded at Bell's idea. All of the monsters had started to surround them.

The party knew that there was no more time for talking, and they readied their bodies for what was coming next.

"Well, then…"

"Yeah."

"…Let's go!"

The Dungeon slowly but surely took away every bit of mental and physical strength that Bell and his battle party had left.

It wouldn't let any adventurer who made even the slightest mistake get away with it.

The Dungeon was very sly. Like a salivating hunter toying with its prey, the Dungeon didn't go in for the kill all at once, but strategically wore its meal down.

Occasionally having monsters howl at them from afar—

Sometimes shaking the ground beneath their feet with strong quakes—

And, of course, consistently birthing monsters at just the right time to cut off their escape—

These little incidents weren't much on their own. However, not knowing what was coming next weighed heavily on the group. None of them could hide their exhaustion.

It was much easier to bring down a castle with a broken foundation. Lost physical strength was not easy to recover. And once they noticed something was wrong, it was already too late.

The prey let out groans of agony, weak bodies hunched over as they fought to catch their breath. Only then did the Dungeon bear its fangs.

"—"

Crack!

A very unwelcome sound reached Bell's ears, his body already on the verge of collapse.

He had lost track of how long he had been half fighting, half running away from monsters. His gaze raced around the tunnel, trying to find the source of the noise.

The walls looked as solid as ever, but the noise was getting louder. The mother Dungeon wasn't about to pull any punches now.

Crack, crack!

The foreboding sound surrounded them, echoing from all sides.

Huh—?

Bell was the first to figure it out.

The sound was coming from above. Welf and Lilly followed his line of sight and gasped.

A weblike network of cracks and fissures sprawled out over the ceiling above them. The parties stood and watched as the web expanded farther down the tunnel in both directions. It was too wide to believe.

Another crack, and more echoes. It got harder to tell the difference between new crevices opening and the echoes with each passing moment.

A piece of rock fell from the ceiling as the entire tunnel groaned, unable to bear the weight any longer.

Bell's body was frozen in place. The boy could feel the blood draining from his head.

—Monsters!

The second that thought crossed his mind…

…The ceiling shattered in a thunderous roar as a swarm of bad bats was born from the tunnel ceiling.

"KYAAAAAAAAAA—!!"

A chorus of high-pitched squeals rang out as the bad bats took wing for the first time.

The dim lights from above were suddenly blacked out by countless shadows in the air.

Shrouded in darkness, Bell and the others could only catch a glimpse of the heavily damaged ceiling.

Until, finally, it caved in.

""""—?!"""""

Bell's, Lilly's, and Welf's eyes practically jumped from their sockets. All of them sprang into action a moment later.

It was a rockslide intended to kill. The three of them made a mad dash forward, trying to escape the onslaught.

One hit after another, new pain erupting with every blow. Their eardrums were assaulted by the thunderous barrage of stones and boulders falling like water. Rocks and boulders just kept coming from above.

There wasn't even a sliver of time to look out for one another.

The three ran as fast as they could to escape the howl of the Dungeon itself.

"Gah, haa…!"

At last the rockslide subsided.

Welf gasped for breath, the air filled with thick dust and debris.

Bell's hands broke out in a cold sweat, but he didn't look in Welf's direction. He could tell by his voice that he was hurt.

There was a small cough in the distance. Lilly.

Wiping away the blood that seeped from the many small cuts on his face, Bell tried to call out to his friends to make sure they were okay.

"Urkh…"

However.

His throat was too dry and full of dust to produce the sound.

"—"

Shapes were coming into focus now that the dust started to settle.

There were several dark shadows climbing over the rubble that sat on top of where he had been standing just a few moments ago.

A pack of hellhounds.

In that moment, Bell's voice was truly gone.

"Garrrrr…!"

All of the hellhounds' heads were low to the ground.

Sparks flew as smoke rose from their mouths.

They started bearing fangs; the rubble underneath their feet was illuminated in red, glowing light.

—*Oh no.*

Lilly turned pale.

She was gripped by the despair of what was about to happen.

—*Can't make it!*

Welf gritted his teeth, as if he were cursing his lack of luck.

This is—

Bell's eyes were opened.

Opened to the strength and number of the monsters.

Opened to the mercilessness of the Dungeon.

Opened to the constant flow of absurdity.

The hellhounds rose and flung their heads forward.

The battle party was lit up by the volley of flames that exploded from their mouths.

The orbs of flame tore through the air, waves of intense heat bursting through the tunnel.

—*The middle levels!*

There was a massive explosion.

© Suzuhito Yasuda

CHAPTER 2 HOW MANY **MEDERS** TO A SAFE **RETURN?**

A small figure ran into the Pantheon—the Guild headquarters.

With twin black ponytails dancing behind her, the figure made her way into the white marble lobby and through a crowd of adventurers almost twice her size.

Hestia didn't care that her skin was covered in sweat or that her breathing was ragged as she darted for the counter in the corner of the lobby.

"Ms. Adviser!"

"G-Goddess Hestia?"

Eina's eyes widened as the small goddess practically tackled the reception desk.

Hestia didn't wait for the half-elf to respond and got straight to the point in a desperate voice.

"Did Bell come here yesterday?!"

"J-just in the morning before going into the Dungeon. I haven't seen him since then…"

Hestia's face contorted as if in pain after hearing her answer.

Seeing a look of confusion on Eina's face, the young goddess immediately started explaining.

"Bell never came home last night."

"!"

"I don't know where his supporter and the other boy are, either. Most likely, all of them are still in the Dungeon."

Welf was a member of *Hephaistos Familia*. Lilly lived at a gnome antique shop.

Hestia had visited both places earlier this morning in hopes of getting information about Bell and the others—just like her, nobody had seen them since early the previous morning.

Eina's face turned a few shades lighter, her emerald eyes wide open as she listened.

Asking the goddess to wait a moment, Eina disappeared from the reception desk like an arrow released from its bow, only to return a minute later.

"I just spoke with the Exchange. No one matching Bell's description went there yesterday."

"...!"

Hestia's blood ran cold.

It was likelier than ever that the entire party never left the Dungeon.

Although, she couldn't completely rule out the possibility that they got mixed up in some incident after they came out. More than anything, she wanted to believe that that was the case.

Especially because yesterday was the day that Bell was planning to crawl the middle levels of the Dungeon for the first time.

Indeed, Bell had said, "I'll tell you what the middle levels are like when I get back!" before leaving yesterday morning.

Hestia had made him promise that whenever he went to a new floor he would contact her immediately once he got back. Yesterday was the first time that he had ever failed to do so.

Hestia was smart enough to realize what this meant, and had been unable to rest the entire night.

Bell and his party had failed to get out of the middle levels.

Her divine intuition only further confirmed her conclusion. The feeling that she was right was driving her mad.

"...Ms. Adviser, please, can you find out if anyone has seen him?"

"Yes, I give you my word. I will ask as many adventurers as possible for information."

Hestia's racing heart seemed to calm down for a moment after making her request. All she could do was sigh and put her next words together in her head.

The goddess was thankful for Eina's cooperation, but she needed more than a promise.

"Also, I'd like to issué a quest. The goal is simple: find Bell."

She didn't have enough time to be picky, so this was the fastest and most effective way to have other adventurers participate.

Eina understood immediately and returned to her desk with a quick nod and came back to the counter with a sheet of paper. She started filling out the registration form with a few quick strokes of a feather pen.

"What do you propose for the reward?"

"Four hundred thousand vals. My *Familia*'s entire savings."

That was the largest amount of money she could prepare right away. Answering a few more of Eina's questions, the two of them worked out the rest of the details.

Lastly, Hestia snatched the pen out of Eina's outstretched hand and practically threw her signature onto the bottom of the form. The registration was complete.

"I need approval from upstairs to post this. Please understand the process will take about an hour. I'll have the quest posted as soon as possible."

"Thanks. I'm counting on you."

Eina gave another quick bow before getting up and making her way to the stairs. Hestia turned away from the counter and headed toward the door.

The goddess went through the doors and onto the Guild headquarters' front lawn. Many adventurers made their way past her, walking by a row of beautiful marble statues. The sky was clear and the streets were relatively quiet, completely unlike the storm that was raging in Hestia's heart.

Miach and Nahza stood next to a beautifully carved monument in the center of the headquarters' front lawn.

"What did you learn, Hestia?"

"Nothing. Looks like they really didn't make it out of the Dungeon."

Miach and Nahza stood in silence as Hestia shook her head from side to side.

Having already heard all the details from Hestia, the two of them knew how serious the situation had become.

The image of the entire party wiped out flashed into the back of her mind.

Hestia suddenly screamed as loud as she could to try to flush it from her head.

"Bell is still alive! My Blessing is still with him!"

He was the only person on Earth to receive her Falna. She could still feel the ichor from her blood edged into Bell's Status on his back—their bond had not been broken.

The other two were surprised by Hestia's sudden outburst. Cautiously lowering her arm, it was Nahza who started the conversation about what to do next.

"Lady Hestia, have you already applied for a quest...?"

"Yes, thanks for your advice, Nahza. It should be up soon."

Miach and Nahza were the reason that Hestia had decided to register one in the first place, despite having almost no information on Bell's whereabouts.

If he turned up out of the blue, then they could all laugh about this later. However, *Miach Familia* had once nearly lost Nahza in the Dungeon in a very similar situation. Hestia needed to exhaust every option before it was too late.

"In that case, I suggest we pay Hephaistos and Takemikazuchi a visit. We need as much help as possible."

"What are we waiting for?!"

Hestia was quick to agree with Miach's suggestion.

They left the Guild headquarters behind and headed out onto the street.

One hour later.

Just as Eina had promised, Hestia's quest was posted on the bulletin board at Guild headquarters.

Amid all of the adventurers looking for a quest to undertake, one in particular found the newly posted quest and leaned in for a closer look.

Without warning—*rip!* She tore the post from the bulletin board.

"Something very bad has happened...Lord Hermes."

Twelve hours earlier.

The Dungeon was silent. With no monsters around, only the moldy smell of the damp air and ash-colored rocks was there to provide atmosphere.

The tunnel was very dim. The only light came down from far above, spots on the ceiling flickering like distant campfires. Only the sounds of heavy footsteps on gravel reverberated through the darkness.

Bell silently made his way one step at a time through the tunnel, his face softly illuminated by the lights above.

A bead of sweat worked its way down his brown, dust-covered face and fell off his narrow chin. It landed quietly at his feet. The cuts covering his head had finally closed, and rivers of dried blood covered his cheeks.

"Hunh…Hunh…" His deep breaths pierced the silence as he adjusted the arm draped over his shoulder.

"Sorry, man…"

"Don't…worry…"

Bell managed to get the words out between breaths, in response to the weak voice in his ear.

Welf wore a very pained expression, his face coated with sweat as Bell helped him to move forward. Bell looked out of the corner of his eye behind Welf and saw Lilly, looking just as ragged as they did, not too far behind. She noticed his gaze and flashed a shaky smile as if to say, "Lilly's okay."

The three of them had managed to survive the hellhounds' volley of fire, although it had been a near thing.

The attack had come from a rather large pack of the monsters. They made their move to escape before the smoke cleared, and their mad dash to safety had been successful.

But they had paid a high price to win their improbable survival. One of Welf's legs had been crushed in the rock slide on level thirteen. It was impossible for him to walk on his own. While Lilly didn't have many visible injuries, Bell could tell by the look on her face that the weakest member of their party had had the most difficult time during their escape. Also, her backpack was in tatters. There was no doubt they had lost a large number of potions and other items.

Bell looked down to assess his own condition after checking up on his allies.

We'd have been wiped out without the salamander wool...

The red fabric still sparkled under what was left of his armor. A fresh bead of cold sweat ran down the back of his neck as Bell thought about what would've happened without it. All of them would be a smoldering pile of ash at this point.

The magical protection that resided within the fairy-made cloth was the only reason that they'd survived at all. The salamander wool had protected their bodies from the intense heat.

Looking at the light burns on his hands, Bell inwardly thanked his adviser over and over.

Eina had saved all their lives.

"Lilly, what items do we have left...?"

"Four potions and two antidotes; no high potions made it..."

Lilly's response made Bell realize just how much danger they were in. Just getting out of the middle levels was going to be extremely difficult.

He tried to do the math in his head—how much distance they had to cover with their current stock of items. All adventurers knew that weapons could break and that healing items were extremely important in the middle levels. The fact that Bell and Lilly didn't have much physical strength left made Welf's condition even more of a dilemma.

Normal potions were designed to restore physical strength. Only high potions and elixirs could clot blood and save someone with deep gashes, broken bones, and other severe injuries. Welf's lower left leg—everything below the knee—was coated in a mixture of dark red and black colors, the bone obviously broken in many places. It was impossible for Bell or Lilly to treat such an injury with the items they still had on hand.

Their formation had lost its only frontline fighter. Surviving in the middle levels had just became a lot more difficult.

And we also…fell.

Bell took a look up toward the lights and could just make out holes in the ceiling as the group pressed forward.

They were on the fourteenth floor.

All of them had fallen through one of those holes. It happened during their mad dash after the rockslide on level thirteen while trying to get away from the hellhounds. No one saw the hole in time, and they'd fallen to the floor below.

They were indeed trapdoors. The shock of falling all that way made standing up again extremely painful for Bell and his party.

All of the holes above them were lined up in a neat little row. However, the walls leading up to them were too high and smooth to climb. Then there was the hole itself; they would slip and fall back down here long before they could reach the floor above. The Dungeon was merciless.

This was the worst possible situation that they could have been in. The group had fallen victim to a "Dungeon Gimmick."

"Bell, Li'l E…If it comes to it, you gotta leave me behind…"

"What does Mr. Welf think he's saying…?"

"No, absolutely not."

They exchanged feeble conversation. Bell readjusted the shoulder that supported Welf after the blacksmith's unnecessary attempt to tell them to save themselves.

They had yet to encounter a monster in the quiet darkness. The only sounds to come through the shadows were made by Bell, Lilly, or Welf. The lights above were only strong enough to illuminate their silhouettes, adding to the feeling of despair that surrounded them.

The sound of the gravel crunching beneath their feet was deafening.

With each step he took, Bell wondered if it would be the one to reveal their position to any nearby monsters.

They had fallen to this floor. Of course the monsters down here would be stronger than the ones they had been fighting on the thirteenth. More of the trapdoors lined this tunnel on both sides. Careful to stay in the middle of the tunnel, every echo sounded like the first warning of a monster's approach. Bell couldn't tell the difference between sounds anymore, his mind completely on edge. Only now did he realize his mouth was bone dry and desperate for some water.

Their path started to curve up toward an intersection. First they turned left, then right.

Plop-plop. All three adventurers' eyes shot toward the source of the sound in unison. It was only a few small pebbles falling from the ceiling. It took all the willpower they had left to slow their racing hearts.

The sound of their own breathing filled their ears. They were tired, but that wasn't the only reason for their shallow, ragged gasps.

It was fear, plain and simple.

Fear of the darkness, fear of what the Dungeon had in store.

Bell thought about how proud he'd felt when he leveled up and became an upper-class adventurer, his name spreading around Orario. He scornfully laughed at himself. Wasn't it Eina who told him adventurers were in the most danger when they thought things were going smoothly?

They were in the deepest pits of hell, all because of one little hole.

Each of them was on the verge of being overwhelmed in a place so deep it had never seen sunlight.

"...A dead end."

Bell managed to stop himself from saying "another."

They were completely lost. Of all the dangers that lurked in the Dungeon, getting lost was the one thing that you needed to avoid at all costs.

The only road markers available to adventurers in the Dungeon were the staircases that linked each level together. However, Bell and the others had fallen through a hole. There were no landmarks or staircases to help them get their bearings. In addition, compasses and other magnetic field–based navigation equipment were completely useless in the Dungeon due to the presence of metals like adamantite in the Dungeon walls.

Without even a map to go by, Bell had no idea which direction would lead them out.

Bell's and Welf's eyes narrowed in frustration as they encountered yet another road block.

"Let's take a rest for a moment."

Lilly took a deep breath and made a proposal as the two young men stood, staring at the solid wall in front of them. They turned to face her and saw that she was soaked with sweat but was somehow forcing herself to remain calm.

By the same token, Lilly's composed brown eyes had a calming effect on Bell and Welf. They were beginning to become desperate, and yet here was this small prum, barely half their size, who could keep a cool head. They both nodded and lowered their bodies to the ground.

Just as Lilly had proposed, the three of them stopped to catch their breath and started trying to figure out what to do from here.

"First, how many healing items do we have? Lilly has four potions and two antidotes. What about Mr. Bell? Mr. Welf?"

"I got nothing."

"I still have a few potions in my leg holster."

Lilly took the potions out of her backpack and passed them to the others. She kept only one for herself. Thinking of the road ahead, Welf was in the greatest need of the healing liquid.

"What about weapons? Lilly lost her bow gun during the fall. Mr. Welf's sword is okay…"

"Bell, did you lose the shortsword, the buckler, and the broadsword?"

"Y-yeah."

Bell was getting more and more anxious as their conversation continued.

The three of them were sitting in a small triangle at the end of the tunnel with only one exit. There was nowhere to run if the monsters found them. On top of that, they had no idea if or when monsters could be born out of the walls surrounding them. Bell did everything he could not to express the fear gripping his chest. Welf and Lilly were no doubt doing the same.

They kept their voices low to avoid attracting attention. Bell reached behind his back and felt for the sheaths of his two weapons, the Hestia Knife and Ushiwakamaru.

"But both my knives are here."

"And the salamander wool is still kickin'."

"Okay...Taking all of this information into account, Lilly believes that our best chance of making it back to the surface alive is to avoid combat with monsters if possible. Only engage if we don't have a choice."

Bell was kneeling on the ground while Welf had his rear end firmly planted on the cold gravel, sticking his injured leg straight out. A fresh wave of sweat rolled down his face as Bell supported him, but he nodded in agreement.

Sitting in front of them, Lilly took another deep breath and worked up the courage to say what had been bothering her all this time.

"Mr. Bell, Mr. Welf, please listen closely. This is just Lilly's gut feeling but...this could very well be the fifteenth floor."

""...!""

Their jaws went slack as Lilly continued her explanation.

"Taking into account how long we were falling, it's very possible we went down two floors. Judging by the color of the walls, the width of the tunnels, lack of light, and complexity of the Dungeon layout, this area looks more like the fifteenth rather than the fourteenth or thirteenth."

Bell remembered being surprised by how long the fall took as well. That was more than enough to convince him that she was right.

That would mean that the road to the surface just became staggeringly long. This was already a hopeless situation had they been on the fourteenth floor, but now they would have to wander around the Dungeon and hope to find the correct path through the fifteenth, fourteenth, and thirteenth floors in order to reach the upper levels. In their condition, that was impossible. They had to contend with strong monsters and complex terrain while dealing with a great deal of physical pain and exhaustion.

That's checkmate. The words came from the back of Bell's mind, a wave of cold dread washing over his body.

Lilly took another breath and kept going.

"This is the important part. It is true that our chances of survival going up are very bleak. However, we do have another option beneath us…We can take cover on the eighteenth floor."

Bell didn't quite understand what she said at first.

Lilly continued her explanation.

"Level eighteen is one of the few floors in the Dungeon where monsters cannot be born—a safe point. It is used as a staging area for expeditions going to the lower levels and beyond. Lilly believes we'll be safe if we can get there."

In a Dungeon infested with monsters, there were very few areas that could be considered "safe." Adventurers had learned over the years that no monsters came out of the walls on the eighteenth floor, and so they used it as a rest area.

The eighteenth floor was the first safe point in the Dungeon after entering the first floor, so it was highly likely that adventurers much stronger than they were there right now. If they could somehow join a group that was heading back to the surface, that would guarantee them safe passage home.

"L-Lilly, wait a second. We have no idea if we can make it out of this floor. If we went farther down…"

"We'll use the holes. There are hundreds of them, and they all lead down. With good luck we can reach our destination quickly. We're lost. Lilly thinks we have a much better chance to find one of the holes than a staircase leading up."

Lilly's logic made sense. Bell had no counterargument and cleared his throat.

Welf fought back the pain in his leg long enough to open his eyes just enough to meet Lilly's gaze and asked a question of his own.

"What do we do about the floor boss? Isn't that massive son of a bitch on level seventeen?"

Even when faced with a thought of one of the most powerful monsters in the Dungeon, Lilly had an answer ready.

"On the day that Mr. Bell slew the Minotaur...Two weeks ago, *Loki Familia* started an expedition. In order to protect a group that large, they would have defeated the monster head-on rather than try to avoid it."

"H-how do you know?"

"Lilly's heard that level seventeen's floor boss, Goliath, is located in front of the entrance to the eighteenth floor. Many powerful adventurers belong to *Loki Familia*. It would be easier for them as a group with the floor boss out of the way."

Lilly went on to explain that leaving the Monster Rex untouched actually put the lower-level adventurers in their group in danger.

"Goliath respawns about every two weeks...There is a chance that we can make it to the eighteenth floor just before it emerges."

There still might be time to pass through a boss-less level seventeen if they moved quickly.

That's what Lilly was implying.

"You're serious...?"

Not up, but down.

That would mean putting themselves in more danger in order to get home safely.

Welf was at a loss for words at the serious look on Lilly's face.

He looked at her with a mixture of shock and awe that she was able to come up with such a daring strategy under the circumstances.

Bell, too, looked at her and wondered how so much courage and spirit could fit in such a small frame.

"...This is only an option. As Mr. Bell and Mr. Welf have said, trying to find a way up is the safer route. There is a chance that we could find another battle party just by walking around."

However, that was completely up to chance.

While it was easy to find lower-level adventurers in the upper levels, the upper-class adventurers strong enough to prowl the middle levels were few and far between. To make matters worse, the layout of the middle levels included intertwining upper and lower tunnels while the higher floors were just one flat, circular maze. It would take a considerable amount of luck to find anyone. That was why

Lilly had mentioned that high-level adventurers gather on the eighteenth floor.

Lilly fell silent for a moment before looking up at Bell with unwavering resolve.

"Mr. Bell is the leader of this party. Lilly leaves the final decision up to you."

All of the air suddenly left Bell's lungs.

Her words ignited a fire within his belly that was hotter than anything he'd felt that day.

Every pore in his skin opened; cold sweat poured down his face.

Bell looked over at Welf. The young man was grimacing in pain but met his gaze and flashed a smile.

"It's up to you. Whatever you choose, I won't hold it against you."

Those words showed just how deep their bond of trust ran.

And at the same time, they closed off any means of escape Bell had from making this decision.

His heart rate quickened.

Party leader…He was the only one who could fill that role.

Lilly the supporter and Welf the smith were lending their talents and abilities to Bell the adventurer. He was the leader, without a doubt.

He had no choice but to rise to this challenge.

…!!

His heart kept speeding up. It felt as though it would tear itself apart at this rate.

This decision would determine his party's fate. He'd never felt such pressure before. His next words would determine whether his friends lived or died.

Fear of losing them made his knees shake. He wanted to cry, to run away, to beg for forgiveness, and to hide from the responsibility.

However—behind all this fear and anxiety, he understood that it was the party leader's job to make decisions like this.

A solo adventurer never felt this much pressure. Every member of a battle party had to trust the leader with their lives.

The opposite was also true. Bell had to trust Lilly and Welf with *his* life. They were the ones who protected his blind side, the ones who covered his back. He had to have the utmost faith in them.

They chose him and believed in him. It would be sacrilege to abandon allies who held him in such high esteem. If there was a time to prove to them that he was worthy of their trust, this was it.

Bell clamped his jaws together and clenched his fists. He breathed in as deep as he could to steady himself.

He built up the courage. Now all that was left was to make the decision.

Go back or press forward.

Depend on luck or blaze their own path.

To go on an adventure or not.

Bell closed his eyes for a moment—opened them.

He looked at each of his party members in turn with confidence and said:

"Let's push on."

The clock on the wall showed that it was early evening.

Hestia was standing inside the Azure Pharmacy, *Miach Familia*'s home.

They sold potions and other healing items in this wooden building. Since many adventurers came here anyway, it worked well for a gathering spot to begin the quest. The preparations for rescuing Bell's battle party had begun.

Along with Hestia, Miach, and Nahza, the crimson-haired goddess Hephaistos was also present.

Across from them stood Takemikazuchi, his long hair tied regally up in three places: on the sides of his head and at the back. The rest of his *Familia* was standing behind him, including Mikoto.

"My apologies, Hestia. It is very possible that my children are part of the reason that yours has not come back."

"..."

Hestia crossed her arms, shut her eyes, and looked away. Mikoto and the others stood behind him, silently staring at the floor as if repenting.

Takemikazuchi Familia's pass-parade maneuver on the thirteenth floor.

Mikoto and the other adventurers had safely returned to their home by the time Hestia came looking for information about Bell. They heard everything—how Bell and his allies were dressed, their features, their formation—and realized what had happened. They hid nothing from their god and told him everything, their faces pale.

Takemikazuchi understood that they had been in a desperate situation, but he had no choice but to apologize for what his followers had done. Hestia's silence was deafening as she realized that they were more than likely the cause of Bell's disappearance.

At long last, Hestia opened her blue eyes and made eye contact with the children on the other side of the room. Miach and Hephaistos stood at her side.

"If Bell never makes it back, I'll hold a grudge against all of you like you'd never believe. But I will not hate you. I promise."

Mikoto gawked at Hestia's words.

Takemikazuchi Familia's hearts were moved by this goddess who, despite her anguish, was able to look at them with resolute eyes and show tolerance. This was the first time anyone other than their own god had had such an impact on them.

Hestia forgave them and made a request.

"As for right now, would you be willing to help me?"

""—On our honor.""

All six of *Takemikazuchi Familia's* members took a knee in one swift motion before lowering their heads toward her.

Takemikazuchi and Miach were taken aback by this group of children's resolve, led by their leader, Ouka, to repay the kindness that Hestia had shown them.

Meanwhile, Hephaistos smiled as her friend gave these children an opportunity to make amends for their mistake.

"Shall we proceed? Time is of the essence."

Miach took a step forward as he spoke. Hestia nodded in response.

"This is a search party, yes? And we know that Hestia's boy's still alive?"

"Yes, he is. Hephaistos, what about yours, Welf?"

This time it was Takemikazuchi who asked the question. Hestia responded and then turned to Hephaistos. The goddess closed her non-bandaged eye and scratched her chin for a moment before answering. Since using her divine power, Arcanum, wasn't an option, she chose to look at the total number of "contracts" that were active, rather than find a specific one, to save time.

"Wait just a moment. Many children have my Blessing, so sensing a single one is rather difficult...Yes, he's probably alive. The number of bonds I have with my children hasn't decreased."

Now Miach had a question for her.

"Can any of your children help us, Hephaistos?"

"Most of mine are currently helping *Loki Familia*'s expedition... Everyone who could make it that far down is there right now. The ones who are available at the moment wouldn't last long in the middle levels, I'm afraid."

Hephaistos turned to Hestia and apologized, but Hestia shook her head to tell her it was okay.

"Looks like we'll have to count on Také's group after all."

"That's fine with me...Ouka and Mikoto will go for sure...Chigusa, can you accompany them as a supporter?"

"Y-yes." A girl whose eyes were covered by her bangs nodded at her god's request.

Ouka and Mikoto were *Takemikazuchi Familia*'s only upper-class adventurers—the only ones who'd reached Level 2. The girl named Chigusa was still Level 1, so she would be deployed as a supporter to supply the others with weapons and potions.

They were the best that the *Familia* had to offer, so they were selected to form the search party.

"Ouka is the only one I've got who can hold his own against anything in the middle levels. The others would just fall behind."

"I think the most important thing for a search party is speed..."

"I agree with Nahza. If we sacrifice speed and maneuverability by increasing numbers for strength, it'll be too late."

"So that means we're depending on these three…?"

Nahza, who had nearly died in the middle levels herself, added her opinion and was supported by Hephaistos. Words spilled out of Hestia's mouth as she again crossed her arms in front of her bulging chest.

That's when they arrived.

"—I'll join you, Hestia!"

The front door was flung open to reveal a charming god standing in the doorway.

"Hermes?! What are you doing here?!"

"Quite the greeting, Takemikazuchi. Of course, I'm here to help my friend out of a pinch."

Hermes glided his way to the middle of the room under the watchful eyes of Miach and Nahza, and smiled at Takemikazuchi. His follower Asfi quietly walked in behind him.

"Hey there, Hestia. Nice to see you!"

"Hermes…Why are you here?"

Hestia wore the same expression of confusion as everyone around her. Hermes walked right up to her with that same dandy smile on his face.

He reached into his jacket and pulled out a sheet of paper—a quest form from the Guild.

"You're in trouble, aren't you?"

"…"

Hermes softly waved the sheet in front of her. The words FIND BELL flashed before her eyes.

Hestia tried to respond, but no words would come out.

"Why would you want to help Bell Cranell, Hermes? Out with it."

"Hey, hey, Takemikazuchi. I'm the one and only Hermes, you know? When one of my buddies is in need, I'll pull out all the stops to help them out."

"Hermes, this is the first time you've seen Hestia since she came to this world, is it not?"

"Some friend you've been."

"Ha-ha, Hephaistos, Miach, aren't you two being a little harsh?"

In addition to Takemikazuchi's watchful eyes, Hermes was now acknowledged by the other two deities in the room. They weren't fooled by his charm. Nahza, Mikoto, and the other humans were completely ignored as the drama unfolded in front of them.

Hermes dropped his jolly bluster for a moment and spoke in a serious voice for the first time since he arrived.

"But my desire to help Hestia is real. I want to save Bell."

He opened his arms and smiled earnestly at each of them in turn.

"How about it, Hestia?"

"..."

Hermes turned to face Hestia last. Smiling with his narrow eyes, the charming deity met her gaze straight-on.

She stared at his orange eyes for a few moments before letting a small "hmph" out of her nose.

"Fine...I'll accept your help, Hermes."

"Great! You can count on me!"

Hermes's charming smile returned after Hestia accepted his offer.

Back to his usual self, he walked over to Miach, who was glaring at him out of one eye, and patted him a few times on the shoulder.

"Are you sure, Hestia?"

"Rescuing Bell and his party is our first priority. The fact is, we need more people."

"...Okay, if you say so."

Takemikazuchi, keeping his eyes locked on Hermes, leaned close to Hestia and whispered into her ear. She responded as quietly as possible.

He decided to keep his mouth shut for the time being, and to do his best to work with Hermes.

"This means that Hermes's followers can join us...Will that be enough?"

"Aren't most of the children in your *Familia* at Level Two, Hermes?"

"Yeah, what about it, Hermes."

"It's just like you said, Hephaistos. Unfortunately most of them are out of town on business—that's why I'm bringing Asfi with me! She's my ace; there's nothing to fear!"

Hermes Familia was registered as a Dungeon-type *Familia*. At the same time, many of its members were involved in other types of business as well. They were famous as a jack-of-all-trades *Familia*. The Guild assigned them an F ranking.

Choosing to believe Hermes's assertion that Asfi's Dungeon range included the nineteenth floor, Miach and the other gods decided to let her join the search party.

The girl breathed a heavy sigh, realizing that her god had just signed her up for the group.

"We'll leave as soon as preparations are complete. Sometime later tonight?"

"Indeed, that will be best."

"Ouka, Mikoto, Chigusa. Make sure you're ready."

""""Yes, my lord!"""""

Something occurred to Asfi while Hephaistos and the other gods were speaking.

She made her way to Hermes's side and said in a low voice:

"Lord Hermes…Just now you said you were taking me along. Don't tell me you're planning to…"

"Of course. I'm coming with you."

Asfi's silver glasses slid to the end of her nose. She quickly pushed them back up with her finger.

"Isn't it forbidden for gods to enter the Dungeon?"

"That just means we can't make our presence known, right? What's the big deal? Go in and get out before the Guild even knows I'm there. I said it before, didn't I? I want to save Bell."

"Don't tell me you've been planning this all along…!"

"Ha-ha-ha! I'm going to need your protection, Asfi."

Asfi's eyebrows arched, and she sucked in her cheeks in frustration as Hermes turned on the charm again with a toothy grin. Suddenly—*whap!*

Hestia just happened to be in earshot of their conversation. Her head whipped around so fast that everyone in the room could hear it.

Her twin ponytails came to life as if guided by their master and wrapped themselves around Hermes's neck.

"Gaoh?!"

"—Bring me with you, Hermes."

The deity bent over backward as Hestia's hair pulled at him from behind. Asfi jumped back in surprise.

Hestia stepped up to his face, her hair not letting him say a thing.

"I'm going to save Bell. I can't just sit here and do nothing while others are out there looking for him."

"W-wait just a moment, Hestia! Calm down!"

Hermes had managed to free himself from enough of the hair to get words out. He flipped his body around to face her.

He made eye contact with her once again and tried to convince her to stay behind.

"The Dungeon is very dangerous. Without our power, one hit from the monster and we're done. But most of all—what would happen if *you're found out*?"

"You think I don't know that?" responded Hestia curtly.

"You're going in after saying all that, aren't you? Another god or two isn't going to make that much difference."

"Ummm…"

"I'm going, got that?"

Hestia's strong tone left Hermes speechless.

A defeated look emerged on Hermes's face as he came to grips with the fact she wouldn't be swayed.

"Somehow I'm not surprised…"

"Don't do anything reckless, okay?"

Just like Hermes, Hephaistos and Takemikazuchi were shocked by Hestia's declaration and could only grimace. "I'm fine!" she said, completely ignoring her friends' concern. The goddess was on fire from within; she was going to save Bell herself.

Miach was about to voice his opinion as well, but it was Nahza who stepped forward.

"What is it, Nahza?"

"Lady Hestia, here…"

She handed her a pouch full of vials, a large amount of potions.

Hestia's expression softened as she looked at the tubes of the red, blue, and green liquids.

"This is all I can do…Sorry I can't join you…"

"This is more than enough. Thank you, Nahza."

Acknowledging the trauma that the chienthrope girl had regarding monsters, Hestia accepted the pouch. Nahza's gaze fell as she apologized, but Hestia just smiled back at her.

"I, too, have something for you."

"Oh? Ohhh?!"

Hephaistos held out a long, thin package wrapped in white cloth. It had a surprising amount of heft to it—so much so that Hestia almost lost her balance when she held out her hands to take it.

Part of the cloth fell away as Hestia shuffled her feet to stay upright. A piece of a dark red blade came into view. Although the blade itself was thick, it didn't look sharp enough to cut anything.

"Hephaistos, what is this…?"

"That boy, Welf, made it. I've been holding on to it for him."

The crimson-haired Goddess of the Forge watched as Hestia took a closer look at the weapon.

"You can use it if you need to…Please give it to Welf once you find him. Also, tell him to stop compromising his allies for his pride's sake."

Hestia slowly nodded at Hephaistos's meaningful words.

In any case, Hestia was grateful for the support from her friends. The other gods in the room smiled and nodded at her.

Meanwhile.

"Well, this complicates things…" Hermes muttered to himself on the outside of Hestia's support circle.

Watching all the good feelings going around, Hermes leaned toward his follower standing next to him and asked a question.

"Asfi, do you think you can protect both of us?"

"Takemikazuchi's battle party will be there as well, but…I can't make any guarantees if they can't keep up."

Asfi told him with the utmost sincerity that she would be able to protect him but couldn't be held responsible for Hestia's well-being. The search party wasn't strong enough.

Hermes mulled over her words for a moment before exhaling out of his nose for much longer than necessary.

"Maybe I should find some more help."

The sun was setting in the west, tinting the sky with red light.

It was around this hour that adventurers called it a day and came out of the Dungeon. Like many of the other bars in the area, the staff of The Benevolent Mistress was hard at work preparing for that evening's customers.

Cat people and humans were dashing all around the establishment, cleaning and organizing everything behind a wooden door with the CLOSED sign hanging out front. Some of them were carrying round tables and chairs; others were out buying ingredients to stock the kitchen. It was a battlefield in its own right.

A certain elf's long, pointy ears were illuminated by red light coming in from the window as she ran a cloth across the surface of the bar counter.

Lyu's ears jumped when she heard a light jingle behind her. Someone had just opened the front door.

"Sorry, I'm coming in."

A lean deity entered the bar.

The reddish light from outside mixed with his orange hair and created a rusty glow around him in the early evening hours.

Hermes grinned from ear to ear as he walked into the building, Asfi in tow.

"I'm so sorry, Lord Hermes. We're not open yet. Can you come back in a little while?"

"Sorry for getting in the way, Runoa. I'll make this quick."

Hermes walked right past the human girl Runoa's objections and right to his intended target.

The other waitresses stopped what they were doing and followed him.

Hermes finally came to a stop in the middle of the bar, directly in front of Lyu.

"…You want to talk to me?"

"Very much so. I need a favor, Lyu."

Asfi came to a halt at his side as Hermes opened his eyes wider than usual.

"There's a quest I'd like you to accept—I need 'Lyon of the Gale Wind.'"

That had been Lyu's alias during her time as an adventurer. It had a savage reputation.

The tension in the bar instantly rose.

The deity and his follower were instantly surrounded by an ominous hiss. The catgirls Ahnya and Chloe, as well as Runoa and the other waitresses, were glaring daggers at them.

There was no escape. Asfi's palms were instantly sweaty from the terrible pressure of all the eyes pointed in their direction. The entire staff of The Benevolent Mistress now saw them as enemies who needed to be eliminated.

The red glow from the windows intensified their perilous atmosphere.

"Are you threatening me?"

Lyu's thin eyebrows curved downward as her eyes bored into the god standing in front of her.

Very few people knew her history, and threatening to make it public served as very good blackmail. She had to know.

Hermes raised both of his hands saying, "No, no, that was not my intention," at the elf as she came right up to his face.

"There's a boy…Bell Cranell, who needs saving."

"…What do you mean by that?"

Hermes explained Bell's situation, and that he wanted her to join the search party.

Lyu's light-blue eyes softened for a moment as she listened, but then suddenly sharpened again.

"Why did you come to me?"

"We're taking some 'baggage' that needs to be protected and we can't count on other gods to provide it. So, I need someone strong but not bound by the rules of a *Familia*. You were the only one I could think of...And then..."

Hermes broke off eye contact with her and looked toward the corner of the room.

"You're a friend of Syr's, right?"

A silver-haired girl stood, dumbstruck, in the doorway leading to the kitchen behind the bar.

She'd arrived just in time to hear what was going on with Bell. Lyu's expression contorted when she saw the look on her friend's face.

The ends of Hermes's lips curved upward. He knew that that last line was far more convincing than anything else thus far. He'd won.

"We leave at eight. Join us; we're waiting for you."

Hermes leaned down to her ear and whispered those words just before leaving.

The god turned around and walked toward the door, escorted by a series of murderous glares as he made his way out of the bar with Asfi close behind.

"Lyu."

"Syr..."

Lyu watched Hermes go, an expression of pure loathing on her face. She only looked away when her friend came up to her side. Syr looked physically ill as she made eye contact with the elf.

A moment of silence passed.

"I'm sorry, Lyu. Save him. Save Bell."

Lyu gazed deep into the silver pools of Syr's eyes.

Lyu could clearly see the fear of losing someone special, as well as a great deal of helplessness. She was particularly sensitive to human emotions. Syr was shivering, practically begging her to go. Lyu forced a smile.

"I am in your debt, Syr. I cannot refuse your request. Nor do I," Lyu continued, "wish for the death of Bell Cranell."

Her voice was clear and steady.

Syr bowed over and over, apologizing many times and, at last, offered her heartfelt thanks.

The other waitresses who had watched everything unfold gathered around Lyu. Ahnya and the others gave their own words of support.

"Leave the bar to us, meow! We'll tell Mama that Lyu had a tummyache and can't work, meow!"

"It's irritating that Lord Hermes can push us around like this… but it can't be helped."

"Mya-ha-ha, Lyu! Save him tonight and he'll owe you forever, meow!"

The airheaded catgirl Ahnya, the smiling Runoa, the scheming Chloe, and all of the other staff members said their piece in turn.

Even the cooks poked their heads out of the kitchen to offer words of encouragement.

Lyu looked at each of them, overwhelmed by their support. Lastly, she smiled and weakly nodded at Syr. Her voice quivered as she said:

"My apologies. Please cover for me."

Lyu sped toward the door, untying the ribbon on her uniform along the way.

Sweat keeps rolling down my face and off my chin.

I think part of it has to do with the stuffy air down here in the middle levels. Of course, I have no idea if I'll get out of this alive, but this humidity is killing me.

Unfortunately, I don't have any choice but to fight my way through it as we press forward.

I'm still lending my shoulder to Welf. Physically, my eyes and ears are on high alert. But mentally, I'm praying my heart out—almost pitifully so—that no monsters show up. Lilly's walking just a few steps back, making sure nothing comes up from behind.

We've covered a lot of distance since deciding to go to level eighteen. Unfortunately, we haven't found a single one of the holes leading down.

I do my best to keep calm and stave off the rumblings of my hungry stomach.

We're alone in this dark tunnel—the one thing that we can't do is start panicking. All of us are on edge, but the moment we give in to the fear will be the beginning of the end for us.

We come to a fork in the tunnel, one path leading left and one path right. At the end of our meeting I told everyone that we should go right whenever we have to make a decision. Just as we agreed, we all go right.

*Haa...haa...*Lilly's small breaths sound painful behind me. I bet she's really tired. Welf's body is pressed right up against mine. It's really hot. But we can't slow down, no matter how much pain we're in.

"...Li'l E, can't you do something about that smell?"

Welf tilts his head and looks at Lilly out of the corner of his eye.

I take a look over my opposite shoulder. Lilly's eyes glaze over at Welf's question—maybe she's lost the will to argue.

"Please put up with it...Lilly's just saying, but the smell is much worse back here."

The "smell" they're talking about is coming from a pouch hanging from Lilly's neck.

It's so putrid that I want to rip my nose off my face. It's amazing I can hold back the tears welling up behind my eyes.

"This stink bothers us, but it's like breathing poison to monsters. As long as nothing drastic happens, the smell will protect us for as long as it lasts."

Just as Lilly explained, this stink pouch called a "malboro" is the main reason why we haven't encountered any monsters for a while.

The thing really works; I'm seeing the effects with my own eyes.

No matter how powerful the monsters in the middle levels are, none of them wants anything to do with this stench.

"You got that from Nahza, if I remember right..."

"Yes, Lilly asked for her help while we were still working in the upper levels..."

Lilly had tried many times to make an item that would repel monsters but failed. So she asked for Nahza's assistance.

Nahza is very familiar with ingredients found outside of Orario. While mixing them with items from the Dungeon, she accidentally created it. Or so I heard.

"By the way, Nahza fell to the floor and rolled around after taking a test sniff."

...Apparently the smell was so bad that poor Nahza was rubbing her nose against everything, desperately trying to get the smell out. I feel sorry for her, just thinking about it—actually seeing it would have been excruciating.

At any rate, the pouch on Lilly's neck has allowed us to avoid any monster encounters. Considering our limited supplies and physical condition, I'm happy to put up with the stench.

Sure, we heard a few howls coming from farther down the tunnel a few times, but they got out of the way as soon as they were close enough to smell us.

"...!"

Ahead of us.

The lights of several glowing red eyes pierce the darkness directly in our path.

The monsters—hellhounds—have us in their sights. I can see three of them, their eyes pulsing with anticipation.

They come to a stop just out of range of the smell, about thirty meders away. I can see them thrashing their heads about, slamming their feet into the ground. They're getting ready to launch their fire attack.

Shit! I brace myself.

If we take the full brunt of their fireballs like this, we're done for. I hear Lilly's body stiffen behind me.

Risk further injury with a head-on attack? Or hit them with the Firebolt first?

Thirty meders...Can I make it up there in time? Can the hellhounds hit us at full power at this range? I don't know what to do! Suddenly—

"Looks like I gotta try...I got this."

Welf's voice came into my ears.

Huh? His right arm shoots forward the moment I look at him in confusion.

The red fabric on the sleeve of his jacket makes a loud "snap" as he extends the palm of his hand toward the hellhounds crouching in the distance.

He utters a short incantation: *"Blasphemous Burn."*

The air in front of Welf's hand instantly ripples, shock waves visible as they boom forward.

A raging torrent of flame—yet somehow silent—rushes to engulf the hellhounds that were mere seconds away from launching their own attack.

"Will-o'-the-Wisp."

Three explosions in the blink of an eye—as the hellhounds' own fire consumes them.

"Ignis Fatuus?!"

Lilly's shocked voice echoes through the tunnel.

I, too, saw the flames the monsters were about to spit at us—and the sudden explosion that followed. I'm just as wide-eyed as she is. The smoke starts to clear. All of the hellhounds are on the ground, their eyes blank.

Ignis Fatuus.

A name for an explosion that results from the inability to control your own magic.

In the Old Age before the gods came to Earth, elves and other magic users created their own spells and tried their own hands at casting Magic.

However, their bodies were at risk until their magic took physical form. It could literally blow up in their faces if they tried to force it out—something very similar to what just happened to those hellhounds.

Thanks to the gods and their Falna, people have a better chance of finding Magic that suits their ability, as well as control it, today than they did in those days. Ignis Fatuus almost never happens anymore.

The possibility of that happening to a monster is next to nothing.

"How about that, it worked..."

"W-Welf, what just happened?"

"My Magic is kind of specialized. From what I've seen, it reacts to magic power and makes it explode."

Will-o'-the-Wisp—anti-magic Magic.

When timed correctly, it can be used against Magic or elemental attacks that use magical power as a counterattack by triggering an Ignis Fatuus. The stronger the magic attack or higher the user's Magic power, the larger the explosion. It could, in a sense, seal Magic power.

As a smith who fights with weapons in close-quarters combat, this type of Magic is a perfect fit for Welf. I can see why he would want it.

"Hadn't tried it on a monster before, but...Worked by the skin of my teeth."

He looks at the surprise on my face and flashes a pained smile.

Apparently he wasn't kidding when he said this was his first time using it on a monster. There aren't any monsters on the upper levels that can breathe fire like the hellhounds. Heck, there aren't any monsters up there that can do anything close to Magic.

Then on the thirteenth floor, when we were about to get roasted, he wouldn't have known the timing for his own Magic. Better late than never.

The spell is very short, but he needs some time to prepare. I guess Welf's Magic isn't perfect.

"Wait, you said 'on a monster'...Does that mean you've used it on people?"

"Yeah. I asked one of the guys in my *Familia* to help me out. Turned into quite the show."

"...Mr. Welf, that's..."

"I know I shouldn't have tried it, but I just had to know what it did. And he knew that there was a bit of a risk, not knowing what would happen...But yeah, it was completely my fault."

Lilly's face became scarier and scarier during Welf's explanation until he finally grimaced and admitted his wrongdoing.

Just maybe, there is a reason that his fellow members of *Hephaistos Familia* don't like him other than his Crozzo blood...

But our path is clear thanks to him. We have another way to keep hellhounds at bay. That's big.

We make our way past their bodies, the monsters dying in front of us. I can hear their faint breathing, but they make no move to pursue us.

We do the same thing to the next monsters we come across.

We avoid all attacks while doing our best to endure with the smell of the pouch around Lilly's neck. I use Firebolt on anything that gets too close for comfort.

Welf takes care of the hellhounds. Now that he knows the timing and distance, any of the monsters that try to use their flaming attack become victims of his anti-magic Magic.

"Welf, here…"

"What's this? A potion?"

I pull a vial filled with a thick red liquid out of my leg holster and hand it to him.

He drinks about half before his eyes open in surprise.

"This is no magic potion. I feel lighter."

I gave him a double potion. It's another of Nahza's creations.

After walking all this way on basically one leg and casting that many spells, he had to have been hurting, but it looks like the potion does the trick.

I breathe a sigh of relief and explain it to him. A genuine smile grows on his lips for the first time in a long time.

"This is good stuff. You have to tell me where I can get more."

"Once we get back, I'll take you there as often as you like…"

I smile back at him as he gives me the rest of the potion. I down it in two gulps.

A new wave of energy passes through my body. My mind and physical strength aren't back up to full, but they're much better than before.

"…Mr. Bell, how about sharing some with Lilly?"

"Eh? We just finished it, didn't we? Don't want to waste any."

"No fair, no fair! It's no fair that only Mr. Welf got some!"

"What're you talking about?"

Finally, a relaxed conversation among party members. A little bit of the tension is gone. Being careful not to let our guard down, we let ourselves relax a bit.

Our Dungeon journey continues, me lending a shoulder to Welf and Lilly watching our backs.

We have hope as we put one foot in front of the other, until—

"There's one…"

I see a hole in the Dungeon floor as I turn a corner. It's right in the middle of the path in this tunnel.

It's almost like it was set apart from the other paths we could've taken. It's a weird-looking, uneven hole, too.

I help Welf over to the hole and we both look down. Lilly isn't far behind and confirms what both of us were thinking—it's connected to a lower floor.

Judging from its depth…probably the sixteenth floor.

We look away from the dark void and exchange glances before nodding to one another.

I put my right arm firmly around Welf's waist and my left around Lilly's backpack.

All of us take a deep breath and jump in.

A golden moon hung in the sky.

The sun completely set, a beautiful night sky spread out over Orario. Magic-stone lamps dotted the city like precious jewels glinting in the night.

The streets were filled with people enjoying one another's company, thousands of dots of light around them. And in the center of the city, a building loomed over Central Park.

A tower stood over the entrance to the Dungeon. Babel.

A certain goddess looked away from it all from the highest floor of the white tower and moved toward a door.

Tup, tup. Her shoes hit the floor as she walked. She tossed her silver hair back over her shoulders with both hands as she went. "Did I keep you waiting?"

She opened a large wooden door after traversing the long hallway. The Goddess of Beauty—Freya—was the first to offer a greeting.

The room was adorned with long bookshelves filled with many expensive and luxurious items. Her favorite attendant, Ottar, and one other god with one of his followers gathered here.

"No, not at all. Sorry for taking up your time, Lady Freya."

Hermes was sitting at a rather strange table designed to resemble an apple. He greeted her with a smile and a jubilant voice. Asfi, however, couldn't hide her nervousness.

Freya glanced at both of them before taking a seat at the table with Ottar at her side.

Each of her movements was graceful and captivating. Her black dress revealed an enormous amount of cleavage as she slid into the chair, her sizable bust swaying. The chair lightly squeaked as she leaned back, silver hair brushing against her white necklace.

Asfi was captivated by her and blushed scarlet red before averting her eyes. Although his follower had been completely taken in by the goddess's beauty, Hermes just kept on smiling in his own charming way.

The two deities sat at either side of the table with their followers standing behind them.

"So, what is it?"

Freya chose to bypass any idle chatter and get straight to the point.

She sat with her shoulders square to him, legs uncrossed with a very confident smile on her lips. Hermes's narrowed eyes opened very wide.

"As I'm sure you're already aware, Bell Cranell has yet to return from the Dungeon. Hestia and I are on our way to help him, Lady Freya."

"And?"

"So, I came here to make a request."

"Why would you bother to come to me?"

Freya's expression didn't change. Both of the gods exchanged glances and smiles.

"You protected him, Lady Freya. At the last Denatus, you protected Bell."

"..."

"He's someone worthy of the attention of someone as beautiful as yourself. So you can't blame me for being interested."

Ten days ago in this very building during the gods' Denatus meeting, Freya had indeed stuck her neck out to protect Bell. More specifically, she stopped Loki from trying to figure out why he'd grown so fast, by pointing out to the others that it was forbidden for them to investigate personal affairs.

Freya had all of the male gods present at Denatus under her spell from the beginning. Her beauty was powerful enough to keep them in a trance and doing her bidding without thinking about her motivations.

Hermes should have been one of them.

"Lady Freya, I'm crazy about you. However, I'm not so far gone that I don't notice something right under my nose."

…In other words, he had been acting.

The other male deities around him were practically falling over themselves with one look at her. All he had to do was blend in.

"Well played," she whispered as she remembered the charming god's performance.

"You're going about this much differently than usual, but I doubt anyone else has noticed."

Freya's "recruiting style" was very well known. Once she'd scouted someone she wanted, she'd make her move immediately.

Despite her usual straightforward hands-on approach, she had yet to do the same thing with Bell. The Freya that Hermes knew wouldn't have wasted time jumping through hoops.

Most likely, the other gods who had been taken in by Freya's beauty wouldn't have noticed that the boy was at the center of her sudden change in strategy.

"Fine, then," said Freya. It was pointless to try and keep up appearances given how much Hermes already knew.

She stopped trying to hide the fact that she was interested in the boy and cast her silver gaze on the deity across from her. It was her way of saying *get to the point.*

"I have no interest in playing with your toy. I just want to see with my own eyes what he can do."

Hermes assumed a serious expression as he spelled it out.

In the blink of an eye, his face changed to that of a beggar on the street.

"So please—please leave my *Familia* alone, Lady Freya?!"

"..."

Genuinely surprised by Hermes's request, Freya sat quietly for a moment before looking down on him like a pathetic worm unworthy of the dirt it was living in. She kept that expression for a long time, and it had Hermes on the verge of tears.

The two strongest *Familias* in Orario belonged to Loki and Freya. If Freya seriously decided to come after them, *Hermes Familia* would be wiped out in no time flat.

That was why Hermes was here—for insurance. Hermes was apparently very fond of his own *Familia*.

At the same time, he wasn't lying—but he wasn't telling the truth, either.

Freya could see it. She knew he wanted to more than just test the boy's power. Her eyes narrowed, her glare getting sharper and sharper...But she stopped.

This is foolish, she sighed to herself.

She realized that trying to shut Hermes down would be a waste of time.

"All right, as you wish."

Freya decided to acquiesce to his request but keep an even closer eye on him.

It was clear to her that Hermes meant no harm toward Bell.

Relief coursed through Hermes's suddenly round eyes as he sank back into his chair. "You have my thanks, Lady Freya! I owe you! If you ever need something, don't hesitate to ask! I'll stop at nothing to—"

"However."

Freya stood up, interrupting Hermes mid-sentence.

Stopping his charm in its tracks, she put her hand on his shoulder and leaned in close.

"It would be wise to remember this: The only one allowed to play with him *is me.*"

Her enchanting voice filled his ears.

Time stood still. A wave of goose bumps overtook Hermes's skin as every hair stood on end. He pulled his mouth into another smile as soon as his senses came back to him.

"Of...of course. I swear to you—"

"That's good. Be sure you do."

Hermes's face glistened with sweat as Freya stood back up with her own charming smile on her lips. She gestured toward the door with one hand and gave a short nod, as if to say, "You may leave."

Hermes cut the good-byes short and took her up on the offer. Freya watched him and his follower go out the door. Asfi had been so intimidated by Ottar's presence that she didn't speak a word as they left. Hermes, however, was laughing at himself, muttering, "Thought I was dead for a moment there..."

Clunk. The doors shut behind them.

"Is this acceptable to you?" Ottar turned to Freya once the other two were out of the room and spoke. "Despite everything he said, things may be in motion that we cannot see. This is just my opinion, but...that god is very suspicious."

Freya giggled softly to herself at Ottar's straightforward warning. "I'll deal with that when the time comes."

She left the table at the middle of the room and walked toward a massive window.

The long, rectangular glass took up most of the wall on that side. She could see the entire nightscape of the city, her feet bathed in moonlight.

"Ishtar has been keeping a close eye on me recently. I'd like to avoid any petty inquiries...If Hermes wants to do something, that's fine."

Ishtar was another goddess of beauty who had attended the last

Denatus. Freya remembered their little argument as she spoke to Ottar.

As long as she knew that Hermes wasn't going to hurt Bell, that was enough for now.

Freya took another step toward the window and looked down.

Every detail of the magnificent city sprawled out beneath her. She could see all the citizens going about their business, nothing more than grains of sand at this height. The many lights that lined the streets intermingled together like brilliant stars in the night sky.

She pulled her head back as something caught her eye.

People were gathering in Central Park.

Freya laughed to herself as she recognized the group right outside Babel's front gate.

"You're late, Hermes!"

Hestia scolded him angrily as he emerged from Babel Tower.

They had gathered in front of the tower's west gate. The curtain of night had fallen over Central Park. The place was very lively during the day, but there was almost no one here now. The pure openness of the park was terribly quiet, and what trees were there were motionless in the night air.

The search party's preparations were complete. Hestia concealed the fact that she was a deity by using a long traveler's robe and a small supporter's backpack strapped over her shoulders. In fact, she looked remarkably like the supporter Lilly. Mikoto and the rest of *Takemikazuchi Familia* were assembled and ready to leave at a moment's notice.

Hestia was tired of waiting. Hermes walked down the front steps with Asfi at his side and a grimace on his face.

"You see, I had a rather loose end that needed tying up…Was easier said than done."

His expression went blank for a moment as he looked at the tallest point of Babel Tower. Coming back to himself, he turned to Hestia and earnestly apologized for being late.

Hestia knew time was of the essence and was just about to give the order to go in.

"...Lady Hestia."

"!"

Mikoto stepped up to her side. Now Hestia noticed, too.

A mysterious person had emerged from the darkness and was walking toward the girls.

The figure was wearing a hooded cape that extended to her lower back. The front of the hood concealed a great deal of the wearer's face; only the lips were visible. Judging by the shorts, knee-high boots, and delicately feminine legs, this person was female.

A long, wooden sword was attached to a belt just under her fluttering cape. Two smaller blades ran down the sides of her thighs.

The female, equipped with adventurers' battle clothes, didn't say a word before coming to a stop in front of the group.

Mikoto moved to protect Hestia, one hand on her katana. Hermes just laughed.

"She's on our side. Strong, too. No need to worry."

Hestia sent a piercing glare in Hermes's direction before taking a look at their new supposed "ally."

A pair of sky-blue eyes emerged from beneath the hood.

With the hooded adventurer joining their search party, the group made their way into the tower.

To save Bell, Hestia and her party entered the Dungeon.

CHAPTER

3

DUNGEON
DEATH
MARCH

Ferocious roars suddenly turned to painful squeals.

The air screamed as it was torn in half by something long and sharp, followed closely by the sound of dying breaths. The wooden sword left afterimages in its wake, looking like little more than a serious practice session.

The movements were unnaturally fast, and she had moved on to the next target before the sound of the crashing impact of the first rang out. Every so often sky-blue eyes flashed from beneath the hood.

Despite being surrounded by more than ten monsters at once, she tore into them with the strength of a hurricane.

"*KYII?!*"

"*GAH—?!*"

An Al-Miraj was struck across the chest when it was too slow to respond to her advance. She sliced another in half with one of her blades, her momentum taking her through a third rabbit monster. All three of the beasts fell in less than a second.

The monsters' net formation was pointless. They weren't fast enough to protect themselves against the hooded adventurer, her cape swirling with each precise movement. Hellhounds jumped for her suddenly exposed back, saliva flying from their bared fangs. However, the hooded female spun like a top and hit their jaws from beneath with her wooden sword. The devil dogs were launched backward, their muzzles completely shattered.

"*KYUAA!*"

Two more Al-Miraj jumped into the fray. Squealing with all their might, both of them were armed with stone tomahawks, this floor's landform weapon.

The hooded adventurer saw the weapons as they were thrown straight at her. She deflected one with a quick whirl of her wooden sword—and caught the second with her bare hand. She spun again and released it without any hesitation.

The monstrous rabbit's red eyes went wide just before it took the tomahawk to the face. The sheer force of the blow launched it straight backward.

The remaining Al-Miraj stood in shock at the sudden disappearance of its ally before a dark shadow descended over it. The creature looked up just in time to see a wooden sword coming right for its face. "*KYU?!*" came its last squeak as its eyes nearly popped out of their sockets. The Al-Miraj fell silent.

"S-so strong..."

"To take on so many of them alone like that."

"W-whoa..."

Takemikazuchi Familia's Mikoto, Ouka, and Chigusa watched the battle unfold before them with bewildered eyes. They might have had different ways of expressing it, but all of them were shocked by the dominant display of strength and skill.

The search party had reached the thirteenth floor.

They had made it all the way through the upper levels in a few short hours in their quest to save Bell and had now reached the middle levels. Their pace was much faster than anyone had anticipated.

This was all thanks to the mysterious hooded adventurer.

She was eliminating monsters on her own before anyone else had a chance to act. Once known by the title "Gale Wind," the female adventurer was on a level far beyond that of Mikoto and the others—Level 4, to be exact.

Even Hermes's ace Asfi watched in awe as the hooded adventurer blazed a trail with unparalleled speed and strength through the upper levels, slaying more monsters in the process than she cared to count.

"*OOUUUUUUUUUUUUUU!!*"

The sound of something rolling at high speed, accompanied by a low roar, reached them. Sure enough, one armadillo monster, a Hard Armored, appeared farther down the tunnel.

Completely unfazed by the wrecking ball rolling her way, the hooded adventurer withdrew one of her small blades. She charged it head-on, blade sticking from the bottom of her hand. Edging out of its path at the last moment, she brought the blade straight through its body on her way by.

The monster's body kept spinning as it fell apart.

The massive rotating flesh hit a rock in the floor, sending four distinct chunks into the air to land at a stunned Mikoto's feet.

"Well, I won't complain about this being too easy. There shouldn't be a problem even in the middle levels as long as she's taking the point position...Would you look at that?"

Asfi had been enjoying the show at the front of their ranks when suddenly a few monsters emerging from the wall behind them caught her attention. *Takemikazuchi Familia* also sensed the danger and immediately moved to protect Hestia and Hermes.

"Excuse me, step this way."

"Eh?"

Ignoring the two hellhounds for the moment, Asfi grabbed Chigusa's shoulder and pulled her back.

Suddenly the ground beneath where Chigusa had been standing swelled and shifted as if a mole were tunneling underneath.

Asfi swirled her white cloak to the side and withdrew a dagger from within.

She didn't even have time to breathe before a Dungeon Worm came bursting out of the wall.

The beast didn't have a head—just a mouth lined with serrated teeth at the end of the wormlike body. It rocketed toward them with its limbless frame writhing in midair. Asfi lined up the cutting edge of her weapon with the oncoming hidden terror of the Dungeon walls and made her move. Meeting the beast head-on, her dagger cut the Dungeon Worm from mouth to tail in one swift motion.

It split clean in half in an explosion of blood. Chigusa's body froze as the pieces of the worm flew past her left and right shoulders.

"Let me handle this."

Asfi turned back toward the hellhounds, both hands now beneath her white cloak.

She had a leather belt wrapped around her thin waist. In addition to her dagger's sheath, several more holsters dangled from the belt. She pulled something from one of them.

It was two small vials filled with a moss-green liquid. Asfi threw them toward the hellhounds.

"*Gu?!*"

"*...gh...?!*"

Both vials hit their marks and exploded on contact, covering the monsters' faces with the green slime. It was sticky and strong, binding the hellhounds' mouths closed before they could unleash their fiery attack.

The monsters immediately started clawing at their mouths, trying to get the green liquid off their faces. Asfi used the opening to withdraw two spiral-shaped darts from a different holster and let them fly.

Both darts pierced the heads of their intended targets. The monsters died instantly.

"I should be more than enough to cover our back."

Mikoto and the others once again stood in disbelief as the items' wielder easily dispatched the monsters around her.

Asfi Al Andromeda.

She was a top-class adventurer belonging to *Hermes Familia*. The title she had received from the gods was "Jack-of-All-Trades, Perseus."

Known as one of the best item makers of this generation, she was one of only five people in Orario who possessed the Advanced Ability "Enigma."

"...Hermes, aren't your children an average of Level Two?"

"Ha-ha-ha, now that you mention it, I forgot to report her leveling up to the Guild!"

Hermes brushed off Hestia's questioning eyes, smiling and answering like it was no big deal. It was obvious to everyone that the girl who just took down three middle-level monsters that easily was much stronger than Level 2. Hermes knew there was no point in denying it.

While they didn't dislike the spotlight, members of *Hermes Familia* preferred to work behind the scenes, unnoticed.

It was very similar to how Hermes himself conducted business.

Hestia knew this from their days living in Tenkai, but she kept it to herself.

"...It's really dark down here."

All monsters taken care of, Hestia's words bounced off the dank walls of the thirteenth floor.

The upper levels hadn't been much of a problem for her, but the distant lights well overhead didn't provide anywhere near enough light for her to see clearly. *Do the children really come down here all the time?* she thought.

Since their basic five senses also became stronger with their Status, this small amount of light was all the adventurers needed. But to Hestia, stripped of her divine power, these Dungeon tunnels were pitch black because her eyes were less sensitive than even the weakest adventurer's. It kept her on edge. It took all the courage she had to put one foot in front of the other.

The darkness was beginning to overwhelm her. Deities were not immune from its effects. Her shallow breaths were getting more and more staggered as she moved the lamp in her right hand left and right as if frantically searching for a way out.

First the light hit the ash-colored stone walls. Then it illuminated landforms—decent-size rocks that could be broken to make tomahawks—before it flashed on a piece of broken sword. *Hm?* She focused the light in that direction only to find the bloody carcass of a hellhound staring back at her. "Eeeek!" she screamed as she jumped back in fright.

"Easy, easy," said Hermes as he caught her shoulders in his hands.

The body sprawled out on the ground was most definitely dead. However, with its magic stone still intact, the beast's body had been left to rot on the ground. The smell indicated it had been dead for nearly a day. Hestia took a deep breath and tried her best to get her racing heart under control. She looked back over her shoulder and could see Hermes forcing a grin in the dim light.

She was slightly jealous of him; he was used to these long journeys and could probably see what was going on. She puckered her cheeks in frustration before looking down at her feet and regaining her balance.

A broken sword and the bloody corpse of the monster. That meant that a clash between at least one adventurer and the monster had happened on this spot not too long ago. At the very least, they knew that the adventurer hadn't had time to remove the magic stone after the battle.

The more Hestia looked at the scene, the easier it was to picture Bell right in the thick of it. A fresh wave of anxiety overtook her.

"…Andromeda, where should we search? We could spend days going in circles down here and never find Bell's battle party," Ouka asked in a low voice as Hestia tried to clear her throat.

He was quite an intimidating man, standing more than 190 celch tall, with wide, muscular shoulders. He looked at Asfi for a moment before returning his gaze to the end of the tunnel.

"Their party was only equipped to spend one day in the Dungeon. Finding a relatively safe spot and staying there indefinitely is not an option for them…I believe something else happened to them— something that made it impossible to retreat."

"'Something else'?"

"Yes. Otherwise their actions wouldn't make sense. With only enough supplies to last a day, they would be overwhelmed in no time down here. Perhaps they fell into one of the holes?"

Mikoto's and Chigusa's eyes went wide as Asfi adjusted her glasses.

"If they did fall too far for them to come back on their own strength, what choices do they have? I highly doubt they're still wandering around in the darkness, at the mercy of any monster that happens to find them. Considering their condition as a party with limited supplies…I'd say they've already been wiped out."

She fell silent after drawing her conclusion.

"Perhaps they abandoned hope of returning to the surface and instead pressed onward to the safe point on the eighteenth floor…I believe that choice has some merit."

"…Would they even try that? That would take some serious guts."

Those who'd experienced the terrors of the Dungeon firsthand knew how dangerous it was to set foot into a lower level with no idea what to expect. If Bell's party fell into one of the holes, they would have been forced into that situation.

Ouka couldn't believe his ears as Asfi offered another possibility.

"In their position, I would go."

A voice as delicate as the tinkling of a bell rang out.

The hooded adventurer had been silent up until now.

Ouka and the other adventurers turned to face her in surprise. She was a good deal ahead of them but somehow within earshot.

"And knowing them—knowing *him*, someone who's already overcome one adventure, I think he would go forward without looking back."

Her soft, refined voice once again filled the tunnel. However, the hooded adventurer didn't say another word.

Asfi looked at the mysterious adventurer's half-hidden face for a moment before turning to her god. "Lord Hermes, what is your opinion?" she asked.

"I agree with your reasoning, Asfi."

"Um, me too…I have a feeling that…Bell is below us…"

Standing next to Hermes, Hestia brought her hands together and thought as she spoke.

Even though she had a direct connection with Bell through her Blessing, that didn't mean that she could tell exactly where he was at any time. However, the bond they shared was stronger than any human relationship, and she could feel the source of their bond coming from beneath her feet.

She nodded to herself slowly as her twin ponytails reached out in different directions, as if searching for him. It didn't take long for both of them to point straight down.

"That's four in favor…That settles it. We'll set a course for the eighteenth floor."

Asfi made the decision for the whole group. Mikoto, Ouka, and Chigusa weren't given the opportunity to speak. Forming a line, they set off to find the path to the lower levels.

The order of their formation didn't change. The hooded adventurer stayed in front with Asfi in the back protecting Hestia and Hermes. Their front line was strong enough to once again blaze a path littered with slain monsters and lead everyone else forward without much need for the other adventurers to draw their weapons.

Armed with spears and shields provided by their supporter, Chigusa, Ouka, and Mikoto were able to protect one another from the occasional sneak attack. With the addition of Asfi's range, their formation had no holes.

"To think a party new to the middle levels would choose to go to the eighteenth floor..."

"Yes, it appears that they're able to make rational decisions under pressure."

Mikoto and Asfi's conversation echoed through the last bit of tunnel before the party emerged into a much wider room.

They had seen many like it before: a large, dome-shaped room with rocky walls. However, this one had a bizarrely shaped hole in the floor with stairs leading down inside of it.

It connected with the level below.

"The usual way is all well and good, but wouldn't it be faster if we went through the holes as well?"

"No, Lady Hestia. The holes in these tunnels open and close on their own, each time making a new path. There's no way to predict where we'd end up if we went in. We would be unable to determine our location...then the searchers would need a search party."

"And we can't ignore the possibility that Bell and his party might still be trying to come up. We might accidentally pass them by. The normal path is our best option."

If they were trying to return to the surface...they would have to use the stairwells that led up as guidance. If they stayed on this path and Bell's battle party were coming up, they could meet halfway. *Hermes Familia*'s reasoning to stay on the main path was flawless.

Hestia nodded in agreement, seeing their point. The hooded adventurer walked over to the hole.

Hestia and the others made their way to the next level, following her fluttering cape as she descended first.

Like a bowstring pulled too far back, they were close to their breaking point.

The tension mounted.

"The stink pouch has run out..." said Lilly with a nervous tremor in her voice.

For Welf, those words didn't just snap the bowstring in his mind. They shattered it.

They were at the end of the tunnel on the sixteenth floor. Welf and the others had been advancing in hopes of finding another hole leading to a lower floor. They came to a stop in the middle of the path. They didn't have much choice.

The air was heavy, their breathing hot. The pressure was immeasurable.

The smell that was keeping them safe from monster attacks had faded away. A bloodthirsty aura had taken its place.

The three of them were no more than sitting ducks. Welf had never experienced this kind of intensity. His ears were so focused on every little sound that something as simple as a step forward blurred his vision. He was far beyond his limit. He had to clench his teeth to keep from passing out under the strain.

Bell's body, the only thing keeping him upright, was also extremely hot. *Snap!* His heart jumped again as Lilly pulled the pouch off her neck and dropped it to the ground.

All of their eyes were focused farther down the tunnel.

They knew that something lurked in the darkness. Every heartbeat sent a shiver down their spines, palms clammy with sweat. Whatever was shrouded in the darkness had an aura so strong that its very presence was torture.

This ain't happening! Seriously, what the hell! Cut me some slack— Welf's mind had reached its breaking point.

Don't know, I don't fucking know! Who the hell survives long enough to be this unlucky?! His thoughts were stuck in a loop. He wanted to ask someone, anyone, if it was really possible for monsters to kill someone without touching them.

Finally—*Thud! Thud!*

The ground shook as new sounds emerged from the black void.

The guillotine was walking toward them. They were the prisoners sentenced to death in this nightmare.

This. This. This is…

Alarm bells were erupting in Welf's head. He grabbed the hilt of his broadsword as if it were his last line of defense. His grip was so fierce that his knuckles turned instantly white.

He squinted his eyes, forcing the muscles in his face to tense up as he tried to see into the darkness. At last, the bright spots in the ceiling burning like torches finally revealed a rusty red body, clear as day.

Its short, violent breaths were accented by each step of its powerful hooves. The lights above accented its burgeoning muscles in stark shadows.

The monster that appeared before Welf had magnificent horns on its head, sticking out like beacons of death.

"—"

The head of a bull on the body of a man.

Standing two meders tall and built like a stone wall.

It held a stone battle-ax, yet another natural weapon, with both hands in front of its face. Its eyes were looking down either side of the blade at its prey.

Welf was so overwhelmed by his first encounter with a Minotaur that he forgot to breathe.

"*UWWOOOOOOOOHHHHHHHHHHHHHHHHHHHHHH!!*"

There was no way to defend.

His will was breaking. First to go was his will to fight, then his ability to face the enemy, then his instincts.

A devastating howl.

It was intimidating enough to bind any living thing's mind and body with fear. Taking the full brunt of the category Level 2 Minotaur's howl, Level 1 Welf was completely defenseless against his own paralyzing fear. He froze in place, his hand still collapsed to the hilt of his sword.

Seeing its opportunity, the Minotaur struck the ground with a mighty hoof and jumped toward him, its massive battle-ax raised high above its head.

Welf could see his own terror reflected in the beast's eyes.

—Death.

Welf accepted his fate; this monster would be his executioner.

A second later—*Slip!*

"?!"

Everything Welf could see was suddenly sideways.

The shoulder that had kept him standing was gone.

Lilly quickly ran up to catch him as he lost his balance. Planting his good knee firmly on the ground, Welf raised his head.

There was a pair of shoulders running toward the beast.

"OOWWWWOOOOOOOOO!!"

The white-haired boy powered through the Minotaur's howl head-on.

Charging forward like a thunderbolt. Swiftly like a rabbit.

Welf's eyes opened as wide as they would go, but before his shaking throat could make a sound—

There was a great flash before him.

"WOOH?!"

The attack hit its mark. The monster's ax fell to the ground with a dull thud.

The boy standing in front of the staggering, bleeding Minotaur with a black knife in his right hand and a crimson dagger in his left—wasn't finished.

He shot forward, blades glinting in the light.

"—*AAaaaaa?!*"

A countless number of lines crisscrossed the Minotaur's entire body.

Violet, then crimson, and then violet again. Each color flashed as the white-haired boy unleashed his fury. He was holding both of his blades backhand as he tore into the creature. It couldn't even cry out in pain under the onslaught.

Lilly and Welf knew one thing as they watched the carnage unfold in front of their eyes:

Bell had snapped.

He charged a powerful enemy without any hesitation. Faster than anything they had ever seen him do—*too* fast. Welf and Lilly couldn't follow the storm of blades he was unleashing. Not giving the Minotaur a chance to counterattack, Bell kept piling on the damage with direct hits to its body.

A continuous barrage that not even eyes could capture.

Extreme speed coupled with swift movements: "Rabbit Rush."

One final flash as Bell cut through the gut of the Minotaur for the last time. Its body falling apart as it took one step back, the beast let out a soft "*Ooooooo*" as it expired and hit the ground.

It was silent and still.

"…!"

Welf and Lilly looked on with awestruck eyes as Bell picked up the battle-ax that the Minotaur dropped and took a defensive stance. They followed his gaze back into the dark void of the tunnel only to see three more Minotaurs emerge.

Their howls combined in a chorus of terror that left everyone speechless. Even Bell had no hope of taking on three of them at once.

But he didn't run away. Suddenly—*ping, ping.*

The tunnel filled with a soft ringing sound like a chime, as little white sparkles surrounded Bell's hands.

—*That's…*

Welf had seen those sparkles before. Those memories suddenly came flooding back to him at the same time that the Minotaurs all charged forward at once.

The attack required ten seconds to build up enough power. Bell braced himself to swing the ax as soon as the attack was ready.

The countdown hit zero. The Minotaurs that had been bearing down on him with horns at the ready took a direct hit.

"—!!"

The tunnel was inundated with a bright light.

It was absolutely blinding. Light seemed to explode from the ax as it stopped the beasts in their tracks, before vaporizing them with a thunderous boom. The explosion took pieces of the tunnel with it.

The aftermath was very similar to the time when Bell had used the same technique to defeat an infant dragon not too long ago. Cracks covered the burned walls like a spiderweb of electricity had torn through the tunnel, floor burned and singed. The path in front of them was littered with smoldering pieces of rock.

At about the time that the last of the smoke and haze cleared...

What was left of the battle-ax fell to the ground in pieces.

Their enemies were gone.

"..."

Welf and Lilly didn't move, just silently stood there unable to speak.

Bell had his back toward them, shoulders rising and falling with each shallow breath.

He had defeated four Minotaurs in a row.

It was an accomplishment that went beyond his Level or skill and put his technique and strategy on display.

That was when Welf understood that all those rumors about the boy defeating a Minotaur weren't just idle gossip.

—*Minotaur Slayer.*

Welf gulped down the air left in his throat, his eyes locked on the boy's back.

"I think it's about time you told me what you're up to, Hermes," said Hestia in a quiet but sharp voice.

The search party pressed forward in the dim light. Hestia matched Hermes's pace while aiming the lamp in her hand all over the place. First toward Ouka and Mikoto, then back toward Chigusa, lighting up all of their faces in turn.

Then she cast the light under Hermes's chin, casting dark shadows across his face.

"How do you mean?"

"The real reason why you want to help Bell."

The search party's current formation was designed to protect the deities in the middle. The hooded adventurer led the way with Ouka and Mikoto on either side of Hestia and Hermes; Chigusa was behind them as Asfi kept an eye on their tail.

Making sure everyone was far enough away not to be overheard, Hestia got in close to Hermes's side.

"Hey, hey, didn't I already tell you? When a buddy of mine's in trouble, it's only natural I help them out!"

"Enough with the act. We've already come this far, what's the point of keeping it up? I want the truth, Hermes."

Hestia pressed hard for answers. Even the blue in her eyes turned a shade more serious than usual.

Seeing the stout resolve in her eyes, Hermes decided it was pointless to resist and flashed a weak smile. "All right then, Hestia."

His already narrow eyes squinted even more narrowly. The corners of his mouth quirked up as he started to speak.

"The reason that I cut my trip so short this time was to do someone a favor."

"A favor…?"

"Yes. That certain someone wanted me to check up on Bell."

This favor was the reason that Takemikazuchi had been so suspicious of Hermes in the first place.

Careful to keep her voice low, Hestia pried even further.

"And who is this mysterious someone?"

"The man who raised Bell. His words, not mine."

This was someone she'd heard about many times—this faceless person who often came up in conversations with Bell. His grandfather.

But according to Bell, his grandfather had already…

"…Bell's grandfather passed away, did he not?"

Hermes leaned down so that he could speak softly into Hestia's ear. "Something unavoidable came up, something that he had to keep secret from his precious little grandson. So he faked his own death and has been in hiding ever since."

She already knew quite a bit about this person from Bell, causing her face to contort as mixed emotions started bubbling up from within her.

"So anyway, he's been keeping a low profile after leaving Bell behind…You see, Bell's title and the fact he's the new record holder were announced at the last Denatos, right? He happened to be sipping tea at the time that he overheard that information. Made for quite the mess, I hear."

Hermes looked like he was thoroughly enjoying himself as he continued his story.

"As you would expect, being a father figure, he wanted to know what his boy was up to. But he couldn't go himself. I just happened to be there and made myself available. I go in and out of Orario all the time, so I was perfect. Isn't that simple?" said Hermes as he extended his finger into the air.

A group of monsters had suddenly appeared in front of their party, and the hooded adventurer moved to engage. The other adventurers quickly snapped to attention to protect from sneak attacks while a one-sided slaughter took place in front of them.

The search party came to a stop. Hestia had been quiet up to this point. Ignoring the sounds of combat, she asked Hermes in a subdued voice:

"So who's the god using you as their errand-boy? There's no way it's—"

"Oh, did I ever say that this person was a god? This was just between you and me, and I'd be grateful if you keep it that way."

Hermes forced a very unnatural smirk.

Although Hestia wasn't thrilled that Hermes dodged the question, she could sense no deceit in his voice. She came to the same conclusion as a certain goddess of beauty had—that he had no intention of harming Bell.

And if his favor story was true, he'd be in a rough spot if Bell didn't make it out of this alive.

"…I understand your situation. However, that doesn't tell me why you're down here. There's no need for you to come this far to check on him. You'd have an unlimited number of chances on the surface, wouldn't you? I have no idea why you're in the Dungeon, Hermes."

Maybe it was because Hermes wasn't at all intimidated by Hestia, or maybe because he wanted to see her reaction, but he told her the truth. However, there is a difference between telling the truth and revealing how deep the truth goes.

Just how far are you willing to go? she thought to herself as she looked into Hermes's unnaturally perfect eyes.

"It's true that I was asked, but I, too, am interested in Bell."

Hermes smiled.

But it wasn't his usual charming smile. It was a softer expression, one that a deity normally wouldn't show.

"I want to see with my own two eyes what he's capable of, Hestia."

The god's orange pupils seemed to sparkle in the darkness as he once again leaned down to Hestia's height.

Then he whispered in her ear.

"I need to know if he possesses what this era requires of him."

Another round of fierce explosions.

A whole pack of hellhounds falls to the ground in a shower of sparks and plumes of smoke. I don't know how many times I've seen it by now—Welf's anti-magic Magic. He still has his hand out, kind of floating in the air in front of us.

His rasping, exhausted breaths are right next to my ear.

"—"

"?! Welf!"

Plop. His neck goes limp, head hitting my shoulder. His body goes slack in an instant. All of his weight suddenly comes down on my shoulder. Bending my knees, I fix my grip and prevent him from falling over.

His face falls in front of mine as I fight to regain balance. Welf's eyes are closed, his face absolutely drenched in sweat.

Mind Down...!

We've depended on him too much. Mental power, or Mind, is required to use Magic. Welf has used so much of it that his body can't take the mental strain anymore. Tears well up in my eyes as I look at his listless body hanging over my shoulder.

All the magic potions and double potions we had are long gone. We can't help Welf.

"…ah."

I hear a long, weak breath behind me just before the sound of something falling over.

I turn my head around just in time to see Lilly's eyes roll into the back of her head as she falls headfirst onto the gravel path.

"Lilly…"

I take a step in her direction. Just like Welf, she's out cold.

The combination of anxiety and fatigue—a new kind of stress we never experienced in the upper levels—must have worn her down.

She's been passing her healing items to us, never taking any for herself. Her Status is the lowest of anyone in our party. She probably ran out of strength a long time ago and has been willing her body forward until now.

"…!"

The only sound left in the tunnel is my own breathing. Suddenly everything looks darker and more terrifying than before.

But it's just my imagination. The Dungeon hasn't changed at all.

This is just, for sure…some kind of symbolism, seeing my fear come to life.

There's no one left to help me. I have to face the terrors of the Dungeon alone. All of this darkness and despair surrounding me is all in my head.

I can hear my heart pounding in my chest. Suddenly the air feels cold. My eyes fly open, scanning the tunnel.

"…!!"

I clench my jaw so hard that my teeth feel like they're going to shatter.

I grab ahold of Lilly's outstretched hand and pull Welf closer.

I have to overcome this fear. I have to confront it head-on before it crushes what little courage I have left.

I don't have enough time to be scared. Move forward. Stand.

All of us are getting out of this alive…!

"Forgive me…!"

Welf's broadsword, Lilly's backpack—they'll just slow me down.

I throw away anything heavy, leaving them with only the most basic equipment, and pick them both up. I get Welf situated over my right shoulder and hold Lilly's small body under my left arm.

Leaving most of our party's equipment behind, I move forward again.

"Gah, uwaa…!"

Welf's arms dangle in front of me, swinging back and forth like a pendulum.

It goes without saying that unconscious people are heavy. But I can carry them, keep moving. It's all thanks to my Status, but I can move forward with the weight of two people in my arms.

Breathe in and out, lift one foot, push off the ground.

I can hear Welf's metal greaves, the armor on his lower legs, clack together with every step I take.

I have to find a hole before any more monsters show up…!

If the monster attacks now, it's over.

Wouldn't be much of a fight, wiped out before I could even move. I can't protect them, and escape would be next to impossible.

A tsunami of cold sweat runs down my body as my muscles scream out in pain. I can't think about that right now. I need to focus all of my strength on pressing forward.

"!"

There's one.

Another tunnel intersects this one, making a four-way intersection. The path to the right ends in about ten meders. But I can just make out an opening in the dim light at the very back of it.

Taking a quick look around to make sure no monsters are waiting to ambush us, I hurry over to the hole.

I step on the lip of the hole and take a look down. Then I take a deep breath and jump.

"—Uff?!"

Air whistles past my ears before a hard impact.

I miss the landing. My feet hit at a bad angle and I lose my grip on Lilly and Welf. Both of them roll forward, their unconscious bodies sprawled out on the cold floor.

Throbbing pain floods my body. I force my shoulders up and crawl over to them. The cool pieces of gravel that were stuck to my face fall off as I go. I can hear them hitting the floor around me.

Finally arriving next to my friends, I grab their bodies and climb to my feet in the darkness. Then I take my first step on the seventeenth floor.

My body...it's too heavy...

My arms and legs feel like they're made of lead.

There's something really strange going on. I've been at my physical limits for a long time now, but this is far beyond anything I've felt before.

There's only one reason I can think of.

"Heroic Desire, Argonaut."

It's this skill that gave me the strength to finish off those Minotaur. I felt like something had been pulled out of me as soon as I launched that charged attack. Like all of my Mind and physical strength had been totally sucked dry.

Of course, an attack that powerful wouldn't come without some kind of price. Doing my best to ignore the side effects of Argonaut, my brain desperately urges my body forward.

"Hanh, hahh..."

How long have I been down here? I lost track of time a long time ago. A full day? It could be longer for all I know. I've never wanted to see the sun so badly in my life.

I'm pretty sure the seventeenth floor is a shade darker than the higher floors. Haven't seen any monsters yet, so I concentrate on my breathing, my chin tight.

Come on knees, bend!

They're screaming out in pain.

My ears are ringing, practically begging to be released from this grueling trek.

I'm trapped, alone in the darkness, searching for an exit I can't see. And even if I find it, is there a light at the end of this tunnel? Is there any hope left?

Part of me wants to give in, give it all up right now.

It's so appealing. Just give up and embrace the end.

"Give me…a break…!!"

I adjust my grip on my friends. Even though the words came out of my mouth, it feels like Welf said them.

I'm the only one left. If I give up now, they die too. My friendship with them is the only thing keeping me going down here at the edge of hell.

Slowly, I make my way through the stagnant air. Every sound, every echo seems to summon the scythe-wielding spirit of Death himself. I can feel him reaching for the back of my neck, fingers brushing against me many times.

I realize something while being pushed this far to the brink:

I'll die the moment those fingers overtake me.

Just like so many adventurers before me who never made it home from the Dungeon.

The tunnels are…converging…

The rock walls seem to open up in front of me, wide enough for large groups of adventurers to easily pass through. The massive tunnel didn't bend or fork, so it was kind of like walking inside a giant snake. The ceiling is extremely high; little beads of light no bigger than candle flames are the only things I can see.

I decide to go toward the wider end of the tunnel. It should lead to the deepest part of the seventeenth floor.

Lilly told me when we decided to go to the eighteenth to look for the widest tunnels, and I'm going to do just that.

The Dungeon is quiet.

…Why?

The seventeenth floor is *too quiet.*

I have no answer. Every little sound seems to echo forever. The pieces of rock that get kicked out of the way roll into the darkness, the sounds of their tumble quietly fading away.

There are no monsters here.

I could feel them around me before, but this place feels empty. It's completely unnatural, going this far in the Dungeon without a single encounter.

It's like they're waiting for something—no, they're afraid of something that's about to *be born*.

The monsters are hiding, staying as quiet as possible.

A cold shiver runs up my spine.

I've got a bad feeling about this.

But I can't stop now.

Reasoning manages to overpower my instincts and drive my feet faster toward the end of the tunnel. The jockey is whipping his horse, pushing onward. The silence is my window of safety. I can still make it through.

I enter a wide-open tunnel area that seems to be designed for an absolute behemoth kind of monster. I rush toward the other side, nearly losing my balance more than a few times as I try to look around.

Then:

"…!"

I made it across.

And into a very wide, very tall room.

The shape of this room is completely different from all the other random and haphazard designs I've seen so far in the middle levels.

The large, circular entrance leads to a rectangular room that has to be at least 200 meders long. This place is even bigger than the Dungeon Pantry. I think it's about a hundred meders wide, the ceiling a good twenty meders over my head.

The walls and ceiling are made of many different-size rocks piled on top of one another—with the exception of the one to my left.

Completely smooth, it looks like someone or something built it with their own hands. I can't believe my eyes. Whoever this massive artisan was, their flat wall ran from one corner of the room all the way to the back. It's overwhelming.

There's a strange kind of beauty to it, but it feels so unnatural. It doesn't belong here.

"The Great Wall of Sorrows…!"

This place—it floods you with a feeling of bewilderment before suddenly vanishing.

It has left so many adventurers with such an empty feeling of

despair that the ones who made it back alive from the seventeenth floor seeing it gave the wall that name.

It's a Dungeon wall that only bears a certain type of monster—the wall of the king.

I gulp down the air stuck in my throat and tear my eyes away from the wall. I have to make my way through.

There aren't any monsters in here. The wall is looming over my left side as I travel deeper into the room, struggling to regain control of my beating heart. I take another look at Welf and Lilly, tightening my grip. Their eyes are closed, bodies limp and helpless.

We can still make it.

We can still make it through here without any problems.

I can see the exit, the entrance to a small cave at the end of the room. If I can just get there—

I brokenly laugh at myself—such a one-track mind—as I set a course for the exit.

Crack!

"—"

I heard it.

That sound.

My head whips to the left.

There it is, right in front of me. My eyes shoot open.

A massive crack runs down the wall from top to bottom like a massive lightning bolt.

"...!!"

My mind goes blank, but my feet speed up.

Holding Welf and Lilly even tighter, I lift my heavy legs as fast as I can.

I'm not even halfway through. The exit is far, too far away. I'm moving as fast as I can but I'm covering no distance. What is going on?!

Crack! Crack! Even more lightning bolts run down the Dungeon wall, deafening echoes filling the room. Pain and fear wash over me as each one hits my ears. The entire room is shaking. A sudden avalanche of wall fragments slams into the Dungeon floor, splitting my eardrums.

This is all building up to one critical point. That's when I feel it—the loudest impact yet.

A deafening explosion.

I can't breathe.

There's a moment of stillness, pieces of the broken wall falling to the ground, a few relatively soft echoes. The wall behind me has been completely destroyed.

Boom.

Something huge has come out of the hole, shaking the room with its first step.

"......"

I stop moving. It feels like invisible strings have latched onto me.

No, stop—don't look!

But my body doesn't listen to reason. My neck seems to twist on its own as it guides my eyes over my left shoulder.

Before I know it I'm facing the beast, my ears ringing in pain.

"......"

I can see it emerging from a large cloud of dust.

It's too big to be real. Thick neck, shoulders, arms, legs. It looks almost human. It's hard to tell in the darkness, but its skin looks grayish brown.

It has greasy black hair coming from the back of its head that's long enough to reach its shoulder blades.

There's one thing I can say with absolute certainty: Of all the living things I have ever seen, this creature is by far the largest.

—This thing.

My entire body shudders.

This isn't the same traumatizing fear that overtook me that day against the Minotaur.

This is awe. The human reaction to realizing the existence of a different scale of power.

The disparity between its existence and mine.

—This is a floor boss.

It's a giant standing more than seven meders tall.

Monster Rex—Goliath.

© Suzuhito Yasuda

"—*Oooo.*"

The dust is clearing more and more every second. Then one of its red eyes—the size of a human head—moves.

My tiny body is reflected in its huge eye. Its whole body turns to face me as the room shakes beneath its feet.

A new flame ignites within me.

My body suddenly free from paralysis, time moves once again.

"*OWOOOOOOOOOOOOOOOOOOOOOOOOOOOOOOOOOOOOOOO OOOOOOOOOOOOOOOOOOOOOOOOOOOOOO!!*"

I take off.

Every fiber of my being wants to be anywhere but here.

The Goliath's piercing roar chases me down the room. The floor jumps beneath me every time the beast takes a step. My ears are overwhelmed by the explosive echoes swirling throughout the area.

Just run. Just run. Just run.

I can feel its murderous eyes lock onto me. Once again I'm being chased by Death himself. Terror drives out any feelings of fatigue or exhaustion. The only two things on my mind are keeping ahold of my friends and getting to that exit tunnel.

The walls of the room rush past me as I make a mad dash forward. The entrance to the eighteenth floor seems to bounce in front of my eyes. But above all else, unfortunately, the giant's steps are getting closer.

Run, run, run, runrunrunrunrunrun!

I let out a scream at the same time the Goliath fills the space with another howl.

A great gust of wind comes from behind me. I get the feeling something is raised far above me, like two hands making one giant fist. An attack powerful enough to pulverize everything is coming in fast.

Even faster, even bigger, one second faster, one step more.

I put every last ounce of strength I have into one kick off the ground.

A desperate dive, an attempt to escape.

I pass through the entrance to the tunnel.

"OOOOOOOOOOOOOOOOOOOOOOOOOOOOOOOOOOOO OOOOO!!"

The brute force of the attack.

The moment I reach the relative safety of the tunnel, a powerful shock wave overtakes me from behind—the brunt of the explosion.

"Gahhh?!"

I'm launched higher into the air.

The immensely powerful wind picks me up and throws me like nothing more than a human-shaped feather.

Then suddenly from behind—*BANG!*

My body slams into the tunnel wall, but my momentum keeps me going.

Another impact, and another as I tumble down the narrow path.

"Geh, uah, gahhh—?!"

Ceiling, floor, and wall zip by, my body bouncing like a little ball.

My eyes spinning, pain mounting from all the impacts, I lose my grip on Lilly and Welf. The three of us tumble together farther and farther down the tunnel.

My mind is in a haze, waves of pain erupting from more places than I could count. Through it all, I get the general feeling that we're going down.

Deeper and deeper into the tunnel, our bodies bloody and broken, until finally—

"Uh—?!"

Whoosh.

Our bodies are practically thrown out of what is most likely the tunnel exit.

We hit the ground at full force and slide to a stop.

I'm on my stomach, and I don't have anywhere near enough energy to move a muscle. I don't think I can even raise my head a single celch.

Everything around me is sideways and tinted red.

Every celch of my body is screaming in pain. I must be in pretty bad shape. The wounds on my cheeks are open again, my head covered in fresh blood.

But I land on something soft, maybe...grass?

Everything around me is bathed in a warm light. What's going on? I have no idea.

"..."

Fssshhh. Is that the sound of leaves rustling in the breeze? Where are my friends?

Lilly and Welf are...here. Both are still breathing. The three of us fell together, side by side the whole way.

I feel my consciousness slipping, but not yet. I can't give in yet!

Not until the two of them, Lilly and Welf...Have to help them. Heal them, fast.

Move, move! I scream at my stone-cold body...Wait, is that someone coming?

"...!"

Shf, shf. That's the sound of footsteps on grass; they're close.

They're right in front of me, looking down on me, their shadow over me.

That moment—my body jolts into action.

Gashi! My right arm rockets forward and grabs ahold of a thin leg.

I can feel the boot shake in my grasp as I weakly raise my head and try to speak.

"Please, save my friends...!"

Like trying to break free, pleading with my very soul.

My eyes shift up to look at my savior.

Shapes blur together into one form with long golden hair.

Everything goes dark.

CHAPTER 4

DUNGEON RESORT?

The first thing I feel is a heaviness, like my body is weighed down.

I don't know how long I've been here. My arms and legs feel like dirt and I keep flowing in and out of consciousness. After a long time fighting the sense of nothingness that comes with a deep slumber, I finally break through.

Everything's all blurry.

I blink a few times to clear my vision. My mind is still blank.

I see...fabric. Probably the inside of a tent.

I'm on my back, looking up at the ceiling.

Just as I start looking around the area—my eyes fly open as the memories flood my brain.

"Lilly, Welf?!"

Our desperate search through the middle levels, the Goliath's appearance, the eighteenth floor. Everything came back at once.

Adrenaline starts pumping through my veins. I don't know what happened; I need to find out.

All of my muscles fire to help me sit up. A fresh wave of pain washes over me a second later.

"_____?!"

I curl into a little ball.

I think it was a scream that came out of my throat. No, the scream came from my entire body.

It feels like every hit I've taken, every cut, scrape, and bruise I've received since entering the thirteenth floor cries out all at once. I'm in tatters; all the abuse has really taken its toll.

I'm writhing in so much pain that I might pass out again.

"Are you okay?"

—Once again, my eyes open.

That beautiful voice came from right beside me. I lay there for a moment, unable to believe my ears before lifting my head.

The first thing I see is a wall of white fabric, probably part of the tent. Then the long, golden hair of an adventurer sitting right next to me comes into view.

"Eh, huh, whaa…?!"

"…Are you all right?"

Her eyebrows furrow in concern as she speaks with that beautiful voice.

A-Aiz…Aiz Wallenstein…?!

I'm not hallucinating! It's actually her!

Why is she here?! I silently scream as my last memories before passing out come back to me.

Long, beautiful golden hair reflected in my cloudy eyes.

I gulp down the air in my throat. The person I begged for help was…Aiz?

I, I grabbed her leg…?! A new firestorm whips up within me as I clench my shaking fist.

"W-why are you here…?!"

"Returning from our expedition…We stopped on the eighteenth…"

Aiz's group, *Loki Familia*, must've come back from trying to explore previously unknown levels deep in the Dungeon. So that means they're resting here at the safe point, level eighteen.

They left on their expedition almost two weeks ago…Considering what Lilly said earlier, we must've just crossed paths.

That was my train of thought as I lay there, marveling at her beauty.

"…! My friends! Are they—?!"

Lilly! My shoulders shake once my brain connects the dots.

—Are they okay?! I'm about to ask as my body flings forward on its own.

My elbows leave the ground, my body straight up.

It feels like something's pushing me from behind. I can't even blink. Suddenly all the pain I was in doesn't matter. My sense of urgency cancels it all out. That doesn't mean my muscles can take it.

I can't balance. The floor is rushing up to my face.

Aiz rises to her knees beside me and holds out both of her arms. *Pwff.*

"..."

"..."

She catches both of my shoulders in her hands. My face, however, is buried deep in her chest.

I can feel her golden hair on my nose.

Her metallic breastplate feels cool on my cheeks. It caught my fall.

I-I'm so glad it was a breastplate and not————there's no time for that kind of thinking?!

"S-sorry!"

My body launches itself away from her faster than the Goliath blasted me down the tunnel.

My face burning red, I get away from her chest as fast as possible. Ignoring the excruciating pain, I bend away to put some distance between us.

My body moves almost like it's a reflex. Losing my balance again, I hit the back of my head on the ground, and stars dance in front of my eyes. To add insult to injury, I yelp in agony in front of Aiz and grasp the back of my neck.

Shame and pain course through my body when...*Swish*. My hair brushes against something.

"Ah...Welf."

He was fast asleep under thick covers right where I fell. Putting up with the pain, I force my body up again and take a good look around. Lilly is next to him on the other side.

I can feel the tension leave my shoulders as I look at their sleeping faces. Finally, relief.

"They are both okay...Riveria and the others healed them."

Upon closer inspection, Welf's right leg and Lilly's numerous injuries have been treated. I don't think our rescuers did anything fancy, but both Welf's and Lilly's wounds have been carefully wrapped in bandages.

"They had taken a lot of damage...but you were in very bad shape..."

Only after she says that do I notice that my head is also wrapped in bandages. She parts my bangs with her fingers and slowly strokes my head.

My cheeks flush pink as I feel her fingertips run through my hair.

And then: "Any pain?" She tilts her head to the side as she asks. That is the final blow.

My whole body turns red.

"T-thank you very much…for saving us, really…"

Somehow I manage to force my body away from her gentle hands and express my gratitude.

Aiz sets her hands in her lap and shakes her head from side to side. "It's nothing," she says with a small smile. I don't know why, but I feel really happy right now.

Then she looks at me with her golden eyes and asks what our plans are from here on out.

She slowly moves her head to look toward the exit of the tent.

"Can you move?"

"Umm…Y-yes."

"Finn told me…Our commander told me to contact him. Come with me, would you?"

Aiz stands up as I give her a sharp nod.

I quickly climb to my feet. She offers her hand to help me up, but I can't afford to embarrass myself even more. Trying to display some amount of manliness, I respectfully decline. There's a new shot of pain…*owwww*…

Focusing completely on my teetering legs, I finally stand straight up. Every muscle in my body is complaining, but I can handle it. I follow Aiz through the exit as she lifts the fabric door out of the way.

"Whoa…?!"

A huge campsite comes into view.

We're surrounded by trees, but the forest isn't that dense here. Tents have been pitched all around us. All of them are facing in toward a central area. Large cargo boxes are sitting on top of tree roots throughout the camp.

Dwarves, animal people, elves…A surprising amount of them are women. Another group of adventurers, a mix of demi-humans, has a very serious air about them. But some are just talking, almost relaxing with one another. Two animal people are sitting beside each other in the grass. A dwarf and an elf, one leaning against a tree with his arms crossed while the other uses her hands to make gestures as she talks...Their armor and weapons show signs of fierce battles, and yet still sparkle. Whoever made their equipment was extremely good at what they do.

A party of adventurers from what could be called the strongest *Familia* in Orario...I can feel the aura of strength radiating from all of them. My body is instinctively trying to pull away.

The members of *Loki Familia* start to notice us.

But they look right past Aiz and straight to me. They don't seem all that happy to see me. Then again, it's only natural, looking at it from their point of view...But what is it...They're looking at me like some kind of enemy. Aiz tilts her head.

A bead of cold sweat rolls down my neck as something occurrs to me. Is it because Aiz has been taking care of me? I'm mulling that spot over as Aiz starts walking. I almost trip trying to keep up.

A barrage of inquisitive looks keeps coming as I move forward. *Yet, this is a forest,* I say to myself as I look at the dim canopy above, trying not to catch the eyes of anyone else. The leaves and branches create a kind of dome canopy over our heads.

However, *sunlight* flashes through the openings.

It feels warm on my face. To top it all off, I think I can see blue through the leaves.

This is the Dungeon. No sunlight ever makes it down here—so why is there shade and a blue sky? I'm so confused.

Is there really a blue sky and warm sun on the other side of those leaves?

"What's wrong?"

"Ah, it's...um, well..."

Aiz must've sensed my bewilderment because she turned to face me.

My confused brain tries to think of how to respond. In the end I can't control my curiosity so I ask her a question.

"This is the eighteenth floor…of the Dungeon, right? Why is it so bright…?"

I look at the sky as I speak. Eina never mentioned anything about this—I bet she'd never thought I'd come this far on my first day in the middle levels—so I'm completely clueless. Aiz follows my gaze, her thin chin rising.

"…Should we take a detour?"

She looks at me again and I clumsily nod.

We turn off our original route and leave the camp area. This part of the forest, completely untouched by humans, spreads out even wider as the canopy towers above us. I don't know why, but I feel like a weight is coming off my shoulders.

I follow her swishing gold hair for a few minutes before the scenery takes my breath away.

Crystals.

Clear and sparkling, they're absolutely gorgeous.

Some of them are really small, no bigger than my foot. But there are some that are large enough that I could stand inside them. A giant could use one of these things as a dagger. Crystals of all shapes and sizes dot the landscape.

My head is on a swivel. The crystals seem to be sprouting in small groups, tall, thin crystals emitting azure light. The entire forest is silently illuminated by their glow. The forest floor is covered in little blue fragments, along with a good amount of moss and tree roots.

It's a mystifying, wondrous sight.

It's impossible not to stand and stare.

The sound of flowing water fills my ears. A small river runs through this forest. Members of *Loki Familia* are drawing water from it. An elf notices Aiz and waves.

It's said that the elves' homeland is somewhere deep in a forest.

Even though I've never seen it myself, I had a feeling it would look a lot like this.

"Ah…"

The forest opens up.

Aiz keeps walking forward, toward a semicircular arch-like exit to the forest bathed in white light. I cover my eyes as they adjust to this new, brighter path.

I blink a few times as everything comes into focus.

"...Amazing."

A wild frontier opens up in front of me.

The first thing my eyes take in is the expansive great plain. My vision is filled with a rich green that I've never seen on the surface. The small shadows moving about are probably monsters. Even here, crystals are scattered throughout the landscape.

There is a pond on my left...On second thought, it's big enough to call it a lake. The perfectly smooth surface is an amazingly pure blue. There are some large rocks—no, islands—sticking out of the middle of it.

The forest spreads out to my right. It's a lot larger than I thought. And then right in front of me, I can clearly see a towering tree jutting out of the middle of the plains.

My eyes follow its massive trunk up and up until...

I happen to catch a glimpse of the ceiling.

"...Ah, aren't those?"

"Yes, all crystals."

Aiz was nice enough to answer my unfinished question.

Just as she said, the entire ceiling of this level is covered in a sheet of crystals.

They go from corner to corner and all the way around, like a field of blooming flowers looking down from above. They are divided into two colors: The big ones in the center are white and remind me of the sun; the ones surrounding them are blue like the sky.

There is no blue sky in the Dungeon.

All the crystals above us make it look like there is.

"The light from the crystals disappears after a while...That's when night comes."

My eyes peel back in surprise.

According to Aiz, the amount of light changes the same way all the time. Right now it's the "afternoon." Apparently it's not matched up with the real sky, though...

It's almost like the Dungeon prepared this by looking outside, I think to myself as I look at the blue crystals.

"…"

The safe point, level eighteen.

A world full of nature and crystals far below the surface.

It has another name: Under Resort.

Plains and a lake, complete with a blue sky. I stand next to Aiz and take it all in.

Back at the campsite in the middle of the forest, there's a tent a bit bigger than the others.

A flag bearing *Loki Familia*'s emblem hangs inside.

And now I'm standing in front of some of the most famous adventurers in Orario.

"Aiz told me about your situation…but I didn't think you had already been carried into our camp."

The person speaking to me has blond hair, very similar to Aiz's golden locks. His eyes are a deep blue, the same color as a lake. Right now, he's doing his best to force a smile.

Just standing in front of this grimacing prum boy is making every hair on my body stand on end.

No, it's not just him. There are two incredibly strong demi-humans behind each of his shoulders. I steal a few glances in their direction, but I avoid eye contact at all costs.

"Oh-ho, this that adventurer you were talking about, Riveria?"

"Indeed, Galess. This is Bell Cranell."

A dwarf built like a stone fortress and a very refined elf. I can feel their gazes; just by listening to their conversation I know they're appraising me, judging me. It's making me even more nervous.

The prum Finn Deimne is *Loki Familia*'s highest-ranking adventurer and field general. The strong, wise dwarf elder is Galess Landrock. And Orario's most powerful magic user is the elfess Riveria Ljos Alf.

The three of them are all top class and are practically the face of Orario's adventurers.

"Th-th-thank you for everything you have done. I-I-I can't thank you enough...!"

I just became an upper-class adventurer myself. But looking at these three—and Aiz as well—there's no doubt they are in a league of their own, far above me.

I'm doing my best to express my gratitude, body low and head down. But for whatever reason I get the feeling that my pathetic stuttering and weakness are only annoying them. Even Aiz, standing right next to me, is looking at me funny.

The skin on my body is red enough to rival the salamander wool covering it.

"Don't be so tense, take it easy. We're all adventurers, aren't we? It's at times like these that we have to help each other out," says Finn Deimne as he stretches his shoulders. "And considering that you're a friend of Aiz's, we can't exactly turn you away. She'd hold a grudge worse than you can imagine. If we didn't do everything in our power to help, none of us would be able to sleep at night."

There's a tinge of humor in his voice. I'm so nervous that I almost miss it. A smile grows on my lips before I know it. Every fiber of my being is telling me to keep my distance from them, but the air feels lighter somehow.

Aiz flashes him a look. I think it meant something like "don't say anything weird." All the tension in the room suddenly leaves. The atmosphere in here is almost comical.

Mr. Finn smiles at me like a boy his age actually would. All my nerves have settled down.

"I believe I understand exactly what happened, but could I hear it in your own words? I'll tell you about our situation, too. Think of it as an exchange of information."

"Ah, sure."

This boy has very good people skills. I feel very comfortable telling him everything. It must come from experience. I nod and start talking.

From the thirteenth through the eighteenth, I spare no detail in my explanation.

"Ga-ha-ha! All the way ta the eighteenth on yer first day! Finn, Riveria, ya were right! This youngster's quite interesting!"

"Galess, this is not a private conversation. Please hold your tongue."

The elf Riveria shoots a one-eyed glare as a warning to the laughing dwarf, Galess.

Actually, I told them that coming down to the eighteenth floor was Lilly's idea…but the dwarf warrior didn't pay attention. Instead, he kept praising me, saying things like, "Got some shifty feet, there, laddie! Escapin' from the floor boss like that!" I can't help but smile back at him.

"As for us, we're taking a rest here. Usually we pass right through the eighteenth floor and straight up to the surface when returning from an expedition…but this time we encountered some monsters with particularly potent venom."

Mr. Finn goes on to say that a good deal of *Loki Familia*'s adventurers, excluding the higher-level ones like Aiz, are infected. Many of them can't move on their own.

Since they were returning from an expedition…meaning that their stock of healing items was very low, they had no way to heal everyone. It was impossible for them to keep moving as a group.

"We sent Bete, the fastest member of our *Familia*, up to the surface to gather some antidotes. With any luck he'll be back tomorrow, but in any case we're stuck here until he arrives."

Apparently he set off to collect the healing items just before we arrived on the eighteenth floor.

We must've just missed him because we used the holes instead of taking the regular path.

"We're very low on supplies, especially food. We'll give you all we can spare, but please understand it's not much."

"N-no, we'll be extremely grateful for anything at all!"

Considering the fact they've already given us a tent to use even though so many of their members are suffering from venom, they've already treated us extremely well. We have no right to complain.

"It's just for a short while, so we will treat you as guests for the time being. As long as you don't try to stir up trouble, you can use that tent for as long as we're here. I'll let everyone know myself."

"…Really, I'm so grateful for everything…Thank you very much."

I thank him, filling my words with as much gratitude as possible.

"You owe us one," Mr. Finn says with a light smile. I say a few more thank-yous as Aiz and I leave the tent.

"Are you sure, Finn?"

Riveria asked Finn a question after Bell left the tent.

Her emerald-green hair swished around her shoulders as she looked down toward the short general.

"It is true that Aiz has taken a liking to him…Plus, there is a member of *Hephaistos Familia* in Bell's party."

"You are certain of this?"

"Yes. One of the smiths told me."

High Smiths belonging to *Hephaistos Familia* had joined this expedition alongside *Loki Familia*. One of the smiths had informed Finn that he recognized Welf when the young man was carried into the camp.

"Goddess Hephaistos doesn't consider any of her followers to be more important than another, yes? I'd hate to get on her bad side just because we refused to help one of them."

"Logical," nodded Riveria with a satisfied look on her face.

Finn swiveled his eyes up to meet her gaze.

"The icing on the cake is that you are interested in Bell Cranell as well, aren't you, Riveria? Aiz has taken an interest in him, so how could you not?"

"…I will not deny that."

"Ga-ha-ha! Look at you, Riveria! Bein' all motherly!"

"No teasing, Galess," she replied, looking somewhat annoyed.

The large dwarf's hearty laughter continued all the same.

"It's good for her to show interest and initiative…Personally, I think this is an opportunity for her. But what about your perspective as the leader of our *Familia*? It's highly likely that the reason that Aiz left home early before this expedition was to meet with Bell Cranell."

Finn, like Riveria, had noticed strange changes in her behavior before the expedition, such as asking how to issue commands to adventurers. They could see the effect that Bell's early-morning training sessions had on the girl.

"Hmm, I think that it would be good for Aiz to change as well… But for now, let's keep Loki in the dark about this."

"Oi, Finn! Ya should challenge Bell Cranell ta a wrestlin' match! It's a style of fightin' Loki was talkin' about. And this geezer would very much like to know how strong he is."

"Hmm…no."

Finn explained that as the leaders of the group, there was no room for carelessness. They could unknowingly put the white rabbit of a boy who was following Aiz around camp in danger.

"In any case, there shouldn't be any problems. Bell Cranell doesn't seem like the kind of human who would go looking for a fight. We'll keep an eye on him for the time being," said Finn, casting his eyes back toward the exit of the tent.

I follow Aiz back to the main camp after meeting with Mr. Finn and the others.

If I had to guess, I'd say there's more than ten white tents set up in the forest. I'm sure there are people suffering from poison inside each of them. Healthy adventurers stand guard outside each tent.

The light filtering down through the branches and leaves from the canopy above is soft. Leaves rustle in the trees above us, but we're not the only ones out and about right now.

"Aiz, good afternoon."

"Good afternoon…"

Members of *Loki Familia* greet Aiz as they walk past.

That's right, she's one of their leaders…

Forgetting something that important sends a twinge to my body. I belong to a different *Familia*, and yet here I am walking with her like this. No wonder I've been getting all these strange looks.

As proof, "welcoming" is the last word I would use to describe their attitude toward me. Men and women either look at me like I'm some kind of criminal or stare at me with very serious eyes.

An elf who just walked by, probably a magic user, didn't stop glaring at me until she passed. I'm scared...!

I'd be overpowered in an instant if I tangled with any of them. They're higher level than me, for sure. And I'm sure they aren't exactly happy I'm walking around their campsite like this.

"Level eighteen..."

"Huh?"

Aiz suddenly speaks with her back to me.

I look up and see that she's looking over her shoulder at me, her face in profile.

"You've...already made it to level eighteen..."

"Eh, umm...Just like I told Mr. Finn, you see, one thing led to another and we just kind of ended up here...We weren't planning on it, though, and we a-almost died!"

I trip over my words as I try to respond and scratch my bandaged cheek.

Aiz spins on her heel to face me, as if she isn't satisfied with such a weak answer.

"Did slaying that Minotaur make you Level Two?"

She's not blinking at all. Her golden stare is rather intimidating, so I nod.

She stays like that for a moment before twisting her body like she's trying to get a look at my back.

Then: *shuffle, shuffle.* She moves to my side. I do my best to shrink away, and break out in a cold sweat.

...Is she trying to look at my Status?

I don't know why I'm getting that impression but once again, *shuffle, shuffle.* She moves once more. So do I. *Shuffle, shuffle*, step, step, *shuffle, shuffle*, step, step. What is going on?

Other members of her *Familia* are watching us. The white-haired boy glistening with sweat and the airheaded Aiz—it must look like we're doing some kind of footwork practice…Out of nowhere:

"Wow—it's really Argonaut!"

A very energetic voice reaches my ears.

Sure, I wasn't expecting anyone to speak up, but it was what she called me that makes my heart skip a beat.

I quickly spin around to face the owner of the voice and see two girls with wheat-colored skin coming up to me.

"Tiona, Tione…"

"You've been busy, Aiz. I hear you've already talked to Finn?"

"I heard you'd been carried in, but you're awake, too! You're one lucky guy, Argonaut!"

Aiz called these two Tiona and Tione…twins, maybe? One has shorter black hair just long enough to cover her ears; the other's is the same color and extends halfway down her back. Their clothes are different, but their faces are almost identical. Their height, too.

Based on how much tan skin is showing, it'd be a safe bet to say they're Amazons. The long-haired one talks to Aiz first, while the one with short hair comes right up to me…However.

She's called me "Argonaut" twice. That's the same name as my Skill. Blood is tearing through my veins.

She knows?! My mind is racing. I open and close my mouth, trying to speak, but nothing comes out. On my third or fourth attempt, words finally emerge.

"A-Argonaut? How do you mean…?"

"Ahh, don't mind her. It's just a name this blockhead came up with to call you."

"All of us saw you fight that Minotaur! And watching you reminded me of this fairy tale I used to love when I was a kid. So, yeah, you were incredible!"

Somehow, my battle with the Minotaur on the ninth floor reminded her of the legend of Argonaut. I take a deep breath and feel the relief wash over me. It wasn't my Skill, but this girl's free-spirited personality that led her to dub me Argonaut. An adventurer's Status, put some

-

l Skills are his lifeline. They're best kept

rselves.

above my

ling.

begin.

onaut is Tiona Hyrute and the long-haired

a minute. The Amazonian Hyrute sisters?

s adventurers just like Aiz?

face-to-face or knew their first names,

o figure it out.

means you've reached Level Two, am

e down a Minotaur on your own, but

"

s from blue

al progres-

g to me that

ile, but to be honest, I can't focus on

ard the wide expanses of healthy,

s nothing to

aceful faces.

or a little bit,

bric wrapped around her chest. Her

her knees, but her stomach is com-

ne's attire looks like little more than

That is to say, there's no safe place to

r Lilly starts

r large breasts sway as she moves or

own…

f overwhelming.

s who are more than likely a few years

ld pass out at any moment.

ound. Know-

weight off m

much as I felt it.

ound the camp with their eyes on us—

m?"

doesn't r

ace in an instant.

n my friends?!"

rong w

, "Ah, there he goes," while I make my

I nearly fall several times as I dash like a madman to [ ] distance between the girls and me.

The forest is getting darker.

The "sunlight" coming down through the many leaves [ ] head is getting dimmer…The light from the crystals is fa[ ]

"Afternoon" in the Dungeon is over. "Night" is about t[ ]

It really is getting dark…

I take a look outside the tent.

There is no red twilight between the two; the "sky" goe[ ] to black. While it does feel a little strange that the natu[ ] sion outside it doesn't exist down here, it's still amazing night can fall in the Dungeon.

I leave the tent entrance and go back inside.

Lilly and Welf are still sleeping. Even though there i[ ] do, I feel like I'm taking care of them as I look at their pe[ ]

The campsite gets livelier as time passes. I space out f[ ] but they're probably making dinner right now.

"Hnnn…"

Welf's body moves. At the same time, the blanket ov[ ] shifting little by little.

Another wave of relief flows through my body.

"…Where are we?"

"Mr. Bell…?"

Both of them slowly blink their eyes as they look a[ ] ing that both of them are alive takes the last bit of [ ] shoulders, and I can finally breathe easy.

I talk to them, my voice loose and calm.

"Lilly, Welf, are you two okay? Do you know who I [ ]

"…Lilly doesn't think there will be a day when she [ ] nize Mr. Bell's face."

"Ah…Li'l E's just as sassy as ever, I hear. Nothin' [ ] Heya, Bell."

A smile works its way across Lilly's lips as Welf responds like his usual self.

I grin from ear to ear and wait for both of them to wake up completely.

They're both a little bit woozy after opening their eyes, but once their heads are clear enough they sit up on their own. They stay on the ground, blankets covering their legs as I explain everything that's happened.

First, that we made it safely to the eighteenth floor. Next, that *Loki Familia* is taking care of us.

I try to be as simple and precise as possible. Both of them sit quietly, staring at me until I finish. Then...they apologize.

"Lilly's so very sorry, Mr. Bell..."

"Held you back there, didn't I...Sorry, man."

"I-it's not like that at all!"

Both of them fall silent as words come pouring out of my mouth.

I sound almost angry as I unleash everything all at once. If Lilly hadn't been there, we would've wandered aimlessly around the Dungeon for who knows how long. If Welf hadn't been there, the hellhounds would've roasted us alive.

Lilly's and Welf's eyes seem to shrink away as they quietly listen to my tirade.

"It's thanks to the two of you, thanks to all of us...that we're here right now, that we survived."

"...Well said."

"We would've died if one of us wasn't here. Lilly agrees."

Their confidence seems to be coming back. Their faces transform from grimaces into actual smiles.

At the same time, I feel a little bit embarrassed about my outburst.

A moment later, all three of us wrinkle our faces as we laugh with one another.

"...Dinner's ready. Are you okay?"

"Ah, yes!"

I jump to my feet in response to a voice coming from outside the tent. Aiz pokes her head in.

Lilly's and Welf's jaws drop as the Kenki appears in front of their very eyes.

"Th-thank you, really. Sharing food with us and all…"

"It's nothing…Can you come outside?"

I freeze for a moment. I've got a bad feeling about going out there, but they've done so much to help us, so…it would be rude not to say hi, wouldn't it?

I look back at Lilly and Welf and use my eyes to ask them if it's okay. Both of them nod.

They climb to their feet and all of us follow Aiz out of the tent and toward the camp.

"Hey, Bell. How do you know the Kenki?"

"Umm…It's a long story."

"Mr. Bell. Please tell Lilly all about it sometime soon."

I'm lending my shoulder to Welf once again and Lilly is smiling beside me, but it's a little frightening.

That story is one embarrassing moment after another, so I'd rather not tell her if I can help it…

The three of us force an empty laugh as we keep up with Aiz.

Lilly and Welf start looking around and taking everything in. We reach the center of camp in no time.

"Humph, it's them…"

A large number of people are sitting in a circle in the open space at the center of their campsite. A few specialized magic-stone lamps are set up in the middle. Bright and flickering, they look almost like flames. If I remember right, this design is called a "campfire."

This big circle isn't just made up of *Loki Familia* members. *Hephaistos Familia*'s High Smiths are here, too. Aiz explains what is going on as Welf recognizes someone in the circle and groans.

"H-hello there……"

All eyes are on us. We make our way to an empty spot and take a seat.

The moment my rear touches ground, *plop*, Aiz sits down on my right. Lilly takes a seat on my left and Welf on the other side of her. We've naturally sat down according to rank…which is kind of scary.

I've sat next to Aiz before, during our morning training sessions…

but it still feels like there's a lot of distance between my idol and me. I don't know if it'll ever go away.

I sneak a peek in her direction. However, she notices right away and makes eye contact. Her golden hair is silky and shiny, like she's just taken a bath. Come to think of it, the air around her smells like a pure hot spring.

"Something wrong?"

"...N-no! Everything's fine!"

I can feel my face heating up, so I break off eye contact before my face starts burning red.

"Everyone, please listen. As I've told many of you, we are hosting some guests tonight. All of them courageously risked their lives to save one another, and managed to safely arrive on the eighteenth floor. I won't ask you to be friendly with them. However, I would like you to respect them as fellow adventurers while they're with us... Now then, let's have a fresh start."

"Wow, he's really good at this..."

Mr. Finn walks to the center of the circle and addresses everyone. He appeals to everyone's pride as adventurers to help avoid arguments and fights. Sounds like Lilly is really impressed by his approach.

At long last, the food arrives. Two or three fruits to a person.

They're red fruits, shaped like gourds. The amber-colored flesh inside looks sweet...I've never seen anything like this on the surface. They must grow here on the eighteenth floor. I carefully take a bite out of the fruit that looks like cotton dipped in honey. No wonder it's been named the "honey cloud."

My mouth is instantly filled with a thick, sweet juice—and I almost spit it out.

It's sweet—much too sweet. I'm not all that good with sweet stuff to begin with, but this is making me tear up. I feel like I'm gonna die! Doing my best to swallow, I take a look around. The female members of *Loki Familia* seem to be enjoying it. Just one bite and their faces melt, their hands on their cheeks. I can tell that shivers are running down their spines.

"Mr. Bell, Mr. Bell? Lilly would be happy to finish that for you, if you don't like it?"

"S-sure. Here…"

"Oh, okay—Ahhhh."

"All right, Bell. Leave it to me, I'll finish it for you…Whew, you were right, way too sweet."

Lilly shifts in front of me and perches like a bird with her mouth open, like she wants me to feed her. But before I can put the rest of the fruit in her mouth, Welf snatches it out of my hand and wolfs the whole thing down in one bite.

Lilly's fuming mad, her face beet red and a little vein popping out of her forehead as she kicks Welf over and over in the shin. He doesn't seem to notice, though, because he's pounding his chest as if the fruit is stuck in his throat.

Aiz watches the events unfold, completely speechless.

"But yeah, I've heard stories about this place…Not the usual Dungeon floor, is it?" The fruit must've passed through, since Welf is taking in the scenery.

All of the white crystals on the ceiling have gone dark, meaning only the larger blue ones are producing any light. The entire forest is covered in a dark blue shadow. A "night sky" not much different from the one outside the Dungeon is on the other side of the leaves above us.

Everyone in the circle around us is illuminated by the orange and bronze light emitted by the campfire-style magic-stone lamps. They're all eating, drinking, and chatting with one another. They look like they're having a great time, their shadows dancing on the trees behind them as several throw their heads back in laughter at the same time. This whole scene looks like a picture out of the tales I used to read—a group of adventurers having a meal together, deep in a forest under a full moon.

Mr. Finn, Ms. Riveria, and Mr. Galess are being served by other party members—more of those red gourd sugar bombs, by the looks of it. I don't know if it's because they're almost finished with their expedition, but the members of *Loki Familia* don't look anxious at all.

I can see that they do have a few people surrounding the camp as lookouts, but everyone else looks like they're on vacation.

"Exotic fruit, a sky...There's supposed to be a town here, too, right?"

"Eh...A t-town?!"

That's a word I wasn't expecting to hear.

A "sky" being this far underground was hard enough to swallow, but an actual town in the Dungeon...

I turn to Aiz without thinking. She looks up from her plate of nutrition cubes and quickly nods.

"...Tomorrow, shall we go?"

"Yes, please!"

I don't think I've nodded my head up and down faster in my life.

This is so exciting! I try to picture this Dungeon Town in my head. What would the buildings look like? What would people do there...? So many questions race through my head. *This must be one of the charms of being an adventurer!* I say to myself as my enthusiasm reaches yet another level.

My face must be beaming right now. Aiz looks at me from the side...I think she's smiling.

"Hiya, Mr. Argonaut!"

I know exactly who it is even before I look up to see Miss Tiona walking this way.

Her older sister Miss Tione is just a few steps behind. The Amazonian twins came right up to me earlier. *Swoop.* They sit down on either side of me.

"What?"

"You *must* tell us your story. Think of it as paying us back for the food and lodging. You wouldn't mind, would you?"

"Please, please!"

Lilly gawked at Miss Tione as she forced her way between us. Aiz just tilted her head to the side as Miss Tiona wiggled her way in. All the breath leaves my body as their skin brushes against me, my body sandwiched between them. My face must be the color of raw meat by now.

Lilly looks pissed, her eyebrows standing on end. Miss Tiona's face appears on my right. She looks really happy and excited for some reason. Then she asks me a question.

"How did you get all of your basic abilities to 'S'?"

My face tries to hide behind my skull.

Muscles kind of twitch their way into a smile as I look to my left. Miss Tione is giggling, her eyes narrowed. The message I get from that look is, *you're not getting away until you talk*.

A new round of questions erupts in my mind: How long ago was my Status exposed? How does she know what my basic abilities were? More and more pop up every second. My heart shakes inside my chest and it won't settle down.

And if I answer her honestly…Would she be satisfied if I bluntly say "effort"? All I did was try to pursue my goal, my idol.

As for said idol, she's sitting with her arms wrapped around her knees and not doing much. However, I can tell that her ears are on high alert…My idol can be cruel sometimes.

Mr. Finn and Ms. Riveria are enjoying the forest view a little ways away, but they do nothing to intervene. Mr. Galess is staring right at me, stroking his beard and taking in every word.

Welf is my last hope. "What, Welfy-boy? You miss us so much that you follow us down here like a lost puppy? How sweet of you." He's surrounded by *Hephaistos Familia*'s smiths.

"Hey, enough! Get lost!" He sounds really angry. Lilly's still fuming, glaring at the Amazon twins and even me.

I'm completely isolated.

Rivers of cold sweat flow out of my skin. I would give anything to pass out right now.

"—GUnuAHH?!"

It comes out of the blue.

"?!"

I know that voice better than anyone, but this is the last place I should hear it.

Lilly and I immediately look at each other. She knows, too. We both firmly nod.

"Excuse me, please, let me through!"

I don't wait for any of them to answer and jump to my feet.

I take off with Lilly right behind me and Welf not too far behind her.

I run headlong in the direction of the sound. The forest quickly opens up. I can see a massive cliff in front of me and the entrance to a circular cave at its base. That's the tunnel that connects the seventeenth and eighteenth floors, for sure.

Loki Familia's lookouts are already gathering at the scene. I squeeze my way past their shoulders and see—

"Owwwww...?! No one ever told me the monsters got that big?!"

"Ah-ha-ha-ha-ha! I thought I was a goner!"

The goddess is on all fours, gasping for breath.

I feel my eyelids pull open. There's also a male deity sitting on the ground next to my goddess, as well as a number of adventurers trying to catch their breath—a girl wearing glasses looks absolutely exhausted.

They must've just barely escaped the floor boss, just like us. I recognize the fear in their eyes.

"...Ah."

The group starts to notice me and the goddess raises her head. She looks around until, *zing*! Her eyes lock onto me.

Her soft blue eyes grow rounder and rounder by the moment. Without warning, she lunges forward, tripping as she tries to run toward me.

"—Bell!!"

"Ouff?!"

The lookouts step aside as she rushes forward. The goddess leaves her feet and comes crashing headfirst into my stomach.

Unfortunately, I was flat-footed and not prepared for the impact. I fall and land hard on my back.

"Bell, Bell! Are you the real one?!"

"G-godeshh...?!"

She's straddling my stomach, patting my arms and legs vigorously until she reaches my face. Grabbing my cheeks, she pulls my face into many different shapes. I reach up and somehow manage to get her to let go.

I'm about to ask why she's here as I prop myself up on my elbows, but she wraps both of her arms around my neck so tight that I can't get the words out, and presses her body against mine.

"…?!"

My eyes are opened wide, skin bright red.

I feel like I'm being squeezed by many soft pillows. I can almost hear the air being pushed out from between our bodies.

The goddess completely embraces me, nestling her head underneath my chin. Hot breath on my neck, all of her weight on my shoulders, and I have no idea what to do.

I try to say something, but what? I open my mouth and close it again more than a few times, when suddenly I hear:

"…Thank heavens."

I can feel her soft voice on my skin.

My nerves calm down, tension draining from my shoulders.

The goddess's body is shaking like a small child's. Her thin arms pull me up and closer to her. I hear something wet coming from around my neck.

There's no need to ask why she's here anymore.

She was worried and put herself at risk to come and find me.

I take a look at one of her black ponytails that's brushing against the side of my face.

Our bodies and minds feel very close, and even our breathing has aligned. The warmth of her body makes me feel like something irreplaceable is being replenished.

Should I hold her? I sit there thinking about it for a moment and start to raise my hands…That's when I notice we have an audience.

They've been here the whole time, quietly watching.

My body goes stiff as a board again as embarrassment floods my system.

My hands are off the ground but not yet around the goddess. With nowhere to go, they just kind of float there.

"Please get ahold of yourself, Lady Hestia."

"Hey! Don't go ruining our beautiful reunion! Gah! Lemme go!"

Lilly has ahold of the collar of the goddess's robe. She does her best to resist, but the prum has a Status. Lilly's stronger. A little girl is pulling another little girl as the latter's arms and legs flail around trying to escape.

Free of the goddess's embrace, I watch the two of them with a bead of sweat rolling down my cheek.

"Mr. Cranell, are you injured?"

"Eh…L-Lyu?!"

An adventurer wearing a hooded cape comes over and kneels next to where I'm sitting on the ground.

Not only do I recognize that voice, but I can make out two sky-blue eyes partially hidden beneath the hood.

There's no mistake. It's the beautiful elf waitress who works at The Benevolent Mistress.

"Lyu, too? Why…?"

"A certain deity was rather insistent I accept a quest. He wanted me to join the search party to find you."

She shifts her light-blue gaze.

I follow her line of sight to the god who was next to the goddess a moment ago.

He's just sitting there, orange hair shifting as he looks around. Slapping the floor a few times with his hands, the deity stands up.

"Okay, I've got a good idea what's going on."

He looks at Aiz and other members of *Loki Familia* in turn, giving each a hearty smile.

Then he notices me looking at him.

He comes over, face still locked in that charming smile.

"So you're Bell Cranell, eh?"

"Y-yes."

I can feel his narrow orange eyes sweeping over me.

My body won't move, mouth won't open. His eyes meet mine and narrow.

"Ahhh…I've been looking for you."

His eyes seemed to smile after he said that.

"The name's Hermes. Nice to make your acquaintance."

"Lord...Hermes?"

"That's me, Bell."

He sticks out his hand without breaking eye contact as I do my best to respond.

It's quite the first impression, this charming smile and handshake. He seems like a friendly deity.

"L-Lord Hermes, if you don't mind my asking, um..."

"The reason I would come this far to help someone I'd never met?"

"Y-yes."

"You see, Hestia is an old friend of mine, so of course I'm going to help her out. She wanted to find you, so naturally I did, too."

He glances over to the spot where the goddess and Lilly are having a rather spirited conversation and chuckles to himself.

Once he looks back at me I bow my head and say, "Th-thank you very much, sir."

It's probably thanks to him that the goddess was able to make it this deep into the Dungeon. I've got a feeling he pulled a few strings to make it happen.

"It's not me you should be thanking, it's them. It's thanks to the hooded adventurer and those children over there that we managed to get this far."

He gestures toward a small group of adventurers still standing at the entrance to the tunnel.

One is a young woman with aqua-blue hair and silver glasses. The other three wear matching armor—probably members of the same *Familia*...

"...Hey, Bell."

I notice them even before Welf points them out.

Those people are—

I've seen those bluish purple eyes. They were filled with tears on level thirteen.

They're the main reason why we're on the eighteenth floor right now...The adventurers who led a swarm of monsters straight into us.

There is a shining emblem on all of their armor: a sword sticking out of the earth.

"—Our deepest and most sincere apologies."

Back in the tent provided by *Loki Familia*.

We've come back here after meeting up with the group led by my goddess.

Lyu, Lord Hermes, and his follower, the girl named Asfi, didn't come with us.

The girl in front of me has her knees, the palms of her hands, and her forehead pressed to the floor in apology.

"Whoa..." The goddess and I take a step back at the overwhelming, almost divine power of her stance.

So this is *Takemikazuchi Familia*'s ultimate technique: the dogeza bow...!

"...All the apologies in the world won't be enough for Lilly to forgive you. We almost died."

"Yeah, this isn't about to go away with a few words."

Lilly and Welf, however, aren't fazed by the full-body bow. They stand tall and speak with a serious edge to their voices. It's a little intimidating, to tell the truth.

Ouka and Chigusa stand behind their straitlaced ally Mikoto, not sure what to do. The girl on the floor raises her head to meet Lilly's eyes. She keeps eye contact as she raises her body into a kneeling position.

"Um, you see, really...We are very sorry..."

"Your anger is justified. You are free to berate us to your heart's content."

The shy Chigusa stuttered as she spoke, her eyes hidden by her bangs. Mikoto, on the other hand, spoke clearly and with great remorse.

Passing off monsters to other adventurers in the Dungeon is normal. So much so, in fact, that many adventurers consider it a necessary tactic for survival. No one expects it to happen to them...but as long as there is no malice to it, all adventurers are expected to accept that they could be on the receiving end of a pass parade at some point. At least that's what I've heard.

However, in our case, coming so close to the line between life and death because of their stunt has left a sour taste in my friends' mouths. Even the goddess crosses her arms and lets out a long "Hmmmm" as the drama unfolds before her.

"I was the one who gave the order. Even now, I believe it was the correct choice."

Said Ouka as his towering frame steps in front of Mikoto.

I gaze in awe at him for a moment. He doesn't shake or quiver at all, a mountain in the middle of the tent.

More than likely…Ouka had carefully considered and weighed all the options. He chose the lives of his friends over the lives of complete strangers.

He was prepared to face this kind of outcome the moment he gave the order, all for the sake of his allies.

I don't know if it's right or wrong…but he made the decision for the sake of his party.

"…You've got some nerve saying that to our faces, big guy."

Welf steps in front of Ouka and squares his shoulders. It wouldn't be an exaggeration to say that the look in his eyes might kill a weaker man.

It feels like a ticking time bomb in here. Everyone's glaring at one another, sizing them up for a fight. But I'm kind of caught in a no-man's-land, looking back and forth at everyone.

*Something bad is going to happen…*I have to find a way to defuse the situation, fast—

"Hello again, everybody. We're back. *Loki Familia* was very understanding of our situation."

So that's where Lord Hermes and Asfi disappeared to. They were getting permission to stay at the camp from Mr. Finn and the other leaders.

"My, my…What's going on in here, Hestia?"

"Oh, you know. This and that."

My goddess's summary is a little bit too brief, but Hermes seems to be satisfied with it and puts on a smile larger than I thought possible.

"No need to think so hard about this! Look at it this way: Mikoto here owes you a big favor. At the same time, you want a chance to atone—am I right?"

"Of course we do..."

"Think about it, Lilly. Should the time come, you can have them bend over backward to help you out of a sticky situation. Doesn't that sound good?"

"...If the time comes."

Lord Hermes moves away from Lilly and Mikoto's staring contest and turns his attention to Welf and Ouka.

"Welf. Sure, this group in front of you got you into one heck of a mess, but they came down here because they wanted to help you. My presence had nothing to do with it."

...A heavy silence falls.

"...I'll play nice. But don't think you've been forgiven."

"Yes...That's fine."

Ouka doesn't look particularly happy, either. Welf steps away and returns to my side.

All of a sudden, the gathering storm clouds have vanished. It might not be anything special for a deity like Lord Hermes...but seeing him effortlessly clear the air like that, I can't help but be impressed.

"Now then, what are the plans from here on out?"

Lord Hermes smiles again and opens his arms as if nothing were wrong in the first place. The rest of us just had all of the anger sucked out of our bodies in one fell swoop; we weren't going to say no.

Lord Hermes gestured toward Asfi. The girl looks a little perplexed but comes forward anyway.

"First of all, concerning our return to the surface...We will leave this floor once *Loki Familia* slays the Goliath. It's in our best interest to avoid danger."

All of us nod in agreement.

"*Loki Familia* will move out two days from now at the earliest."

"Which means we have a whole day to kill…Since we're already down here, why don't we do a little sightseeing on the eighteenth floor?"

Looks like everyone likes Lord Hermes's suggestion.

This may be a safe point in the Dungeon where no monsters are born, but it's still the Dungeon. We decide to stick together as a group. Considering that Aiz had promised to take me to the town tomorrow, we agree that that's where we would go.

Our planning session ends rather quickly. Now all that's left is to get some sleep.

"Oh, that's right. Welf."

"What is it, Lady Hestia?"

The ladies had claimed the right to sleep inside the tent, so the men were on their way outside to keep watch and find a comfortable place to lie down when Welf was pulled aside.

The goddess also calls over Chigusa and receives a long, weapon-like thing wrapped in white cloth from her.

"This is something Hephaistos was holding on to. She also had this to say. Let me see…'Stop compromising allies for your pride'… or something like that."

"…"

Welf falls silent as he takes the weapon from the goddess and quietly walks outside.

"Welf?"

"…It's nothing. Don't worry about it," he responds to me, but he never takes his eyes off the cloth-covered thing in his hands.

"Night" on the eighteenth floor has ended. It's "morning" now.

Loki Familia was nice enough to give us some food for breakfast. Aiz leads us toward the town, just as she promised she would. Miss Tiona and Miss Tione must've had some free time as well because they're coming with us.

…Lyu's not here.

I wonder why. We talked briefly yesterday, but she never came to the tent. Lord Hermes did say that she had something she needed to take care of and not to worry, but it feels strange. I follow Aiz out of the camp with Lyu on my mind.

The town has a lake view…or rather it was built on the main island in the middle of the lake. We move out of the forest covering the southern part of the eighteenth floor toward the lake in the west.

"Um, Goddess…"

"Hm? What is it, Bell?"

"Something about you seems different since you got here yesterday…"

Aiz and the others have gone ahead. The goddess is right next to me, so I ask her a question.

It had been bugging me for a while, but now is the first chance I had to ask. "Ahh," she responds and grins back at me. "All gods and goddesses have a special aura. I'm concealing mine right now—so nothing knows that I'm here."

Aura…The way for the people of Gekai to know that the person standing in front of them is a deity. It's almost like a glow. At some point I'd heard that when a god uses their divine power, Arcanum, their aura goes into overdrive and other deities know about it. Basically, everyone would know that they had violated their own rules, and they would be exiled back to Tenkai—.

"Generally speaking, gods and goddesses aren't allowed in the Dungeon."

"Can I ask why?"

"Because it would be bad if *they* found out."

Who are they? I tilt my head in confusion. But I have a feeling that I shouldn't press her for an answer, so I let it drop.

"I know we're headed to that massive lump of an island…but how do we get across the lake?"

"There's a really big tree lying on its side that makes a bridge between the two. Look, see?" Miss Tiona answers Welf's question without hesitation. I look to where she's pointing…and sure enough, there's a tree big enough to see from this far away on top of the water, connecting the island to the rest of the Dungeon floor.

The immense rocky island seems to grow by the second as we get closer. The tree bridge has been stripped of all leaves and branches and is basically just a giant log. I follow the girls onto it, looking at all the footprints on its surface. It's not at all flat and there's no railing whatsoever; I really have to focus to stay upright. It's not just me, either—I catch the goddess just as she was about to fall off the tree.

"Morning" is not quite as bright as the "afternoon" in the Dungeon, but the light coming from the faintly glowing crystals on the ceiling is warm. There's enough light for me to see my reflection on the surface of the water beneath me.

"If there's a town down here, wouldn't you guys have been better off staying there instead of the woods...?"

"They'd rob us blind, so no."

Miss Tione immediately put my question to rest. That begs a new question on what she meant by that, but I keep my mouth shut as we reach the island.

The road leading to the town is a steep one. The island looks like a mountain from far away, but from here it looks more like a cliff. Small plants and crystals jut out from the cracks in the stone wall. We climb high enough to get an incredible view of the entire floor.

"Yeah. Now that's what I call beautiful."

"*Huff, huff*...ha, wow. This is amazing."

Lord Hermes seems perfectly fine, while my goddess is gasping for breath, but both of them have the same reaction to the scenery. Don't get me wrong, the rest of us are absolutely astounded. We can see everything from here.

There are no walls or rooms on the eighteenth floor, it's just a fat cylinder with a domed top. The crystals cover every inch of the ceiling and spread all the way to the other side of the floor.

The tunnel to the seventeenth floor is on the southern edge of the forest. *Loki Familia*'s camp is in that area. The forest itself extends far into the east and has many rivers and springs throughout the greenery. The trees thin out considerably in the north. I don't know if it's because the rest of the land is an open plain, but the dark shadows roaming around really stand out. There's nothing else they could be but monsters.

"Monsters come to this floor, just like us..."

"It would be appropriate to say that this is their haven, not ours."

Aiz and Asfi explain that the monsters come here looking for all of the abundant fruit and fresh water.

The colossal tree I saw before stands in the center of it all. It's the only place higher up than the island in the western lake that we're standing on.

That's the true identity of the eighteenth floor, a wilderness deep underground.

"Lilly's never been far away from Orario but…this is very pretty."

"No, you can travel far and wide and never find a view that will rival this one."

"…Reminds me of the mountains in our beloved homeland in the East."

"Yes…"

First Lilly and Mikoto, then Ouka and Chigusa. It's impossible not to be moved by the natural beauty surrounding us. I'm doing my best to engrave this view into my memory.

We leave the cliff overlooking the eighteenth floor and follow what's left of the path to the top of the island.

"Whaa…!!"

An arch-shaped gate decorated with flags at the end of two rows of wooden pillars greets our eyes.

HELLO FRIENDS, WELCOME TO RIVIRA! is written in the common language of Koine across the top of the gate.

"Better not let that fool you. They're just warming you up, making you feel good before coming for your wallet."

That's the second time Tione has warned me to be careful here. In any case, we pass through the gate.

The town is on the very top of the island, mixed in with beautiful white and blue crystals and the natural scenery.

The "buildings" are nothing more than shacks made out of scraps of wood and large tents with signs on them. A few of them are built into large cracks in the walls of stone and tunnel entrances. The town's hotel is like that, too. Since the town is built halfway into the cliff next to a relatively flat area, many stairs are necessary to help people go from shop to shop. No matter where you go around town, the pristine lake below and the amazing backdrop of the eighteenth floor are always in view.

The rest-stop town surrounded by rock and crystals…Rivira.

"This town is run by adventurers, of course. There are no bothersome rules or regulations here, so everyone is able to do business as they please."

The goddess, Lilly, Welf, and I look around the town and listen to Asfi's explanation.

She says that this town in the middle of the Dungeon was once controlled by the Guild as a frontline base of sorts. Adventurers themselves took over the place after the Guild gave up trying to maintain it. The reason that this spot was chosen out of everywhere else on the eighteenth floor was because the lake and rocky cliffs provided protection.

With the exception of the south gate, where we came in, the north gate, and the east gate overlooking the lake, the town is surrounded by a thick wall. It isn't much compared to the wall surrounding Orario outside, but the crystal and rock structure looks plenty sturdy.

Many adventurers use this town as a base camp for repeated trips below the eighteenth floor. Rest up, go dungeon crawling, come back, and rest up again…It's not uncommon for people to follow that cycle until they physically can't continue anymore.

"So do the monsters not attack this town?"

"Of course they do. Just last month it was overrun and they completely destroyed everything."

"That was a close one! We just happened to have front-row seats!"

The Amazonian twins respond awfully casually about something that should be really scary. My mouth twitches just thinking about it.

"But all the adventurers here are really good at running away. They wait for a little bit after an attack, come back, and rebuild."

"Set up, get smashed, set up again…It happens over and over."

According to them—despite this being a safe point in the Dungeon—the town of Rivira is under the constant threat of monster attacks. Even though all of the residents are upper-class adventurers, the town is reduced to rubble as soon as an irregular monster shows up. But as soon as the monsters go away on their own, the adventurers come back to set up shop again.

The current Rivira is the 334th reincarnation.

The town's namesake comes from a great female adventurer named Rivira Santilini, who helped establish the first one.

"Excuse me, Miss Asfi. There are tons of crystals all around town…"

"Indeed. Any of the crystals that are found on the eighteenth floor can be turned in for money at the Exchange aboveground."

"—Mr. Bell, let's collect as many as we can before we leave!"

Lilly's eyes sparkle as she smiles at me while we walk into the town's main square.

"We'll only block the road if we try to stay together like this. Let's break off into smaller groups and have a look around!"

Lord Hermes gestured all around the square as he spoke, and all of us agree with him.

No one is allowed to travel alone, so we start making our own groups.

"All right, Bell. Let's go out on the town together! You there, stay away!!"

"Eh, Goddess, what are you…?!"

"…"

The Goddess growls at Aiz, grabs my hand, and pulls me farther into the town.

Due to the nature of the town of Rivira, almost all of the structures in town were shops.

Of course, there were a few cramped hotels and a tavern here and there, but weapon and item shops dominated the streets. Every single establishment was owned and operated by adventurers.

Only adventurers and a few supporters filled its streets. Being upper-class adventurers, their armor and weapons were also top-notch—as well as equipped to be used at a moment's notice. Two-handed swords, halberds, and full-plated body armor were everywhere. It was a much more extreme version of "Adventurers Way" on the surface.

Only monsters would stand a chance, trying to assault a town with residents who were as heavily armed as these people.

"You?! Why are you here?!"

"G-Goddess, please calm down...?!"

"Ha-ha, the more the merrier, am I right?"

Bell walked along a twisting path of rocks under a blue sky composed of crystals that look like they could fall at any moment.

Aiz was leading the way, followed closely by an angry Hestia, as well as Hermes and Asfi behind Bell. Everyone was taking in the sights and sounds of the prospering town. However, the landscape was so uneven that large crystals and even trees needed to be used as ladders to get from one section of the town to another.

"Um, these items on display...Aren't they a bit...expensive?"

"That's one of Rivira's features..."

Bell's eyes had been running over the price tags of weapons and items in the windows of the shops they passed, and he asked Aiz about it. The very same equipment was available on the surface with one or two fewer digits in the price.

Asfi and Hermes explained as the group entered a new street.

"Things like weapons, items, and food are sold at many times their original price here."

"It's not easy to get these things in the Dungeon, so most adventurers break down and buy what they need no matter the cost."

Just as Hermes said, supplies were very difficult to obtain. The business owners of Rivira knew that and took advantage of the adventurers who failed to prepare enough stock.

"Water is expensive in a desert...It's the same thing."

No matter where anyone travels around the world, there will be places where they can get specific items much cheaper than others and vice versa.

Spend a large sum of money on an item that could save your life, or save that money for later and risk death.

The adventurers who passed through Rivira were all forced to make that choice.

Everything right down to magic-stone lamps was extremely expensive.

"Lilly can't believe this! Twenty thousand vals for a backpack... absurd!"

"That much for a grindstone? You've got to be kidding..."

Lilly flung her new oversize backpack over her shoulders, fuming with rage. Welf had considered buying a grindstone at one of the weapon supply shops in town and came down with a bad case of sticker shock.

There was no one outside the shops trying to attract customers; instead they sat comfortably in a chair in the back of their establishments as they blurred the line between a profitable business and outright stealing.

The town's beauty could do nothing to hide the greed of its inhabitants.

"This is why we're camping in the woods rather than staying here overnight."

"The amount of money required for everyone in our expedition to stay at one of those hotels would be outrageous."

Tiona grinned as she interlaced her fingers behind her head when she saw the look on Welf's and Lilly's faces. Tione let out a long sigh in disgust. The two Level 1 adventurers were trying to replace everything they'd lost on their journey to the eighteenth floor. The Amazonian twins offered to help them find what they needed.

"This is exactly why Lilly hates adventurers! They are so obsessed with money that they'll jump at any opportunity to take advantage of someone else."

"There are many things I'd like to say to a certain money-obsessed prum that I know...Li'l E, you should open a shop down here!"

"..."

"Hey, don't take it seriously."

All that they had learned was they would leave empty-handed if they tried to purchase something for the established retail price.

"Th-that's an Exchange…"

"They really can get away with anything down here…"

"…W-wow."

A sign decorated with drawings of a Minotaur and purple stones stood out from the other shops on the street. Its purpose was to encourage people to sell their magic stones and drop items.

Mikoto, Ouka, and Chigusa stared in amazement at an adventurer who was trying to sell the fang of a giant monster to the Exchange. The man was dissatisfied by the amount the clerk offered for the drop item he'd hauled all the way up here. Despite all the angry yelling, the clerk just shrugged his shoulders and said, "You can take it somewhere else." In the end, the adventurer agreed on a price, sold the fang, and stomped away with his fists clenched and face boiling with anger.

It was a very simple system. The adventurers who ran this Exchange would buy drop items and magic stones for less than half their value and sell them to the Guild for full price when they returned to the surface. Of course, the adventurers who sold the items would get upset, but they realized that there was a limit to how much they could carry. It was better to sell off their extra items here than throw them away. This also gave them the opportunity to continue crawling the Dungeon for more magic stones and drop items to take to the surface.

From the buyer's perspective, it was an easy way to get valuable items and profit from them.

"This is a scam…"

"Captain Ouka, you are correct, but please be prudent."

The compensation was low, but no fights broke out over it.

The owners were quite strong—strong enough to keep the other storeowners quiet—and ran the most profitable business in Rivira.

One such owner noticed Mikoto, Ouka, and Chigusa. He glared at them while tapping a massive club against his shoulder. The three adventurers quickly took their leave.

Buy low, sell high.

It wasn't just the motto of the adventurers in the town of Rivira, it was their way of life.

"...But Hermes, no adventurers carry large amounts of money down here. How are they supposed to buy anything with prices this high?"

Bell's group, just like Lilly's and Mikoto's, had seen the high prices. It was Hestia who asked the question that was on everyone's mind. She had found something...a small bottle of perfume. Her eyes were locked on it even as she spoke.

Hermes gestured toward the man sitting at the back of the shop who took out a piece of paper and requested a signature.

"Just like that, they put it in writing. The shop gets the adventurer's signature and their *Familia*'s emblem to create an IOU. They come to collect the money later."

There were two payment options in Rivira: trade items for merchandise directly or by signing a payment contract.

It would be cumbersome and even dangerous to carry large amounts of money into the Dungeon. To get around this, a *Familia*'s emblem was used as credit. Then someone representing the shop would return to the outside and show up at that *Familia*'s home, the emblem in hand.

The opposite was true with the Exchange in Rivira. The shop had a representative on the surface where an adventurer could take a receipt issued by the shop to receive their money.

For that reason, suspicious persons who refused to identify themselves could never do business in this town.

"You haven't made an emblem yet, have you, Hestia? It'd be a good idea to do that; it would help Bell out a lot, too. An emblem works like identity verification; there are places in Orario where they come in handy."

"Ohhh, an emblem...I see..."

Hestia folded her arms and looked up toward the ceiling.

While her lack of followers was a problem, the thought of Bell having his own emblem made Hestia excited. She stole a glance at the *Familia* emblem sewn into Asfi's battle cloth, winged traveler's hat, and sandals, and had fun envisioning the emblem she could create for him.

She was lost in thought when suddenly—*thump*.

"You got a problem?"

"Ah...Sorry!"

Bell was quick to step in front of Hestia and apologize. He bowed a few times before looking up at the adventurer's face and saw a scar that he remembered from somewhere..."Huh?" He remembered where at the same time that the scarred adventurer did.

"You...No way...!"

"That's him! Mord, that's the brat from the bar!"

All three were human men. The one with the scar was named Mord, and his two companions were behind him.

The three of them had been present at The Benevolent Mistress during Bell's leveling-up party. They'd incurred the wrath of Lyu and the other staff members before being chased out.

Bell watched in horror as Mord took on a much more frightening visage.

"The hell're *you* doin' here...!"

Mord's anger from the bar incident must've been directed at Bell because he started to reach for the boy.

However, he caught the glint of golden hair out of the corner of his eye. The Kenki was watching.

His eyes flinched even while his teeth were bared in Bell's direction. He felt Aiz's empty golden gaze wash over him. "Tsk!" The man clicked his tongue as he backed away, his allies in tow.

"Hey, hey, Bell. You're not going out and picking fights with adventurers like that, are you?"

"No, it's not like that..."

"So, what happened between you and them? Strangers don't get that mad at each other on sight."

Trapped between Hestia's and Hermes's questions, Bell forced a shaky smile and explained what happened.

"Ohh?" said Hermes, his ears perking up in the middle of Bell's story.

"So, those children consider Bell an enemy..."

He took a look at the three of them, getting smaller as they walked down the other side of the path.

The view of the eighteenth floor from the town's central square is absolutely breathtaking. There's a cliff right on the other side of this railing and the lake is far below. I doubt anyone could survive falling off. Even the craziest of daredevils wouldn't even think of trying this one.

We all met up again after exploring the town in groups, but I came over here to check out the scenery by myself.

Lord Hermes offered to buy everyone a "Dungeon Sandwich" at a nearby café. The goddess and the others are eating there now. Sandwiches with liberal amounts of fruit between two slices of bread... including the honey cloud. I had to escape.

Also...The Dungeon heals itself after taking physical damage, so it's impossible to break ground and build something sturdy or blast away rock to hollow out an area for a shop. They have to use the terrain as is. Although, I've heard that some rather enthusiastic adventurers brought building materials down from the surface and used them in combination with the natural features of the eighteenth floor to make a stove. I don't know if they're passionate or just crazy...but the fact remains that the town of Rivira has fresh-baked bread and other food readily available. It's selling quite well, actually.

"The deepest town in the world, huh?"

A town run entirely by adventurers.

It's literally the frontier base for Dungeon exploration.

Many adventurers use this area as a place to organize their final plans for journeying into the lower levels. Of course, this is just for upper-class and top-tier adventurers who are up to that challenge.

That's where *she* is—at an extremely high level, one that I can only look up at and admire.

I take another look at the vast open space that is the eighteenth floor, while standing behind a railing made of rusty old swords and broken spears.

"Ah…"

I hear footsteps and immediately turn around, only to see her… Aiz is walking toward me by herself.

My body freezes as she comes to a stop in front of me. But her eyes, they're looking past me and off into the distance.

"What were you looking at…?"

"Eh, um…Well, I-I was looking for the entrance to the nineteenth floor."

I panic when she asked the question out of the blue and that's the best I could do.

She walks up next to me and points somewhere on the eighteenth floor. She must've believed me. I force my body to turn around and take a look.

"The Central Tree…"

"The big one in the middle…The one right there?"

"Yes. The entrance to the nineteenth floor is between its roots…"

Her fingers, wrist, and elbow all extend straight toward the base of the behemoth tree.

As if to reinforce what she was saying, black shadows emerge from the roots almost on cue. The monsters take a quick look around before splitting up, a few heading north and the rest going east.

"…Um, Aiz, why did you come out here?"

"Because you weren't with everyone else…So, um."

…She was worried about me.

Those words send my beating heart into a tailspin.

Even just thinking about them makes me blush. She's right there, looking at me with those golden eyes. We're standing close enough that I could reach out and touch her, easily. I can feel the blood coursing through my veins. It's hot.

"…Did you want to be alone?"

"I-i-it's not like that! I'm really happy that you're here—No, wait—what I mean is, um—"

The look of concern on her face makes me so nervous that I can't speak straight, to the point that the truth comes out. It's too late to try to fool her with a loud voice.

I quickly try to hide my face behind my right shoulder and cautiously peek out.

Once I finally do get a look at her…her eyes are wide open and she's smiling. If I'm not mistaken, Aiz is blushing.

"Bell, you're always so nervous…"

Her words are warm and filled with caring, like the way that she would speak to someone close to her.

She said my name. I can't talk. My chest might explode.

My spirit is shaking to its very core.

I've never…felt like this before.

"…"

This is not good. My resolve is wavering.

If she keeps standing this close to me…

Even though I've never accomplished anything, even though I'm way out of my league, if my knees get any weaker in the warmth of her presence…

I might just give up pursuing her.

I quickly look down, hiding my eyes behind my bangs and blushing like no other.

My spirit is singing throughout my whole body. I squeeze my eyebrows together in a desperate attempt to keep myself steady.

All the butterflies in my stomach are making their way up my back. I can feel their heat as they move.

Then without warning:

The goddess suddenly jumps into my line of sight, as if she were trying to tear us apart.

"—Wow, what a view!!"

"Wha—?!"

Flip! I take my eyes off the ground and, sure enough, the goddess has wedged herself between us.

Aiz looks just as surprised as I am. The goddess is forcing a smile, her eyes half lidded.

"No fair, Bell. Going to such a beautiful spot and not inviting me! We are more than just *companions*, you know!"

A ping of fear courses through my skin as I repeatedly apologize to the goddess's smiling face. The way she emphasizes the word "companions" is absolutely terrifying.

"So as you can see, Miss Wallensomething, get lost! Don't get in the way of our family time! This is reserved for just Bell and me!!"

"U-um..."

Shove, shove. The goddess keeps nudging Aiz's breastplate with her hand and Aiz has no idea what to do. I move in to try and stop her.

I manage to fit myself in front of the goddess—she's almost *growling*—even as she keeps looking at Aiz menacingly. Sweat won't stop pouring down my face.

"...? Goddess, are you wearing something new?"

"Oh, Bell! You noticed!"

She spins toward me, her expression completely different. She thrusts a small, open pouch out at me. There's a clear vial inside.

"Isn't that...perfume? Is this the one that you saw earlier...?"

"That it is—a girl has needs, after all! Don't tell me you want some stinky, sword-swinging girl at your side, Bell?!"

She really does smell good, but I sensed something evil in her words. Aiz blinks a few times, brings her arm up to her nose, and— *sniff, sniff.* She smells like pure water, though...Why is the goddess being so aggressive today?

She tells me she borrowed Lord Hermes's emblem to buy the perfume. She's spent more than a day in the Dungeon, so I can't blame her for being a little bit self-conscious about her aroma.

"Wha...Aiz, you defeated a floor boss by yourself, right?"

I have to clear the air, change the subject at any cost.

Also, I...need to hear this for myself.

The goddess's head spins around to look up at her. Aiz just tilts her head to the side and nods with a quiet "Yes.

"But it was only because I had Riveria's help..."

"Even still…"

"…Yes, I slew it."

—All I was able to do was run from the Goliath.

—She stood up to one of them, alone, and won.

She's still far away, far above me. In fact, the obvious distance between us is so great I wouldn't be surprised if the girl standing here is an illusion. I got a little bit of notoriety, so what.

I reconnect with my true, cowardly self, as well as with what I'm aiming for, what I want to be.

"Nothing to worry about, Bell! With the two of us working hard together for long enough, you can do it!"

The goddess suddenly raises her voice.

I admit I'm a little bit flustered, but that makes me happy to hear.

I can work harder, become stronger, and reach my goal.

However, for the goddess's sake, for my family, I won't overdo it. I won't leave her behind.

The promise I made a long time ago echoes in the back of my mind. I look at both of their faces, Aiz's and the goddess's…All I can do now is focus all of my energy on getting stronger.

It seems so clear again.

"Wallensomething, no wandering off again without my permission!"

"I am sorry…?"

Aiz and the goddess seem to be having some kind of argument.

I lower my eyebrows and force a smile. But before long, all my worries leave me and I smile for real.

"Afternoon" began on the eighteenth floor the moment Bell and the others returned to *Loki Familia*'s forest camp.

The light that came from the white and blue crystals covering the ceiling had noticeably intensified in the span of a few minutes. Monsters roaming the northern area of the floor howled as if celebrating the Dungeon's gift.

"Hey, let's all go take a bath!"

Tiona excitedly called out to everyone just before reaching the center of camp. All of the trees around them were bathed in the early afternoon warmth of the crystals above.

The group was just about to go their separate ways when she made the suggestion. First she looked toward Aiz and Tione, but also extended the invitation to Hestia and Mikoto's group.

"Again—? How many times will it take until you're satisfied?"

"What's the problem? There's plenty of time. And the water feels *amazing*."

"Besides, wouldn't the sight of Lady Hestia's boobs make you go insane?"

"F-fat chance! W-why would it?!"

The twins' comical argument showed no signs of slowing down. Not too far away, Lilly looked up at Hestia.

"What should we do, Lady Hestia?"

"Wellll…Of course, I *would* like to wash up a bit…"

Hestia looked down at her dirty clothes and less-than-clean skin.

Of course, her journey to the eighteenth floor made her sweat more than she'd like to admit, and she'd fallen to the ground so much since she'd arrived here that her normally white clothes were now a few shades darker. Even if washing them was a lost cause, she at least wanted her body to feel clean.

"How about you Mikoto, Chigusa? Want to come bathe with us?"

"If I am welcome, I would like to…Chigusa?"

"M-me too…Y-yes."

"What about Miss Asfi?"

"…Lord Hermes."

"Ahhh, sure, sure. I'm well-protected here, so you can relax for a while."

Lilly looked up at Asfi when she asked. Hermes didn't even look around when his follower asked him for permission, instead just waving his hand as though he didn't care one way or the other. "Well then, I shall join you," said Asfi as she pushed the bridge of her silver glasses higher up her nose.

"Aiz, too. Let's go!"

"Sure..."

"Invite Leene and the others, too. We'll take turns as lookouts."

Tiona embraced Aiz from behind, smiling brightly. The blond girl nodded and the rest of the women started to move out of the camp.

Tione went around the camp to invite a few more female members of their battle party to come with them. Being naked and defenseless in a forest where monsters lurked was a very scary idea.

Tiona led the group out of camp and into the forest, all of the men staying behind.

"Ta-da, here we are!"

"""""Whoa...""""""

Hestia, Lilly, Mikoto, and Chigusa responded in unison.

The first thing they saw when they came into a clearing was a waterfall standing ten meders tall.

The water came down with enough force to release a fine mist, cooling the air around them. Their skin was covered in small beads of moisture in no time flat.

Tiona had taken them to an isolated lagoon at the base of the waterfall. It was completely encased by a wall of trees and crystals. The canopy of a large tree covered the lagoon from above. The azure color of the water's surface sparkled in the afternoon light, reflections dancing on the trees surrounding them. They had found a hidden jewel within the forest.

"Isn't this great? Found it myself the other day!"

"Agreed, this is a very beautiful spot..."

"Lilly has a question, if you don't mind, Miss Tione. Where is this water coming from?"

"It's different from glacier runoff or melted snow. There's a special crystal even deeper in the forest that constantly produces pure water. It's much cleaner than the water outside. You can drink it, no problem."

Conversations between Tiona and Mikoto as well as Tione and Lilly filled their companions' ears as the group made their way toward the water.

There was no shyness or hesitation among them at this point.

They shed armor and clothing while talking as if around the dinner table. Tione's full, luscious breasts and Tiona's sleek, slender body emerged. Mikoto and Asfi pulled off their clothing and set it neatly on the ground beside them. Chigusa, blushing from head to toe, was the last to start disrobing.

As for Aiz…After a series of clicks to detach her armor, she gently grabbed her underclothing. There was a certain pair of eyes on her—Hestia watched closely as Aiz exposed her curvy, yet well-defined feminine form.

A moment later, the goddess practically threw her garments to the ground.

"Heh-heh……Looks like I win!"

"Are we competing, Lady Hestia…?"

The short goddess puffed out her chest, looking around triumphantly.

Aiz's undergarments hung loosely in her grip as she looked down at the extremely confident deity with confusion. Lilly was about to remove her panties when she, too, turned to look at the young goddess with tired eyes.

"Guess what? These hair bands were a gift from Bell! A present to show his affection!"

"Lady Hestia, would you mind sharing more of that story…!"

Lilly drifted closer as Hestia removed the hair bands and held them out for everyone to see. Even Aiz perked up a bit to get a better view.

All of the girls gathered around, talking excitedly as they took their first steps into the lagoon. Their lookouts stood at the edge of the clearing, ready to protect their friends from anything that came too close.

"…Now should be good."

Lord Hermes nods to himself as he whispers those words.

"Huh?"

"Bell, would you join me for a moment?"

We were just kind of hanging out around the camp, but Lord Hermes came up to me with a serious look on his face.

He keeps his voice low, as if he's trying not to be overheard.

"I've been waiting for this chance. No, it wouldn't be an exaggeration to say that this chance is the reason I'm here...A chance to be alone with you."

He's been waiting for a chance to talk to...me...?

He must have something very important to talk about. At least that's what I'm getting from how he's acting. He's turned off all of his charms, his orange eyes looking straight ahead without blinking.

I've never seen Lord Hermes like this. I gulp down the air in my throat. I can see Welf and Ouka off on their own in different areas of the camp. They haven't noticed us.

Feeling a little uneasy, I slowly nod.

"Join me," Lord Hermes says as he starts to move. No one moves to stop us as we leave the camp and enter the forest.

"...Um, Lord Hermes? Where are we going?"

I had followed him quietly for a while, but he's not slowing down. All I can do is direct a question at the back of his head.

We're pretty deep into the forest now. There's no one anywhere near here, so it should be safe for us to talk about anything.

"...This already looks good," says Lord Hermes as he stops in front of a tree.

Its trunk and branches look very strong and sturdy. Lord Hermes suddenly starts climbing it. It looks like he's done this a few times, to say the least. He uses his long arms and legs to work his way up the trunk.

"Now, Bell, get up here." I zoned out there for a second but quickly respond to his call and follow him. Two people climbing a tree in the middle of nowhere—I'm sure this is a very bizarre scene.

"E-excuse me, Lord Hermes?"

"Just as I thought. Have a look, Bell. These branches are strong enough to walk on."

Just when I thought he was going to tell me what we're doing here, he grins at me with twinkling eyes.

I take a look from this high spot in the tree canopy, and sure enough there is a small network of sturdy tree branches that form a hidden path. I'm completely clueless as to why he pointed that out to me, but suddenly he laughs with a "Ho-ho!" and steps out onto the first branch.

"L-Lord Hermes, didn't you…want to talk to me about something?!"

"Talk? I never said anything about talking, my boy."

"Wha…?" I start to say, but Lord Hermes pushes aside some leaves and steps onto the branch of another tree. We move through the canopy, the light shifting above us, filtering through the leaves as the branches shift under our weight. This is worse than the tree bridge to Rivira; keeping my balance takes every ounce of concentration.

"Why are we up here?!" My frustration gets the better of me as I try to keep up with him—he comes to a sudden stop and looks back at me.

Hermes gives me a very manly grin, then jerks his chin in a certain direction to draw my attention.

Dossshhhh. I can hear a waterfall.

"We've come this far. You should've figured it out by now—We're peeping."

"?!"

I freeze as my eyes fly open. Lord Hermes takes on an air of providence with his next words.

"All those girls down there are taking a bath, you know? It's practically our duty to have a look, don't you think?"

"No, I don't!"

"No need to shy away, Bell. Seriously, I bet Hestia scrubs your back in the shower every night already."

"That has never happened!"

What is this god saying?!

"Ah-ha-ha-ha-ha-ha!" He's laughing at me. I don't think he believes me, either. My face pulses with heat as Lord Hermes turns his back to me and quietly sneaks forward, almost floating down the path of branches. He must know exactly where he's going because he's not hesitating at all. I've heard of people being desperate, but this is insane!

The sound of rushing water is on the other side of the wall of leaves by the time I catch up to him.

"This is wrong—let's turn back, Lord Hermes! We shouldn't be here...!"

"Bell, top-class adventurers will hear us if we make too much noise."

He cups his hand over my mouth and points down. My eyes follow straight to—a group of heavily armed female adventurers. They must be keeping an eye on the forest.

I back away from his hand and look up at him. His smile is absolutely radiant. I've never seen a perverted smile look so appealing.

It could be because of the sound of the waterfall or how wide these leaves are, but it seems that Aiz and the others, including the lookouts, haven't noticed us yet.

"Lord Hermes, Lord Hermes, this is bad, they'll tear us to pieces...!"

"This is pitiful, Bell. *Peeping is a man's due!* Just think of it as you and I are sharing a particularly delicious bottle of wine...Didn't your grandfather teach you anything?"

The two of us advance slowly down the branch, whispering to each other, when suddenly a shiver goes down my spine.

Peeping is...a man's due?

I feel like something is waking up inside me. Something from a long time ago, something from when I was a kid. What was it Gramps was trying to teach me back then? My surroundings suddenly don't matter as my memory kicks into high gear.

Everything comes out at once, like mist from a black jar—especially when I hear Aiz's innocent voice coming from below—but I use every fiber of my being to seal that black jar shut.

"*Let me out—!*" The words seem to come from behind the seal in my head. If I'd hesitated for a moment, I'm sure I would've been overpowered by the wicked urge held within. But my reasoning in the now wins the day. I reach out and put my hand on the shoulder next to me.

"L-let's go back, Lord Hermes!"

I lean forward as if to stand up and start to pull him away from the waterfall.

"Ah, if you move too much…"

Just then.

Crack. The branch beneath us screams out in pain. It starts moving up and down.

The large branch that has been supporting our weight breaks at its base next to the tree.

Lord Hermes manages to shift his weight to an adjoining branch, but I'm off balance and on two feet. *Whoop*—

I fall straight into the open air.

"—*Daaaaaahhhh!!*"

With nothing to stop me, I fall face-first into the body of water below.

Splash! The water explodes around me as I make impact.

"Blugh, glub, glublubb?!"

Luckily I fell into a relatively deep part. I frantically kick my arms and legs to get back to the surface. My face erupts out of the water and I take many deep breaths.

Water's in my lungs, making me panic. I pick a direction and flail my arms and legs in a desperate attempt to reach land. Finally my feet touch the bottom, then my hands.

Khaa, khaa! After a fit of rough coughing, I finally catch my breath.

"…Argonaut?"

My body shivers at the sound of the voice coming from just above my head.

I stare at my reflection in the light-blue water for a moment before slowly, very slowly lifting my eyes.

"What, did you want to take a bath, too?"

"Such a calm face…You're quite good, aren't you?"

U—waaaaaaaaaaaaaaaaaaaaaaaaaaaaaaaaaaaaaaaaaaaaaaaaaaaaaaaa!!

The Amazonian twins are right there. Tiona is leaning in toward me with curious eyes while Tione is behind her, running her fingers through her long hair.

They're completely naked and not trying to hide anything, their wheat-colored skin completely exposed.

—Have Amazons no shame?!

"Wha-wa-wa-wa…?!"

"Eh? Ehhh…?!"

"Don't tell me…Lord Hermes?"

To my right, a very pink Mikoto stands completely still as Chigusa swiftly hides her body underwater.

Asfi is next to them. She doesn't have her glasses on but that doesn't stop her from looking up into the tree, beams of rage blasting out of her eyes.

Rustle. The branches around the area I fell from start twitching.

"Bell, it's children like you…!"

"W-what do you think you're doing, Mr. Bell?!"

To my left, the goddess has her hair down and her feet on the bottom of the lagoon. Half of her bulging chest is hidden under the waterline as she yells at me with a red face.

Lilly's the same way, screaming in a high-pitched voice.

"…ah."

And directly in front of me…

Aiz is standing with her back to the waterfall, hugging her body to hide her chest. Her cheeks are a light shade of red.

Water is dripping from her wet golden hair, tracing its way all the way down to her legs.

I turn a deep red as the image of Aiz's naked body is burned into my eyes.

The next moment, my head explodes.

"S-SOOOOOORRRYYYYYYY!!"

I launch myself out of the water and race past the lookouts in the blink of an eye, taking off into the forest as fast as I can.

I charge into the forest with reckless abandon.

More distance, faster, forward! A big tree stands in the middle of my path so I take a hard right. I cut over to the forest floor, running like a scared rabbit.

But then I notice something important.

"I—I'm lost..."

At long last, the flames burning within me cool enough for me to think straight. I take a look around and see that I don't recognize anything. The trees and crystals in this area don't look like the ones close to the campsite; the canopy is thinner and brighter, too.

Am I in the southern part of the forest? The east? Maybe the southeast?

I try as hard as I can to remember how the forest looked from the town of Rivira this morning, but I can't remember any details. I don't think anyone could remember the layout of an area after only one day.

I have no clue where I am.

"Guaaa..."

"B-bugbear...?!"

I quickly jump out of sight after catching a glimpse of a bearlike monster sitting at the base of a tree.

If I remember right...their Strength and Defense are on par with a Minotaur. But what really makes them dangerous is deceptively high Agility that doesn't match their large body size. First appearing on the nineteenth floor, they corner their prey before tearing it apart. The thought of an agile Minotaur is absolutely terrifying. This particular bugbear must be hungry, or it's found its favorite thing in the world, because it's completely distracted by the fruit on the lower branches of the tree. It's got one honey cloud in its massive paw and another in its mouth.

I clasp my hands over my nose and mouth while trying to get my beating heart under control. Turning my back toward the tree, I slowly shimmy around the trunk and wait for the bear to leave.

T-this is bad, really bad...!

An impending sense of danger, being lost in a forest filled with monsters, takes over me.

Aiz said something earlier today about the adventurers in Rivira regularly culling the monsters on the eighteenth floor to keep their numbers down. Unfortunately, I don't think they come this far out in the woods—why would they? That means there are more of them out here than closer to town.

I'm lost and more than likely surrounded by monsters. This is a very, very dangerous situation.

If I don't get back to the campsite by "night"...!

I press forward, my eyes playing tricks on me, making the forest look like an ominous swamp, my ears on high alert.

Wait...What's that?

A different kind of sound sends my mind into a whirlwind.

This isn't the quiet murmuring of a stream, but like water being poured out of a glass...Very unnatural.

I can't deny that there's a chance that a monster is making the sound at a nearby pond. In fact, that's probably it. But I'm hungry and my throat is dry enough to rival a desert. I decide it's worth the risk and walk toward the sound of the water.

A pile of logs greets my eyes as I turn a corner. They're blocking the area between two trees on the ground, but I can climb up and over them. Keeping an eye on my footing to avoid the clumps of moss, I work my way to the top and through the opening, toward the source of the noise. *Kaw, kaw!* Two bird monsters fly off in the distance.

The foliage around me becomes thicker, the path darker. But before long, everything around me starts taking on a light-blue hue.

The trees stand like vertical columns, crystals shining beneath my feet as if guiding me forward...

"—"

The forest opens to reveal a small pond.

All words leave me as soon as I lay eyes on the middle of the body of water.

There is a *fairy*.

She doesn't have a thread of clothing, only milky white skin— her slender back to me as she washes her body. She cups her hands together and carefully lifts the water above her head before letting it run through her hair.

This looks like a page out of a fairy tale, no joke.

A bathing fairy. A chance encounter deep in the woods with a beautiful water spirit.

This is no different. She's frozen the flow of time, but for some reason I can make that connection.

Blip, blip. The water makes soft splashing sounds as the fairy moves. She has a slender but muscular frame and long, pointed ears.

I stand with my hand resting on the tree beside me, dumbstruck as I take in the view. My brain doesn't have the ability to produce any kind of emotion when faced with this kind of beauty.

But wait, in those fairy tales, right about now...

The person who sees the fairy taking a bath suddenly gets hit with an arrow—

"—Who's there!"

Light flashes.

A sharp voice and a white blade were thrown at me at the same time—a dagger buries itself in the tree next to my face, above my hand. *Shing!* My ears finally register the sound of the blade piercing tree bark. Gulp. I swallow the air in my throat.

The elf's sky-blue eyes lock onto me. Lyu's eyes.

She has her left arm wrapped around her chest, hiding it from view. Her right hand, the one that threw the dagger, is still extended as she glares straight through me...Her eyebrows sink the moment that she realizes it was me who was peeping on her.

"Mr. Cranell?"

"...S-SORRYYYYYYYY?!"

All of my muscles snap to life at the sound of my name. I jump back and away before landing on all fours and executing *Takemika-zuchi Familia's* trademark facedown bow.

I slam my face into the ground, trying to apologize.

What am I doing, WHAT AM I DOING?! I've made the same mistake *again*?!

That's twice in a row?! I scream at myself over and over. Lord Hermes must never know.

My ears burn red as I clamp my eyes shut. "Haa..." I hear her breathe out.

My shoulders shudder in fear as I wait for her next words.

"Please turn your back."

"Y-yes, ma'am!"

I keep my head down, rotating on my knees. The edge of the pond leaves my line of sight; tree roots take their place. At that point I raise my upper body and sit as still as stone.

I can hear the sound of cloth behind me as rivers of sweat run down my face. My cheeks blush. She's putting on clothes.

"You may turn around."

Slowly, carefully I shift my knees around. Lyu's wearing the same battle cloth that I saw her in yesterday.

Hip-hugging short pants and long boots. She's wearing that cape over her shirt but the hood is down. The beautiful elf and I make eye contact.

"First, I would like to hear your explanation."

"Y-yes!! Well, you see, it's like this...!"

Lyu walks right up to me and I stand while stuttering, trying to tell her what happened...but the truth is too embarrassing. What am I supposed to say? That I was discovered watching the other girls bathe and then came here?!

I have to think of something else...No.

Her sky-blue eyes are looking right through me; she'd spot a lie instantly. And that would make her even more furious.

My jaw flexes open and closed a few times before the words start to come out. She listens quietly as I confess to every moral outrage I've committed in the past hour.

I thrust my head down below my waist as soon as I've told her everything there was to tell.

"I understand your situation, Mr. Cranell. Allow me to guide you back to *Loki Familia*'s campground after this."

"...Y-you'll forgive me?"

"There is no need for forgiveness, for you are not at fault. A grudge against you would be misplaced."

"H-how do you know I'm not lying...?"

"Mr. Cranell...Modesty may be a virtue, but please stop regarding yourself as inferior. It's a bad habit."

I apologize to her once again. Lyu sounded a little angry there.

Looking down on my abilities...So she's angry at me for the way I think about myself?

Lyu walks toward a different tree, leaving me standing there for a moment. She must've stashed her wooden sword and other weapons there before getting into the spring.

Lastly, she affixes a small pouch to her belt underneath her cape. "My apologies for the wait," she says as she comes back.

"...Um, this is a little late, but thank you for coming all this way to rescue me. This floor is pretty far down..."

"No, please don't concern yourself. I was planning to come to this floor regardless. The distance is not a problem."

My eyes flicker a little bit wider. I wasn't expecting a response like that.

Lyu continues talking anyway.

"I have something to take care of before leading you back to the campsite. Can you spare some of your time?"

"Ah...Sure."

She says a quick thank-you and starts walking.

I catch a glimpse of the side of her face before following her.

"Lyu...were you, um...in the forest this whole time?"

"Yes."

"Why didn't you join everyone at the campsite? There're monsters out here! Wouldn't it be much safer with—"

"I had an errand to attend to. And I didn't want others to see my face."

She said everything evenly and without emotion, just like usual.

Lord Hermes said something before, she who had "reasons"...Is this what he was talking about?

"I assume that god Hermes has informed you about my past already."

"No, nothing…"

"…Really?"

"Y-yes."

"It seems I have come to the wrong conclusion…" Though she's looking the other way, I can sense the pained smile on her face. "We've already come this far. There's no point in hiding anything at this stage. Follow me."

What is it…? Does she have some kind of connection to this floor?

All I can do is just follow that cape and think about the moment when she said she was once known as an adventurer.

Lyu must know this area extremely well. She's walking with purpose as she makes sharp turns at specific trees and crystals as if following a set path. We walk for about twenty minutes without encountering any monsters before arriving at her destination.

"This is…"

What greets my eyes after emerging from a narrow tunnel through the trees is a graveyard.

There's a small open space surrounded by thinner trees and absolutely stunning crystal formations.

A series of wooden crosses, broken tree branches held together with string, are lined up in the clearing and bathed in the crystal light shining through the canopy above.

"…Mama Mia occasionally gives me time to bring them some flowers."

Lyu goes to each of the grave markers and carefully sets a flower in front of them.

Was gathering these flowers her "errand"?

She reaches under her cape to the small pouch and withdraws a bottle—she pours a little bit of the wine onto each of the graves.

"Lyu, what is this place—?"

"All that remains of the women who fought by my side. My *Familia*."

She quietly looks back at me as she speaks. I feel like I've just been hit by a ton of bricks.

Her sky-blue eyes draw me in.

"Another with knowledge of my past has emerged. It's only a matter of time before you find out...I would regret not telling you myself."

She says it's a bit selfish of her, but asks for my permission.

I nod back at her.

"My name appears on the Guild's blacklist."

"?!"

Then she says something unbelievable.

"My position as an adventurer has been revoked. There was a time that a bounty was placed on my head."

She hid her face and she didn't stay with us at the campsite...Is that why?

"I once belonged to *Astrea Familia*...She is the goddess of justice and order, and I idolized her from the day we met."

Lyu Lyon. That's how she was known. Her title, "Gale Wind."

A hooded adventurer shrouded in mystery whose full name was unknown.

"Apart from activities in the Dungeon, my *Familia* took it upon itself to eliminate those who try to rob Orario of peace. For that reason, we made many enemies."

She says that as recently as five years ago, Orario was inundated with an "evil" that threatened the city.

Swearing upon Astrea's crest, a winged sword of justice, Lyu and her allies fought to purge the city of that cancerous presence and protect those vulnerable to it.

"Until, one day, a *Familia* that had taken up arms against us set a trap in the Dungeon. I was the only one to escape alive...Unable to retrieve their bodies, I collected what articles I could and buried them here."

"So that's what these graves are...?"

"Yes. These women were fond of this location."

She tells me that they would always casually joke, saying if they died, they wanted to be buried here.

I can't imagine what images must be running through her head. She looks toward the ground, her lower lip quivering.

"...I went to Astrea as the sole survivor and told her everything. Then I pleaded with her to leave Orario by herself. I begged her for days, and at long last she obliged."

"Y-you helped your goddess escape?"

"No, not that."

Lyu's voice snaps, saying her reasoning was much more selfish as her fists clench.

"I didn't want her to see the passionate, violent creature I was becoming."

She says that she didn't know how to control the emotions that were overtaking her at that time.

"I had to avenge those who had fought beside me. I set my sights on the *Familia* that ended their lives and swore to take revenge alone."

"A-alone...?!"

Attacks under the cover of darkness, ambushes, traps. She used all manner of sneak attacks to eliminate them one by one—until that *Familia* was wiped out.

A large and influential group in Orario was torn out by the roots and utterly eliminated at the hands of a single elf.

"My actions had nothing to do with justice. Filled with a lust for revenge, I tracked down each member and erased them along with anyone connected to them...Even the slightest suspicion was enough."

That's what landed her on the Guild's blacklist.

In her quest for vengeance, she earned the hatred of not only adventurers but merchants, smiths, and townspeople. They were the ones who issued the bounty.

The reward for her capture kept growing and growing...The Guild had no choice but to punish her despite the surrounding circumstances. Especially considering she had bared her fangs at groups connected to the offender. After all, they sold the items and weapons used to kill her family.

With the goddess Astrea outside the city walls, her Status remained intact as the "Gale Wind" covered Orario in a storm of fury.

"…So, what happened after that?"

"I collapsed. With all targets eliminated, with no one left, alone in a back alley."

She must've accepted death the moment she swore revenge.

Her quest complete, her goddess gone and friends dead, there was nothing left for her in this world.

"Covered in blood and dirt on the side of the road…It was a fitting end for someone who had committed atrocities such as I."

"…"

"However…"

"—*Are you okay?*"

A warm hand had reached out to take hers.

Syr found Lyu in that back alley and saved her.

She listened to her story—everything Lyu had done, over and over—and managed to bring her back from the brink.

"After rescuing me, Syr convinced Mama Mia to employ me as a waitress at The Benevolent Mistress……I also keep my hair dyed."

Since she'd always worn a hood and gone by the name Lyon during her time as an adventurer, the chances of her being discovered were very low as long as she changed the color of her hair.

In a soft tone, Lyu goes on to explain how she became her current self.

"…I apologize for soiling your ears."

"Wh-what?"

"In short, the elf you see before you is a shameless, violent criminal…I have betrayed your trust, Mr. Cranell."

She looks at me with the same calm expression, even though she's confessing all of her crimes to me. I clear my throat.

I don't know how to respond, so I just say the first thing that comes to my mind:

"Lyu…*Please stop regarding yourself as inferior.* I'll get mad at you."

Her sky-blue eyes open a little wider.

She stands still for a moment before finally saying:

"That was…very clever."

Only very slightly, but her lips soften.

She isn't smiling by any means, but her eyes don't look as piercing as they normally do.

All I did was repeat her own words back to her, just stole the line, but her reaction makes me feel good. Why wouldn't it? Her usual ice-cold expression just warmed up a little.

A tranquil mood overtakes us in the middle of the graveyard, surrounded by green leaves and crystal light.

"…Can I ask…"

"What is it?"

"Can I ask why you came to Orario?"

This is my best chance.

My best chance to find out why Lyu came to the place where people go to follow their dreams.

I want to know why she and I met in the first place.

"…"

She opens her mouth very slightly before looking up toward the ceiling.

Then Lyu squints her eyes to protect them from the beams of light penetrating the canopy above.

"…We elves are a race known for our good looks."

Her eyes barely open, she wanders around the grassy Dungeon floor.

At long last, Lyu continues her story.

"Myself and others have been praised for our beauty. However, is that really true? Extremely proud and revolted by anything unclean, we do not allow others to easily touch our skin…"

"…"

"There are some who believe other races to be dirty on the surface as well as within, and refuse to interact with them, isolating themselves in their home forests. At the very least, most of the elves from my home forest believed as such…

"However," she continues.

"Only recognizing their own beauty while looking down at everything else as if it were nothing more than trash…A thought came to me."

Lyu once again looks up to the light.

"That the beautiful, magnificent elves were actually the most revolting."

Knowing the value that elves place on interpersonal relationships, I bet she was the only one who felt that way.

Among all those elves, so full of pride, she was the only one to question their logic.

"As soon as that idea took hold, it was impossible to remove. I became embarrassed of my own motherland, so I left…and eventually arrived in Orario."

"By accident?"

"Not exactly…I heard many travelers say that Orario was home to gods, humans, and other fairies, a place full of life where people gather. I thought that if I were there, I might be able to find something…No, that's not it."

She looks into the palms of her hands as if she's remembering her first days in the city.

"I wanted companions worthy of my respect who felt I was worthy of theirs."

It was the one thing that she didn't have growing up in elvish culture with elvish customs.

People who placed no value on race or looks, but on content of character. Friends who would laugh alongside her.

"I came to the city with high hopes…but they were quickly dashed. I didn't expose my skin to anyone but other elves. My face always covered by a hood, I slapped away any hands that reached out."

Elvish culture was too deeply ingrained…Lyu couldn't turn over a new leaf.

In this new place, she was constantly stared at because of her beauty, and she couldn't take it.

Elves don't allow someone they don't trust to touch their skin. She couldn't fix that and other elvish teachings that had been drilled into her head since childhood—it must've tormented her.

"What a jest. I left my homeland because I couldn't stand my own kind, and yet in the outside world, I was no different from them. So I cut myself off, creating a wall."

So that was why she kept her hood up during her time in Orario.

She was disappointed in herself for realizing she was exactly the same as the elves back in the forest.

From her point of view, *she* was the one looking down at people.

Her inborn disdain for other races came full circle, back to herself. It became self-loathing.

"I didn't change. I was still an elf, nose high in the air with pride."

"Lyu..."

"However."

Her tone suddenly changes.

Then she walks right up to me, face-to-face, and gently grabs my hand.

"—Huh?"

"Just like this, there was someone who took hold of my hand, who I could touch."

She's shaking my hand.

Her fingers feel so small and delicate that I'm afraid they might break off if I shook back. And yet, her skin is very soft and supple. My cheeks blush before I know it.

"This is my second time with you, yes? Do you remember?"

"Y-yes?!"

"The day when you lost your knife and were desperately searching."

I'm too stunned to figure out what she's talking about at first, but then the feeling of her skin on my hands triggers a memory. The day when Lilly, disguised as a dog person, stole the Divine Knife. That's what she's talking about.

I clearly remember happily embracing her hands because she had recovered the knife.

"I was very taken aback. Taken aback that I didn't immediately throw the human who had suddenly grabbed my hands onto the side of the road."

Her face forms an expression I've never seen on Lyu before: a mischievous grin.

I wouldn't have been able to say anything if she'd sliced me in half… Only now does the realization hit me. My cheeks and ears are burning, but I do my best to force a smile.

"You are the third person who I did not immediately punish for touching my skin."

She says that with her hand still firmly grasped around mine.

—*Eh? Your name is Lyu? That's too hard to say. I'll call you Lyon from now on!*

The first, the bright and cheerful girl who invited her to join her own *Familia.*

—*Are you okay?*

The second, the nice girl who extended a warm hand to her cold fingers, the waitress who gave her a place to be.

And the third is…

"Please don't make such a confused face. I feel like you're making sport of me."

"S-sorry!"

"I am joking…I have been following your actions closely since we met. I've come to understand your weakness, your sincerity, and most of all your spirit."

"Lyu…?"

"Mr. Cranell, you are kind."

Completely overwhelmed by this new aura radiating from her eyes, I can only respond by saying her name.

She blinks her eyes closed, the blue orbs hidden from sight for a moment, before slowly opening them up again.

"You are a human worthy of my respect."

Lyu…smiles.

Her thin eyebrows relax as the edges of her feminine lips curl upward.

My whole body blushes pink as she faces me with a smile as pure and clean as a white lotus.

"…Uh."

"Mr. Cranell?"

I know it's a little late, but now I truly know why the smile of an elf is a dangerous thing.

The smile of a refined elf while knowing their usual demeanor day in and day out is particularly brutal. It's a trump card powerful enough to make my knees go weak despite having my own aspirations.

Elvish beauty isn't all just on the surface.

A smile that they give only to their most trusted companions.

My eyes are filled with the light beams from above and the tranquil colors of the graveyard and flowers, but most of all, the beautiful smile on her tilted head.

Now I think I know why other races have a thing for elves.

"Ow, ow, ow…What would you do if you broke my face, Asfi?"

"You reap what you sow."

"Night" had already fallen on the eighteenth floor of the Dungeon.

Two figures quietly made their way out of the forest campsite: Hermes and Asfi.

"A god no better than a Peeping Tom…Have you no shame!"

"Peeping isn't that big of a deal for us…"

Bell, who had gone missing after the peeping incident, returned to the campsite shortly before dinner. The fact that he was led to the scene by the deity—and that he practically buried his face in the ground bowing—allowed him to escape with a harsh verbal warning. Only Hermes, the instigator, was physically punished.

"…Well then, where are we going on this pitch-black night?"

"On a pitch-black night like this, there's only one place to bring a lady. Isn't it obvious?"

On the other side of the grasslands before them, the lights of the town of Rivira shone like a beacon from the west.

"To a tavern."

"Damn it!"

Inside one of the few taverns in a small niche of Rivira.

Built inside of a naturally occurring crevice in the cliff face, the bar floor was covered by a dirty rug and had only one table with a few chairs. The walls were dotted with portable magic-stone lamps. Even in here, crystals grew on one of the walls and a few spots in the ceiling.

One man slammed his mug down on the table inside this bar that was a little bit different from most adventurers' usual watering holes.

"Take it easy, Mord."

"Shut it! That brat, I have no freakin' idea how he got down here... Too damn cocky!"

"That jealousy I hear?"

That line got a chuckle out of everyone around the table, other than Mord.

Only a select few upper-class adventurers had the ability to come to Rivira, meaning that the more time you spent there the more you got to know the residents who did business.

The customers at this bar might have been from different *Familias*, but they were on good terms with Mord's group.

"The hell you laughin' about?! That piece-of-shit rookie hasn't done nothing, levels up in a few months, and now his ass is all the way down here?! How stupid are we, workin' hard for years just to make it this far!!"

Recounting the events at The Benevolent Mistress, Mord wasted no time in pointing out the source of his rage.

All the people here were part of an exclusive club of upper-class adventurers within Orario. The thought of some newbie walking the same streets was something he couldn't take lying down.

Even more so that some of the gods themselves were talking about this particular rookie, this "rabbit."

The bar became quiet enough to hear a pin drop when Mord's rant finally came to an end.

"Even got himself some high-quality salamander wool...Damn that kid, I wanna tear his head off."

Mord spat in anger before taking another swig from a particularly potent ale, even by Rivira's standards.

"But Mord, no matter how much you want to knock 'im down a peg—how? He's with the Kenki."

"One of Hermes's and also…Takemikazuchi's group, too."

Mord's companions sat on either side of him, trying to make him see reason.

"The guy wouldn't be here without them…Don't you think the Little Rookie realizes that?"

"Enough small talk! Are you gonna help me or not? Which is it?!"

Their words had done nothing more than make Mord even angrier.

The adventurers sitting around the table froze in place; the fury emanating from the man's eyes wouldn't let them move. They knew that at any moment Mord could draw out any of the weapons hanging from his waist if the thought crossed his mind.

"If we could get him alone, lure that punk-ass brat away from the others…"

Bell had stood out too much.

He'd come too far into the middle levels too quickly after leveling up.

Quickly enough to draw the attention, and outrage, of other upper-class adventurers.

"O-oh, you boys are really living it up in here!"

Twitch. Every set of eyes in the bar fell on the entrance.

They saw Hermes, walking in like he owned the place, followed quietly by Asfi.

"…What business do you have, Mr. Deity? If you're looking for a drink, it'd be better to go back up top."

"Ha-ha, I just heard some sneaky plans in the works and couldn't help myself."

Step. One of the adventurers put himself firmly between the god and the exit.

He knew their plan. Hermes had been with Bell, and would no doubt warn him. The god couldn't be allowed to escape.

*Things like this happen all the time these days…*Asfi lamented as she hid herself in Hermes's shadow.

"So, what's it to you? You gonna try and stop us by yourself?"

"What gave you that idea? Do as you like. Ignore me and keep forming a plan."

"Whaa?" Mord's jaw dropped in disbelief.

"I happen to like children like you. This world would be so boring if everyone played nice."

Hermes's eyes arched into a smile as he chuckled to himself.

Just for a moment, Hermes flashed his true character—one who enjoyed all of the charms of being on earth as a god.

He wasn't showing tolerance for good and evil. He actually was good *and* evil.

Mord was left speechless by this presence before him, something far more mysterious than any monster.

"You want a chance to attack Bell, yes? In that case, why don't I tell you our plans for tomorrow?"

"…How do I know I can take your word, Mr. Deity?"

"Hey, hey, this is Hermes you're talking to. I don't lie to any children."

A few of the others around the table tried to get Mord's attention, but he ignored them and took Hermes's offer.

"I'm not in a position to help you directly…Oh yes, if you need a 'lucky charm' of courage to vanquish your foes, I have a little something you can borrow."

With that, Hermes turned to Asfi, who handed him an item. Hermes took it and presented it to Mord.

It was a small helmet. Based on its design, it looked more like a hat with a small brim around the front.

Its color was the same as the dirt found deep in the earth, black as coal.

"And this is…"

"A magic item forged by the one and only Perseus. It'd be easier to show you what it can do."

Mord's words left him as he watched others put on the helmet. He couldn't believe his eyes.

A magic item created by one of the most celebrated item makers in

Orario. Perseus's items were said to grant the user Magic and Skills through the power of "Enigma."

"Seriously, I can use this…?"

Mord's voice shook as Hermes nodded with a "Yeah.

"However, on one condition…"

Mord took the item in one hand and held it to his chest, his eyes gleaming.

"Entertain me. Give me a show I won't soon forget."

CHAPTER 5 **THE OUTLAWS' PARTY**

© Suzuhito Yasuda

Bell Cranell

Level 2

Strength: G 267 -> F 365   **Defense:** H 144 -> G271

Utility: G 288 -> F349   **Agility:** F 375 -> E 469

Magic: H 189 -> G270

Luck: I

(Magic)

"Firebolt"

- **Swift Strike Magic**

(Skill)

"Argonaut"

- **Charges automatically with an active action**

Hestia informed Bell of his new Status inside their tent.

"Hmm, this is your first big jump in a while…"

"Y-yes it is…"

There were no pencils or paper for her to write down his status in Koine, but just as Hestia had said, Bell's basic abilities hadn't improved by this margin since he'd leveled up. Apparently traveling from the thirteenth floor to the eighteenth floor and narrowly escaping a floor boss gave him enough excelia to receive a big boost.

"Your abilities did go up, but you got quite a bit of high-quality excelia, too."

"Huh?"

"You've done something *great*. It means you're one step closer to leveling up again."

Hestia giggled at the stunned look on Bell's face.

Overcoming countless brushes with death on the journey to the eighteenth floor must've been what did it.

Accomplishing something great, overcoming an extraordinary obstacle—these things were required to level up and couldn't be done by continuously defeating low-level monsters. Bell mulled over these thoughts in his mind as he re-equipped his armor.

"Loki's children are busy getting ready. We should get out of their tent as soon as possible."

"I think so, too."

Today was the day that *Loki Familia* would leave the eighteenth floor. The antidotes had arrived late last night from the surface, so they were finally able to leave as a group. The sounds of *Loki Familia*'s adventurers disassembling the campsite rang out from all around their tent.

Bell gave a quick wave to Hestia, who was still cleaning up the equipment she needed for updating his Status, and stepped outside.

"Why the hell is rabbit boy here?! No one told me a damn thing!"

"Because we knew you'd react like this, Bete. Now come on, let's get going!"

"Hey, hands off, idiot Amazon!"

Bell walked through the area surrounded by people busily folding tents and toward the spot where *Loki Familia*'s leaders were gathered just outside of camp.

"A-Aiz!"

He noticed a girl with long golden hair standing apart from the others and called out to her.

The girl who turned around was fully equipped for battle, breastplate snug over her chest and saber hanging at her side.

"Are you leaving already?"

"Yes...I was asked to join the forward party."

Due to the large amount of party members needed for an expedition, these groups were required to travel in smaller parties starting on the seventeenth floor, to avoid blocking the passageways. *Loki Familia* had been split in two.

Aiz, along with Tiona and the others, was assigned to the first group.

However, Bell's group would be returning to the surface along with the second party.

"U-um…"

"?"

Of course, this meant that Aiz would be part of the battle to slay the Goliath lurking just upstairs.

Bell felt ashamed that he could only wait for them to carve a safe passageway for him. It reminded him just how much further he had to go to catch up to her.

He knew just how useless these words were, but he went ahead and said them anyway.

"…Please be careful."

"…You, too, be careful."

Aiz's normally expressionless mouth curled a bit as she responded.

"See you again," she said softly. She joined her companions as they set off toward the tunnel opening that led to the seventeenth floor. Bell stood there and watched her leave until every single member of the forward party had disappeared into the tunnel.

"Mr. Bell, shouldn't we be getting ready?"

"Ah, yes!"

He heard Lilly call out to him from behind and quickly turned to face her.

They made their way to the center of the diminishing campsite, checked to make sure their bags were completely stocked, and took a look at their weapons.

"Yo, Bell, pass those over here!"

"Sure. Thanks, Welf."

Bell took his two knives out of their sheaths and handed them to the red-haired boy, who quickly ran them across a grinding stone. Bell watched as the Hestia Knife and Ushiwakamaru shone brighter and brighter with each passing moment, their cutting edges revived.

Mikoto walked up next to the mesmerized Bell, her blades already sharpened and equipped.

"I apologize, Mr. Welf. To sharpen our weapons as well as yours…"

"No big deal. This is my job, after all. Another three or four is a piece of cake."

"Did you end up buying that stone in Rivira?"

"Nah, I lowered my head and called in some favors…"

Welf jerked his head toward a few of the remaining High Smiths in the camp in response to Ouka's question.

The prices had been so high in Rivira that all Bell's group could afford to buy in the town were an old broadsword and Lilly's new backpack. Both had been purchased using Welf's *Familia*'s crest, so he was already feeling the empty space in his wallet.

The sword in question, as well as the long weapon wrapped in white cloth, lay on the ground next to him as he worked.

"I've been wondering…Where are Lord Hermes and Ms. Asfi?"

"Lord Hermes said he wanted one more chance to go exploring. He told Lilly to go back to the surface with everyone ahead of him. Asfi looked very tired and frustrated at the situation."

"Quite the hard worker…"

Mikoto, Lilly, and Welf's conversation made Bell think about Lyu. She, too, was planning on going back alone, at least that's what she had told him last night after safely escorting him to the campsite. Considering her situation and Status—Bell's jaw had dropped when she told him she was Level 4—her plan was no surprise.

Everyone's splitting up, Bell thought to himself as he looked up at the "Morning" ceiling above the forest.

"Okay, all set…"

Putting the last of the potions she received from Nahza into her pouch, Hestia stepped outside the tent.

The thick forest canopy blocked a great deal of the morning light coming from the crystals above. All she could see was the dark green of the forest surrounding her. The campsite was almost deserted, only a few random boxes still on the ground and no people in sight. Hestia was just about to call out to Bell to have him help her fold the tent.

"…? Is someone there?"

Swissh, swissh. The sound of someone stepping through the grass caught her attention and she turned around. But all she saw was trees and the dark green shade they provided. No one was there.

Maybe some leaves fell? she thought to herself as she looked toward the upper branches.

"—Muguu?!"

Something suddenly clamped itself over her mouth.

But it didn't end there. She felt a thickly armored arm wrap around her and something solid press against her back. Her eyes frantically darted all over, desperately searching for something that couldn't be found. It was almost as though she were acting out a scene in which she was being restrained.

Then her feet left the ground as her small frame was hoisted into the air and moved away from the campsite.

An invisible human?!

Almost as if confirming her speculation, a strange object that looked like a fistful of paper appeared out of nowhere beneath her, hit the ground, and rolled to a stop. She flailed her body, kicking her legs as potions inside her still-open pouch fell onto the grass.

"*Mgghh?!*" Hestia's muffled screams went unheard as she was carried off into the forest.

"Goddess? *Goddess?*"

Bell looked from left to right, calling out to her.

Everything in order for their return to the surface, the boy realized that Hestia was not there. He returned to the tent where she had just updated his Status. He left soon after, scratching his head once he realized she wasn't there, either.

"This is strange..."

Bell did another lap around the campsite, his right hand on the back of his head. Only a few of the tents were left; there was nothing to obstruct his view. Even though there were many trees in this area, none of them was thick enough to completely conceal the goddess's small body.

However, there was no way she could have just disappeared.

"Maybe she went to see others off...?"

Bell turned toward the tunnel that connected to the seventeenth floor with an even more confused look on his face. The trees became much thicker only a few steps out of the campsite, enough to block his vision. Even though it was relatively safe in this area, it was also true that monsters lurked in these woods. And it was very unlike Hestia to disappear without saying a word to anyone...These thoughts and others passed through Bell's mind.

"Eh...?"

He found it immediately.

It was a small grassy area just a little ways from the campsite. There were many vials of potions scattered on the ground and a small ball of paper.

Bell came to a sudden stop, his eyes practically jumping out of his head at the scene before him.

"Aren't these...?!"

He picked up the closest vial—a double potion made by Nahza, one that Hestia had carried with her from the surface. Bell fell to his knees, forgetting to breathe. The way the vials of potion were sprawled out on the ground gave him a hint as to what had happened to Hestia.

His head snapped up, his eyes scanning the surroundings. The feeling that something bad had happened washed over him as he reached for the crumpled piece of paper.

...*Little Rookie. I have your goddess. If you want her back, come to the crystal on the east side of the Central Tree, alone*...

Bell's eyes went wide in shock upon reading it before jumping to his feet.

A crude map was scribbled at the bottom of the message. Bell took off at full speed, the paper firmly in his grasp.

"Ah..."

Chigusa caught a glimpse of Bell out of the corner of her eye, but he had been oblivious to her presence.

Who would do something like this, and for what?

A new wave of confusion thundered through Bell's head. Not a monster, but an adventurer just like him had put his hands on Hestia. There was only one thing he knew for certain: The adventurer in question wasn't playing around. His actions and the note were enough to figure that out. Enough to make him dizzy.

Was Hestia okay?

That question lit a fire within him. He carved through the forest at full speed, leaving nothing but dirt and sweat in his wake.

Bell ran. He emerged from the forest and into the great plain on a course directly for the Central Tree in the distance. *Thump, thump, thump.* He coaxed even more speed out of his legs. Monsters in the area noticed him and gave chase but couldn't keep up. The white rabbit left all of them in the dust.

"—JYAAAAAAAAAAAAAAAAAAAA!"

Several large shadows blocked his path.

A group of medium-size, two-legged insect monsters called mad beetles stood their ground. Bell thrust out his right arm in response.

"Firebolt!!"

The electric inferno emerged from his palm the same instant that Bell's voice erupted from his throat. A heartbeat later, Bell broke through the hole in the mad beetles' formation and kept right on going.

"Hee-hee, this is awesome…The real deal."

Mord fought back tears of joy.

He held a black helmet in the shape of a hat in his hands.

He looked down at the magic item made by Asfi, aka Perseus—"Hades Head"—with the eyes of an adventurer who had just struck gold.

"Hey, you over there, release me! You think you can get away with this?! I'm a goddess, you know?!"

Mord looked over his shoulder at the source of the protests.

They were somewhere in the middle of the southern forest on the eighteenth floor of the Dungeon. Crystals were scarce in this area while thick grass spread out between the trees. Hestia lay beneath one of the big ones, her hands and feet bound with rope.

"My apologies, Lady Worship. Please forgive my sloppiness."

"You don't feel sorry for anything at all, now do you…?!"

There were two more adventurers standing around the tree, the same ones who'd sat next to Mord at the bar in Rivira.

They surrounded Hestia on her left and right, watching her.

"Disappearing and reappearing out of nowhere, is that your Magic?! Why did you bring me here?!"

"Ha-ha-ha, I can't answer all those questions at once, Lady Worship."

Mord kept the Hades Head out of Hestia's line of sight as he turned to face her, a faint grin on his face.

The power of the magic item he received from Hermes granted the wearer invisibility. Requiring no Mind or physical strength to perform a Skill, the person remained invisible as long as the item was equipped. Mord used this ability to kidnap Hestia from the campsite and bring her here.

It was easy for him to find an opening once he knew that Bell's group, along with *Loki Familia*, would be busy preparing for their return trip today.

"We have nothing against you directly, Lady Worship. So please don't worry. None of us is stupid enough to raise a hand to a deity. The repercussions are just too scary. So won't you please quiet down?"

"What reason do I have to be quiet, now that I know you won't hurt me?"

"Hee-hee-hee, Lady Worship. Please forgive me, but if you aren't quiet…I'll be forced to cut that beautiful hair of yours, or maybe those clothes, until you shut your mouth."

Mord grinned as he pulled a longsword hanging from his waist halfway out of its sheath. Hestia fell silent. Her shapely breasts shook under the one thin layer of fabric keeping them contained, as if expressing the fear that overtook her.

Mord was satisfied by the look of distress in the small goddess's eyes and thrust the blade back in. Leaving the others in charge, he once again turned his back to her.

"Hey, we're not finished here! What are you trying to do?!"

"…I'm going to teach a member of your precious family a lesson."

Mord's teeth flashed as he grinned at Hestia's wide eyes.

"The boy's got a thing or two to learn about the code adventurers live by."

"You find them?!"

"No, Mr. Bell and Lady Hestia are gone!"

Lilly's voice shook responding to Welf's call as the young man ran up to her.

Not much time had passed since Bell took off by himself to find Hestia. Lilly was the first to notice his absence and asked for help searching the campsite and the surrounding forest.

Lilly hunched over, trying to catch her breath. Mikoto and Ouka joined them.

"This is not good. If we don't find them soon, *Loki Familia* will leave us behind."

"There is no time…"

The two of them were still looking around the forest even as they spoke.

Although *Loki Familia*'s second group had agreed to escort them back to the surface, they were under no obligation to wait. With no formal agreement to hold them back, they would start their journey according to their schedule. The window for the young adventurers to join up with them was closing with each passing second.

Welf furrowed his brow and said:

"This ain't like Bell and Lady Hestia, especially not at a time like this."

"That would mean…something has happened to them?"

Lilly said what all of them were thinking. The four quickly formed a circle, stress and anxiety overtaking them. It was written clear as day on their faces.

"Can we request assistance from Lord Hermes and Ms. Asfi?"

"They could be on the other side of the forest by now. With no way to find them, we lose too much time."

"Ms. Lyu…No, the hooded adventurer. Does anyone know where she is?"

"Only Bell would have any idea where to start looking."

Welf started swearing to himself, frustration overtaking him as he folded his arms. That was when a new voice reached the party.

"E-everyone—!"

Chigusa came running into view from between the trees north of the campsite, frantically waving her arms. "What's wrong?" "Did something happen?" Rather than try to explain, Chigusa led them to the spot where the vials of potions littered the ground.

"Aren't these the ones that Hestia received from Nahza…?"

"Oh, and also, I saw Mr. Cranell run off that way. He looked very distressed…"

"…Lilly thinks it's safe to say they've got mixed up in something bad."

Said the prum as she reached down to inspect the potions for any kind of clue.

"Indeed, it seems unlikely that a monster did something to Lady Hestia. So that means this was the work of other adventurers?"

"Kidnapping? Without any of us or *Loki Familia* noticing?"

Welf and Mikoto's conversation going on over her head, Lilly's hand shook as she found something.

"This is…"

"Found it…!"

Bell saw a large blue crystal reaching up toward the ceiling as he made his way among the trees.

Stuffing the map down the front of his shirt, Bell picked up his pace. The ground was uneven with thousands of thick roots. He tore through the forest with powerful strides as if guided by the wind.

The Central Tree was due east of the crystal landmark that stood directly in front of him. He squinted his eyes as the crystal's glow grew more intense with each step. The trees thinned out as he emerged into a very open and bright location.

"He's here, Mord!"

An adventurer hidden in the shade of one of the last remaining trees saw the boy and called up toward the crystal.

Bell came to a stop. The adventurer who emerged from behind the blue crystal was none other than the person who he'd bumped into in Rivira, Mord.

"That was fast, Little Rookie!"

"…The goddess?!"

He immediately figured out that the man in front of him was the one responsible for Hestia's disappearance and wasted no time asking him about it. Mord moved out from under the shadow of the crystal, his lips forming a toothy grin.

"Yer Lady Worship was nothing more than bait to draw you out, little punk. We haven't done jack shit! After all, who'd be stupid enough to hurt a god? They can hold one hell of a grudge!"

Bell's eyes sharpened. He was their real target.

"Why…What do you want with me?"

"You must have some idea. You can't seriously be that stupid, can you, record holder?"

The man's voice was laced with a thick, cold hatred. It told Bell everything he needed to know.

The reason that the man had gone as far as capturing Hestia to lure him out was…

"You alone?"

"…Yes."

"Is that so? Well, I brought some insurance, just in case."

Rustle, rustle.

Upper-class adventurers emerged from behind trees and under grass. There were too many for Bell to count offhand, at least twenty in all.

Mord's group moved to surround Bell, his body tensing up on the spot.

"Don't have a heart attack, they won't touch you—follow me!"

Mord jerked his chin over his shoulder. Bell had no choice but to do what he was told. The squad of adventurers wasn't far behind—*clack, clack*—tapping their exposed blades against their armor as if waiting for the fun to begin. Bell kept his mouth shut and tried to ignore the thinly veiled excited smiles that surrounded him.

His first priority was to rescue Hestia, but that was impossible under these conditions. He didn't know where she was being held, and no one here was about to let him have a look around. Bell came to the conclusion that he had no choice but to listen to their demands for the time being.

He had fought enough monsters to be calm in the face of danger. However, he didn't recognize the quiver running through his limbs at this very moment as fear.

"This place…"

Mord led Bell to a small plateau.

The surface was almost perfectly smooth, with a circular area slightly higher than the rest. About seven mcders in diameter, it was unmistakably a stage designed for an audience.

"Up, now." Once again, Bell did as he was told. Mord was close behind. The squad of adventurers surrounded the stage. There was no way to escape.

"And now is when the fun begins. We duel."

"Duel…?"

"That's right, a duel! And the pathetic loser has to do whatever the winner tells him…When I win, I'm takin' all of yer good-looking equipment and selling it for profit."

The scars on Mord's face warped as he grinned yet again, as if to say, *you might as well hand everything over now.* The look in his eyes and the tone of his voice showed extreme confidence.

The winner would take everything from the loser. Bell needed a moment to let that archaic and violent rule sink in. He narrowed his eyes, eyebrows sinking as low as they would go.

Steadying his breath, Bell responded with as much resolve as he could muster.

"Release the goddess if I win."

"...Sure, sure. *If* you win."

Mord's face went blank for a moment when Bell issued his demand. However, a thin, cold grin reappeared on his lips in no time, his eyes glaring.

The surface of the stage was covered with loose dirt and small pieces of crystal. The imposing form of the towering blue crystal stood not too far away. Bell and Mord took their places in the middle of the arena, pulling weapons from the sheaths around their waists.

The type of weapons they carried gave clues about each of the combatants' fighting styles. The Hestia Knife in his right hand and Ushiwakamaru in his left, Bell fought with a combination of high speed and an overwhelming flurry of knife strikes. The crowd of adventurers around the stage started whistling and hollering as Bell took a defensive stance.

As for Mord, he slowly withdrew a great sword that he kept strapped to his back, longsword still at his waist.

"But don't get the wrong idea, ya punk-ass brat."

He rested the gigantic sword on his right shoulder and reached behind his back with his left hand.

Then he laughed. Dark and evil, his eyes glinted at Bell.

"This is a show—where I beat the livin' shit out of you!"

He thrust the massive weapon into the ground.

The force of the impact was enough to crack the stage as well as send up an explosion of loose dirt and debris. Bell felt the ground shake through his boots as Mord disappeared from sight. "Dammit, man!" came the angry voice of an adventurer behind him as he took a face-full of the dust. Bell quickly jumped away from the cloud to gain some distance, set his feet, and watched carefully.

"Huh...?"

The dirt cloud was gone, but Bell couldn't believe his eyes.

The great sword was still stuck in the ground, but Mord was gone. Not left or right—Bell quickly scanned the audience to see if he was trying to sneak up on him from behind using them as cover. Mord wasn't there.

Above. His eyes went wide as he looked toward the ceiling—but the blow came *from the side.*

"Ge-HA?!"

Something about the size and shape of a fist swung in from the right side of his head. It was powerful enough to take Bell off of his feet. He quickly recovered, rolling a few times before jumping back up. Bell quickly looked around the stage, doing his best to ignore the throbbing pain in his right temple. But Mord was nowhere to be seen.

Bell had just enough time to register confusion before the next hit came.

—A jump kick?!

Whoosh. He could hear air whistling by his ears a moment before the heel of a sabaton iron boot buried itself in his chest. Eyes flying open as all the air in his lungs was expelled, Bell was once again launched backward. Landing flat on his back and fighting for breath, Bell quickly rolled away from the spot after sensing a violent aura coming right for him. The place where his head was just a moment ago suddenly crumbled. A stomp attack had just landed.

Absolute hell was waiting for him as Bell climbed back to his feet.

An unrelenting storm of punches and kicks were unleashed on his body.

"HAAAAAAAAAAAAAAAAAAAAAAAAAA!!"

Blood and dirt flew with every blow. Left-right, right-left. The audience roared with excitement as Bell was pushed closer and closer to the edge of the stage. Their arms waving and fists pumping, Bell was caught in a fierce whirlwind of bloodlust.

The boy was seeing stars every time a blow landed, but he came to realize that he couldn't see the attacker.

Struggling to stay conscious, Bell focused on the area directly in front of him and tried to assess the situation. This wasn't a Skill— maybe Magic? He had never encountered anything like this and was much too slow to react. Taking punch after punch, explosions of pain erupted all over his body.

The force of each hit sent his body right and left, flicks of blood scattering across the stage floor.

"Smash his head in, Mord!"

"Amazing! We can't see 'im either?!"

"Rip that smart-aleck rabbit's nose clean off his face!"

There were still sounds. Iron boots were clicking, the air was rustling.

However, all the noise surrounding the duel canceled them all out. Bell had no way to predict where Mord's next blow was coming from.

Even shifting his body when he could feel the attacker's aura did little to protect him. The amount of damage Mord had inflicted using this strategy had completely negated Bell's Agility advantage despite their Statuses and Levels being fairly equal. Bell's half-a-second delayed reaction was becoming his downfall.

Mord used Bell's lack of knowledge as a shield and didn't give him any time to react.

"Get back in there!"

"…?!"

Bell had been forced all the way to the edge of the stage. One of the onlookers shoved him back toward the center. Leaning forward to catch his balance, Bell took another direct shot to his ribs from Mord's knee.

His consciousness was unstable. But the pain from every punch and kick was not the cause.

It was the spite, malice, and hostility of people.

Bell had never encountered anything like that before. Not once had he been trapped in a whirlpool of hate and jealousy. This was his first time confronting the darker side of humanity.

—It was making him dizzy.

Jeers and insults were hurled at him from every direction, joyous laughter and piercing glares as well. Light-headed and with a twinge of fear, Bell realized that this stage was in a completely different world from the one that he knew, the warm, supportive realm that he called home.

It was an adventurer's baptism of fire.

This was part of being an adventurer, a rite of passage. Now, this was what made an adventurer.

Wine and women, riches and titles were all required to make an outlaw's party.

Bell gritted his teeth in a desperate attempt to stay conscious even as the blows kept coming.

Bell and Mord's very one-sided duel was surrounded by a ring of excited adventurers yelling at the top of their lungs.

Two sets of eyes watched the "show" created by the outlaws from a safe distance.

"You have vulgar taste…Do you seriously find watching this kind of fight interesting?"

"Harsh, Asfi, very harsh."

Hidden in the canopy on the edge of the forest overlooking the stage, Hermes shrugged as his follower glared at him with unyielding eyes.

"You said that you wanted to see the power of Bell Cranell with your own eyes…Did you come all the way down into the Dungeon to see something like this?"

"Actually, I was hoping to see him fight a floor boss, but that didn't work out so well."

A shade of disappointment filled Hermes's orange-colored eyes as he watched Bell jerk and shake below. "This is even more sadistic," Asfi responded with a tone of sadness in her voice.

"Going out of your way to give them my helmet, informing all of those adventurers…I'm beginning to think you have a grudge against him."

"Oh? I'd call it tough love."

"It's impossible to call this love."

"Now hear me out. Sooner or later, adventurers were going to bare their fangs at Bell. You said it yourself, he wasn't well-liked, yes? Bell was naïve, and at that rate he would eventually meet up with something far crueler. Vulgar or not, I wanted him to understand this side of humanity."

Asfi fell silent at her god's level of tolerance and acceptance of all types of people.

Not only did Hermes inform them of a way to get Bell isolated, but he'd also provided a magic item that allowed them to avoid any entanglements with the Kenki. He'd even asked them to entertain him with a show.

This might have gone too far to be a simple test for Bell, but perhaps it was exactly what he was hoping for.

"But while I can't deny I'm enjoying this on some level, I've done something terrible to Hestia."

"...And if the boy should fall here?"

"Then he didn't have what it takes, that's all."

Hermes didn't take his eyes off the fight, even as he responded without hesitation to Asfi's questions.

Until finally, he lifted his eyes to a different angle and said:

"But even now...both Bell *and the others* shine brightly with the thoughts of their friends."

"—Found 'em!"

Welf signaled to the others as soon as he caught a glimpse of a large group of adventurers.

There were three people behind him: Ouka, Mikoto, and Chigusa with her backpack. *Shf-shf-shf*, all of them quickly ran through the grass in the forest to meet up with him. Moving as a group, they analyzed their surroundings and made their approach.

"*Loki Familia* really did leave us behind."

"Let's consider our options after we have safely recovered Mr. Bell and Lady Hestia."

Mikoto and Ouka exchanged words while equipping themselves with short bows and arrows from Chigusa's backpack.

"Just to warn you guys, I'm pretty useless against people that strong. All I can do is seal their magic!"

"That's plenty."

Ouka nodded at Welf before joining Mikoto behind a large tree root. The two of them made eye contact for a moment and jumped into the air, unleashing arrows toward their opponents.

"Oi!" "What was that?!"

"The ones who were with the Little Rookie! How the hell did they find us?!"

Although the shots came from behind them, the upper-class adventurers drew their weapons and deflected the arrows with ease, proving their skill. Mikoto and Ouka fired four arrows per second, creating a rain of unrelenting projectiles. The adventurers who had been watching the fight quickly broke away from the stage and ran toward the source.

"This was part of the plan anyway! Wipe them out!"

"Who the heck would be intimidated by Takemikazuchi's banner, huh?!"

The fastest of the upper-class adventurers quickly maneuvered through the arrow rain, shouting threats as they went. Ouka saw the first few break through their ranged attacks when he fired his last arrow. He discarded his short bow without hesitation.

"Chigusa, a spear!"

"Sir!"

Taking one from her a second later, Ouka moved to engage.

"Too slow, nimrod!"

A werewolf with particularly high Agility sidestepped Ouka's first strike. Smiling as he made it past the first defense, the werewolf turned his claws on Mikoto, who had just thrown down her own short bow.

"—Yah!"

"?!"

Seizing the opportunity, Mikoto quickly grasped hold of her attacker's wrist and flung him cleanly over her shoulder.

The werewolf landed square on his back. Before he had a chance to register the pain, however, Ouka stomped straight into the werewolf's gut with all of his might.

"*Gheh?*"

"We are followers of *Lord Takemikazuchi*, yes?"

The werewolf's body flinched in response. Ouka and Mikoto's teamwork had put one of the upper-class adventurers completely out of commission.

Being a god of combat, Takemikazuchi made sure that all of his followers were proficient with many types of weapons, even empty-handed fighting styles. Not limited to just bows and spears, Ouka and Mikoto were able to adjust their battle style to fit any situation.

With their supporter Chigusa by their side, the two of them were able to respond to the newcomers as well. Using a mixture of techniques and battle savvy, the three of them moved to find the most advantageous position to continue the fight.

"The sons of bitches are hard to put down...!"

"Idiots! We've got the numbers! Surround and overwhelm them already!"

The last of the upper-class adventurers arrived to join the fray, yelling at those who were already engaged in combat.

Welf looked on, overwhelmed as adventurers just kept coming.

"Hey, there's too many of them!"

"We'll have to use the trees to our advantage...Stay close!"

Ouka's voice was steady and in control despite the twenty enemies brandishing their weapons in his direction.

Welf took his place to form a four-man cell as they used the landscape for protection during the brawl.

"Hey, what's going on?!"

Hestia's eyes went wide as the sounds of battle echoed through the forest.

She could tell that this was no skirmish but something much, much bigger. The sound of clashing swords and small vibrations through the trees was more than enough to make her shiver in fright.

She had a bad feeling that this had something to do with the "lesson" Mord had planned for Bell. Something bad was happening to him, she knew it. Fighting hard against the ropes cutting into her wrists and ankles, she desperately tried to get answers from the men Mord had left behind.

"Ahh…Sounds like they're having a good time…"

"Dammit, I wanna go watch…"

"—Hey! No ignoring gods! That's an order!"

The two adventurers sitting on the ground on either side of Hestia just stared blankly back at her. "Urrggghhhaaaaaaa!!" she yelled as her face bulged with rage. Unfortunately for her, her small build was not the least bit intimidating. Her captors weren't sure how to react.

"!" "Who's there?!"

"Huh? Huh?"

Hestia looked left and right in rapid-fire succession as the adventurers suddenly sprang to their feet.

Rustle, rustle. They quickly spotted movement in the thick bushes just beyond their hiding place—two long, white ears emerged as a rabbit poked its face out from behind the leaves.

"B-Bell?"

"'Course not!"

"Al-Miraj, eh?…Scared the shit out of me."

The rabbit monster flicked its head from side to side, its red eyes scanning the surroundings before it hopped out of the bush. Holding a honey cloud in its small hands, it quickly bounded through the area and out of sight as if looking for more fruit.

One of the adventurers breathed a sigh of relief, but then suddenly furrowed his brow.

"Wait a second, why would there be an Al-Miraj on the eighteenth…?"

That particular rabbit monster only appeared on the thirteenth and fourteenth floors of the Dungeon. Monsters tended to attack anything they perceived as a threat, including other monsters. So how could one Al-Miraj, a fairly weak monster, make it all the way down to the eighteenth floor on its own? The adventurer couldn't shake the feeling that something was amiss.

He stepped away from Hestia and toward the spot where the rabbit disappeared when suddenly—*splat splatt!*

"Huh…?"

"*Ghaa.*"

Something hit him square in the chest. Honey-colored juices ran down the front of his armor. He looked toward his ally; the man had been hit in the head with the same thing.

The moment the two of them realized they'd been hit with fruit, the ground shook as a tree collapsed behind them.

The two of them slowly turned around to find...

"*Guuraa...*"

Three bugbears, each drooling with hunger.

""—UWAAAHHHHHHHHHHHHHHHHH!!""

"ROOOOAAAAARRRRRRRRRRRRRRRRR!!"

The three monsters howled in unison and set their sights on the fruit-covered adventurers. They were after the honey cloud, but it was suddenly mobile as the adventurers took off in the opposite direction. The bugbears gave chase, leaving Hestia by herself, blinking in confusion. *Boing, boing*, the Al-Miraj came back to the clearing and stopped in front of her.

"Oooooh! I taste horrible, so don't eat me!"

"—Stroke of midnight's bell."

The voice came from inside the monster's body. Hestia watched in shock as the Magic was lifted.

"Even monsters would get sick if they tried to eat Lady Hestia."

"Supporter!"

A cloud of gray ash surrounded the rabbit's white fur. As soon as the cloud cleared, there was no monster, only Lilly in its place.

She had fooled the adventurers using her Magic, Cinder Ella, which could transform her body into anything she could clearly picture in her mind, even monsters. The technique that had served her so well during her days as a thief allowed her to sic monsters onto her adversaries.

"You're alone?! No, that's not important. How did you find me?!"

"Lilly was with Welf until she figured it out right before finding Mr. Bell. Lilly found this place because...of the perfume that Lady Hestia put on this morning."

Because someone had taken Hestia against her will, chances were she was being held as a hostage. Lilly had connected the dots, broken away from the main group, used her Magic to transform into a monster, and rescued the captured goddess.

She found the bottle of perfume that Hestia had purchased in Rivira among the scattered vials of potions. The smell led her straight to Hestia.

"Lilly's Magic can copy physical forms as well as basic characteristics of the target. Lilly can't get any stronger than her Status, but copying an inborn sense of smell is possible."

"Th-that's convenient! Shape-shifting magic!"

Certain types of animal people were known to have particularly sharp senses with the assistance of their Status.

Lilly's sense of smell had been enhanced by spending time disguised as a chienthrope and a werewolf. That's what tipped her off.

"Mr. Bell is fighting at the base of that large crystal. Let's get going."

"*Yes!*"

Lilly cut Hestia's bonds with a knife and the two of them ran headlong toward the crystal.

"*Blasphemous Burn!*"

Anti-magic Magic—Welf activated Will-o'-the-Wisp, causing the three adventurers who were conjuring Magic to be overtaken by Ignis Fatuus. Three explosions erupted around the battle.

The afflicted adventurers collapsed to the charred patches of ground at their feet, smoke wafting from their mouths.

"One of those bastards has some frickin' weird Magic!"

"Smash him first!"

Mord's two buddies, human adventurers, converged on Welf.

"You wouldn't gang up on a smith, would you…?!"

Two Level 2 adventurers advanced on the Level 1 Welf. While he had time to set his feet, the two of them were far too fast for him to counter. He barely managed to use the flat side of his broadsword as a shield.

The two blades clashed, sending the strongest shock wave Welf ever experienced through his body. His defensive stance broken, the young man had no time to regain his footing because the second adventurer had already launched his own assault.

"Eat this!"

"—?!"

The man's iron boot carved an arc through the air and came down hard into his right shoulder, cutting into Welf's salamander wool jacket. He managed to avoid a deadly strike by shifting his body to the left, but the strap used to hold his broadsword snapped in half.

The broadsword's sheath and the weapon wrapped in white cloth fell away from his body.

The sheath simply fell to his feet, but the weapon fell down the steep hill at his back and into the thick forest below.

Time stood still as Welf watched it tumble farther and farther away, helpless to retrieve it. He took an iron boot to the ribs and fell down a second later.

"Geh—?!"

"It's over!"

Welf felt the impact throughout his back and saw a sword coming straight for his chest—then suddenly a strong gust of wind—

"Haggh?!"

The blade of Lyu's wooden sword.

Welf watched in amazement as the man who was about to kill him took a hard hit from behind and collapsed like a bag of dirt.

"I thought the forest was too loud…So this is what's going on."

"You…!"

The one who saved Welf was none other than the hooded adventurer.

She kept her wooden sword pointed toward the ground and stared down the remaining adventurer.

"W-who the hell are you?! A friend of this punk?"

The man menacingly brandished his sword, but the girl calmly put her hands on either side of the hood and pulled it back.

"Apparently you didn't learn your lesson. We shouldn't have held back the first time."

"—Gaaaaaiiiigh!!"

The man let out a scream as if he'd seen visions of his own death the moment that the hooded adventurer's face—Lyu's face—was exposed.

He had been with Mord at The Benevolent Mistress when the waitresses overpowered them. He screamed because the most frightening and violent among them, the elf, had now appeared right in front of his nose once again.

A look of despair overtook him as he turned to run, but Lyu showed no mercy and struck him down before he could take a step.

"I apologize for my tardiness. My blade shall assist you."

"Uh, yeah, thanks."

Lyu pulled her hood back over her face and swished the cape. She advanced on the group attacking Ouka and Mikoto. Their enemies dropped like flies, on the ground seconds later and moaning in pain.

Welf looked through the forest, the ground littered with fallen upper-class adventurers, for a moment before looking in the direction that the white-wrapped weapon had fallen.

"..."

He moved up to the edge as if it were a wall and looked over.

He glared down the hill like it was his father's sworn enemy for a few seconds.

Turning his back to it, he rushed off to rejoin Ouka and the others.

Impact after bone-crushing impact echoed through the clearing.

Bell bobbed and weaved, the outside of his arms pulsing with pain as he stood his ground.

The ring of adventurers who surrounded the stage was already gone. The sound of weapons clashing and roars of battle could be heard in the forest not too far away. *Takemikazuchi Familia*, with the assistance of Welf and Lyu, was putting up quite a fight. Bell and Mord's duel continued on the suddenly quiet stage, its audience nowhere to be seen.

One scream, and then another. The outlaws were dropping fast.

"...?"

There was an invisible attack, a solid fist on the end of the meaty arm that tore through the air. The blow landed squarely on the outside of Bell's skinny arms.

There was also a sense of confusion—Bell could feel it coming from the opponent he couldn't see. Mord took a step back, changed his angle, and unleashed a flurry of powerful kicks.

Block. Block. Block.

Although his defense wasn't perfect, Bell had a good idea where the attacks would come from, as well as their timing. The boy showed no signs of losing his footing.

His ruby-red eyes had a lock on where Mord's invisible body was at every moment.

The invisible presence shook once again. *Thump, thump.* The sound of iron hitting stone reverberated through the air as the invisible man jumped backward to gain some distance. *This can't be right*, he thought to himself as he set his feet and held his breath. He completely hid his presence from Bell, like an assassin on the job.

Once he was certain that those ruby-red eyes hadn't followed him, Mord snuck around Bell's right shoulder and charged.

"—!!"

Bell's body reacted in an instant. He swung his left leg back and to his right with the utmost confidence.

It was a long, sweeping kick with his well-armored heel leading. His left foot cut through what looked like open air.

Whok! His greave hit the chin of his assailant.

The confusion turned to shock. The invisible presence backed away to avoid yet another counterattack, shaking—Mord's eyes burned with pure rage as he roared with anger.

"H-how can you see?!"

Bell *couldn't* see him.

Mord's aura of fury and confusion engulfed the air around the stage. Bell could not see him, and yet he was looking right at him. In truth, it wasn't the man's aura that Bell was sensing, but the intensity of his eyes.

—Just like the *intense gaze of another*, the feeling of being judged.

In the past two months, Bell had noticed the gaze of a certain pair of silver eyes always following him. The feeling of being watched had heightened his senses tremendously. He didn't know who it came from, but it would strike without warning, making him jump in surprise. His sensitivity had dramatically increased after feeling it brush across his shoulders so many times.

The intense stare of a deity had had a great impact on the boy who was already much more cowardly than other humans. He was nothing more than a rabbit looking for cover.

Mord's "gaze" of malice was like a beacon—as were the two sets of eyes looking down at him from the trees. Bell could feel them all.

He knew where the enemy's eyes were looking, he knew where they were looking from, he could "see" where his enemy was.

The fact that Mord was invisible was irrelevant. It was the intensity in his eyes that gave him away.

"Damn it, damn it, damn it all to hell!"

The sound of a sword being drawn.

Mord had been enjoying himself, punching and kicking Bell to his heart's content up until now. Playtime was over, time to kill. The weapon, just like his body, was invisible due to the power of the Hades Head.

Bell's eyes flew open. Sensing his opponent's charge, Bell dove headfirst to the side. He heard the air whistle just as he got out of the way of the sword.

Bell rolled a few times on the surface of the stage. *Snatch!* He flung out his right hand in mid-roll and grabbed a handful of loose dirt and small blue crystals before regaining his feet.

"I'm gonna slice you like a—"

Screamed Mord as he raised his sword and charged in for another attack.

Bell once again picked up his attack angle from the man's gaze and clenched his right fist, grinding the crystals and dirt into a fine powder.

A heartbeat later, he threw the powder straight into Mord's path.

"Wha?!"

The blue powder hit Mord square in the face. Thousands of pieces of crystal spread out over his body.

The man's ghostly blue outline appeared in the center of the stage. Even the sword came into view. Bell now knew exactly where he was.

Bell squared his shoulders toward his mostly invisible opponent, the twinkling blue crystals guiding him.

"Heh!"

"Ha, hooooooo!"

Bell drew Ushiwakamaru, flipped it to a backhanded position, and charged headlong toward his opponent. Mord raised his long-sword and brought it down on the white rabbit.

Bell saw the twinkling blue outline of the weapon coming down diagonally from the left and deflected it using the crimson blade in his left hand.

The blades collided in an explosion of sparks; the screech of metal on metal pierced the air. A sudden crack sounded from the invisible but sparkling blue longsword. Suddenly, a piece of it appeared out of nowhere as the blade snapped in half. The force of the blow pushed Mord back a few steps. He froze in shock, holding what was left of the sword in his right hand.

However, Bell didn't stop.

Planting his left foot directly in front of his enemy, Bell used the clock-wise momentum from the previous swing to jump and spin into the air.

His right foot whipped through the air with the strength and speed of a tornado, the technique he'd acquired from Aiz.

"Graaaagh!!"

His right heel made contact with the side of Mord's head.

"GAHH?!"

He hit the same place that Mord had attacked first, the right temple, with his own armored boot.

The man's body was thrown back by centrifugal force, the motion accompanied by yet another cracking sound. Except this time, it was coming from the magic item he was wearing, the Hades Head.

Cracks covered the helmet like a spiderweb before it shattered into pieces. Mord's body reappeared at the same moment.

He landed on his back, his fists shaking in anger as he once again made eye contact with Bell.

"Wh–at the…fuck!! Rot in hell, you bastard!!"

Mord clutched the side of his head as he climbed back to his feet, bloodshot eyes never once leaving their target.

Bell's body was in rough shape. Cuts, bruises, and blood covered his arms and face as he steadied his breath and took another defensive stance.

The sounds of battle still raged around them as they stared each other down, getting ready for one last charge to settle this.

"Stop—this—*now*—!!"

Cling…Everything fell silent.

Even Mord and Bell froze in place with their fists raised and looked in the direction the loud voice came from.

Standing there for all to see was Hestia. Lilly was standing next to the small goddess as she looked out over the battlefield.

"Bell, everyone, I'm okay! This battle is now pointless! All of you, stand down!"

Bell felt a wave of relief wash over him upon hearing her voice, and he let his arms slowly drop.

Welf's group also sheathed their weapons, following the goddess's wishes.

On the other hand, Mord's rage did not subside. Veins throbbing on his face, he turned to face his allies, who were at a loss as to what to do.

"The words of a goddess don't mean shit! End them, all of them!!"

Most of the upper-class adventurers were on the ground and writhing in pain thanks to Lyu's counterattack. But they'd already come this far; they couldn't turn back now. The adventurers rose to their feet as Mord turned back toward Bell and set his feet to charge.

However.

"—You will stop."

The entire floor seemed to fall silent with those words, the air eerily still.

Mord and all of the adventurers' bodies stopped moving as if they were being restrained by unseen chains. The color leaving their faces, many sets of eyes locked onto Hestia. Their throats quivered in fear. Even Bell and those who came to help him were lost for words at the power exuding from the expressionless goddess.

This was the power that made the people of this world bow down to the gods. They had no choice but to lower their heads to a being from the heavenly plane of Deusdia.

Hestia unleashed her godly providence not for her own benefit, but to stop the children from hurting one another.

"Put down your weapons."

"Uh, ah…"

Bell had never seen Hestia look like this, or use such a persuasive tone.

Mord and his adventurers could only grunt and moan as they stepped backward, overwhelmed by the immense pressure being emitted from the goddess's blue eyes.

"…uwaHHHHHHH!!"

One of the upper-class adventurers turned tail and ran. Then a second and a third, the others watching and contemplating their options. Suddenly, everyone started a full retreat. "W-wait, you idiots!" screamed Mord. It didn't take long for him to join them.

A distinct calm filled the forest, as if the storm had passed.

"—Bell, are you all right?!"

"Ughaa?!"

Bell still couldn't move even as Hestia tackled him to the ground. Time came back to him. The goddess sat on top of his stomach as she took one of Miach's high potions out of her pouch, popped off the lid, and poured it onto Bell's face. "Bwff?!" Bell spat in surprise even as the sweet liquid flowed into his injuries and healed them. The potion made its way into his bloodstream and through his body, healing his other wounds in the process while restoring his strength.

"Uwahhhh, I'm sooooo sorry, Bell! It's my fault you ended up like this—"

"Ah, no, Goddess…I couldn't protect you in the first place, so… Please don't cry."

Bell didn't know how to react as Hestia collapsed onto his chest, tears pouring from her eyes. He slowly wrapped his arms around her, as if trying to comfort a crying child. Just moments ago, she was unmistakably a deity from another world. But now she was looking very human. Bell didn't know what to think anymore.

The gods were still worthy of the awe and reverence of the children of Gekai even with their divine powers, Arcanum, sealed.

This was because their life on Gekai was nothing more than a game to them…They could still unleash their divine providence and force everyone around them to bow down. But at the same time, they cared about the children who had pledged to follow them, and they wanted to assist in their life stories.

Bell looked down at the deity who had used her power not for her own gain but to save people just like him…Hestia looked up, eyes filled with tears. At that moment, Bell felt something new for his goddess, an even deeper connection.

"You in one piece, Bell?"

"Welf…"

"Lilly understands the situation, but please don't act alone! Mr. Bell had plenty of chances to ask us for help!"

"Mmm—" Hestia once again buried her face in Bell's chest as Welf and Lilly appeared on the stage. The red-haired young man was doing his best to force a smile as Lilly scolded Bell. The boy apologized and thanked them both. Mikoto and her group watched from a distance, smiling at the bonds of friendship that held the battle party together.

"…Hmmm. Sorry, *Takemikazuchi Familia*, I've caused trouble for you, too."

"Not at all, Lady Hestia. We were happy to help."

"Thank you for your help too, Hood."

"Hood…"

Hestia had stopped crying and stood up, finally acting like the goddess she really was. Her face hidden under the hood of her cape, Lyu mumbled to herself as everyone's shoulders relaxed.

A soft breeze came to the forest with the battle finished. Everyone there had a genuine smile on their face.

Then: "Anyway, how should we—" Hestia began. That's when it happened.

"Eh—?"

The ground beneath their feet shook.

No, the entire floor was shaking.

"Q-quake?"

"No, this is…"

"The Dungeon is shaking?"

Chigusa, Mikoto, and Ouka spoke to one another with their eyes on the ground.

Zhaa, zhaa—the vibrations became more intense, causing the leaves to rub against one another.

"This is…*a bad tremor.*"

Bell realized at the moment that those words left Lyu's lips…

An Irregular was about to occur, and this was a warning sign.

Every feature of the eighteenth floor seemed to shiver around them—the next moment…

Something above them cast a massive shadow over the stage.

"…The hell is that?"

The words fell from Welf's mouth as he looked upward.

The entire ceiling of the eighteenth floor was covered in millions upon millions of crystals, each providing light. The largest one of these, the "sun" of the floor, had something inside it.

Something big. Something moving.

A piece of it reflected onto every surface of the massive white crystal, as if it were inside one big kaleidoscope. It was blocking the source of the light, each one of its movements casting a shadow across the vast landscape.

Just like the others, Bell had noticed the thing inside the crystal and watched it closely as the biggest tremor yet overtook him. All of the adventurers present on the stage took a defensive stance, their hands going for their weapons out of reflex.

Then—*crack.*

It appeared.

The thing was still moving inside the crystal, but a thick line had appeared on the surface of the crystal itself.

"A crack…?! Monster?!"

"That's impossible. This is a safe point!"

Several pieces of crystal fell away, glinting in the sky as they fell to the ground.

More and more lines appeared on the surface of the crystal as Mikoto and Lilly practically screamed at what they were watching.

The black thing inside the crystal was doing more than wiggling; it was punching and kicking from within. The figure seemed to grow with each passing moment.

"Aw, c'mon…No way. This is my fault."

Whoosh. Every head snapped in Hestia's direction.

Completely ignoring the stares of the people around her, Hestia didn't take her eyes off the ceiling and continued:

"That was almost nothing…There's no way?"

The echoes of the cracks were getting louder, as though they were attempting to crush everything beneath them. Hestia watched in disbelief.

"*I was noticed…?!*"

"No, this isn't Hestia's fault."

Hermes watched the entire floor continue to shake from his perch on top of the tree.

"Lord Hermes, what did you do this time?!"

"Of course, none of my little amusements could trigger something like this."

Asfi's lack of trust in her god came out in her voice as she unloaded all of her frustration at the top of her lungs. Hermes, however, kept his eyes on the black shadow inside the crystal.

"Ahh, Uranus…Haven't you been listening to the prayers? I didn't hear anything about this."

Hermes's eyes narrowed in frustration. He was so upset by his predicament that he practically spat the words out of his mouth.

"Stop ignoring me and please tell me what's going on! What is that thing?!"

"Out of control, I'd say. And for some reason it's more sensitive than usual. And it's noticed our presence."

Hermes once again ignored Asfi's borderline panicked confusion and continued talking quietly, almost to himself.

"The Dungeon *hates it*, you see. It hates the fact that gods are all the way down here."

Hermes continued to watch the ceiling despite the suspicious look he was getting from Asfi. She opened her mouth to speak but was suddenly interrupted by the sound of another loud crack.

The monsters lurking in the forest chose that moment to howl at the "sky." The sound of their vicious howls mixed with the cracking sound coming from above and resonated through the whole landscape.

"Asfi, go to Rivira and call for reinforcements."

"Reinforcements? Don't tell me we're going to have to fight that thing? Not run away?"

"Certainly looks that way…"

Hermes let his words trail off. A moment later, a new series of echoes joined the chorus from the south—a rockslide.

Asfi's head snapped in that direction. The pupils of her eyes shrank behind her glasses.

"The tunnel, our only escape route, is blocked…I don't think it wants us to get away."

"—?! I've had it! If I don't get out of this alive, I'm haunting you until the end of time, Lord Hermes!"

Asfi flung herself out of the tree with reckless abandon. Hermes watched her go, his shoulders slumping out of sympathy for her situation. He looked back up toward the ceiling once she was out of sight.

"Well, then…"

The cracks were growing, scattering like a spiderweb of lightning. A rain of crystal shards fell to the ground below.

The thing stuck its face out from the top of the crystal, shaped like an open lotus flower, with a thunderous boom.

Hermes watched in awe, frozen to the spot, before cracking a smile in spite of himself.

"Yep, that's a floor boss."

The monster thrust its face out of the bottom of the heavily damaged crystal.

It was almost as if a severed head had been placed on the ceiling of the eighteenth floor. However, this head was most definitely alive. Its massive eyes glared at anything that moved as it stared down from above. Its shoulders and chest emerged with another explosion of crystal shards shooting out in all directions. With most of its upper body free, it opened its gigantic jaws.

"OOOOOOOOOOOOOOOOOOOOOOOOOOOOOOOOOOO OOOOOOOOOO!!"

A booming roar made the entire floor tremble. The otherworldly monster, a Goliath that surpassed the seventeenth floor's version in every way, was born into the safe point of the Dungeon.

The Goliath slammed its fists into the crystal until its legs started to emerge and gravity took care of the rest.

It fell toward the ground like a black meteor, surrounded by twinkling crystal shards, large enough to engulf any humans in its path. Flipping its feet downward in mid-fall, the beast landed with a loud crunch directly on top of the Central Tree.

The resulting shock wave was deafening. The trees roots were crushed under the monster's weight. In fact, the trunk was thrust halfway underground as the colossal tree buckled under the giant's weight. The crystal shards weren't far behind, slicing into the trees and tall grass of the plains, embedding themselves in the ground.

The "blue sky" was gone. The crystal that supplied the most light to the floor—the one the Goliath just smashed to pieces—had lost its luster. A shroud of darkness fell over the eighteenth floor. What was left of the broken crystal faintly glowed in the middle of the sea of blue crystals. An unnatural night with a full moon had come to pass.

An irregular Monster Rex stood in the middle of it all.

The monster slowly lifted its head as it stepped down from the tree.

"...Wh-wha...?"

The people with the best view of the Goliath's landing were Mord and his group of adventurers.

They were running away from the edge of the eastern forest and toward the plains. Unfortunately for them, they were coming up on the Central Tree when the first crack rang out.

The Goliath on the seventeenth floor had skin the color of ash; this one was pure black, with eyes the color of blood. It loomed over Mord, unblinking.

"—OOOOOOOOOOOOOOOOOOOOOOOOWWWWW!!"

"H–HYYEEEEEEEEEEEEEEEEEEEEEEEEEEEEEEEEEEEE EEE!!"

Everyone in Mord's group had been waiting for another party to defeat the floor boss on the seventeenth floor to gain safe passage. Engaging this new beast in combat wasn't an option. The group scattered in all directions, desperately trying to escape.

"What the hell is that...?!"

"Black Goliath...?!"

Bell's party had emerged from the forest and stood in shock of what greeted their eyes.

The Goliath made its move toward Mord's group as Welf and Lilly spoke to no one in particular. Even from this distance, Bell could tell that this Goliath was much more agile and powerful than the one he'd encountered on the seventeenth floor.

"That monster was probably sent to kill me...No, sent to kill the gods who came too deep."

The Dungeon had sensed the presence of the deities and had sent this monster specifically to assassinate them.

The others didn't completely understand what was going on. But every single one of them gulped as soon as Hestia told them that this floor boss was more than likely after her.

Although the beast was extremely powerful, it chased after anything that moved. Perhaps it was born too quickly to inherit the intelligence of other floor bosses.

"…W-we have to help them?!"

Bell was just as shaken as Welf and the others. But the sight of the other adventurers in danger helped him control his fear as he braced his legs to spring forward.

"Stand down."

"?!"

Lyu grabbed Bell's hand from behind.

The boy could see her sharp sky-blue gaze coming from underneath her hood.

"Do you really intend to assist them? With this party?"

Her expression was so blank, her very words seemed cold as she asked what should have been an obvious question.

Their party had only five upper-class adventurers to take down what was most likely at least a Level 4 Monster Rex. The difference in their strength was astronomical.

But most of all, was that group of outlaws worth saving at the potential cost of his friends' lives? Lyu's body language accented everything.

The boy's eyes opened a little bit wider as a look of uncertainty passed over his face.

But it lasted only for that instant.

"Let's help them."

Lyu's eyes narrowed at the boy's quick decision.

"You are unfit to lead a party."

Being who she was, Lyu's criticism cut deep.

Then he met her sharp gaze for one moment—and she smiled.

"But you are not wrong."

With Bell's expression fresh in her mind and a grin on her lips, Lyu raced away from the forest and toward the Goliath with her cape fluttering in her wake. She was the first to move to help the other party.

Bell's heart twinged for a moment before he took off after her at full speed.

Then Lilly, Welf, Mikoto, Ouka, Chigusa, and lastly Hestia.

No one voiced any disagreement, only exchanged glances and nods.

Sorry—and thank you. Their hearts and minds were unified.

Bell yelled:

"Let's go!"

Seven figures left the forest and entered the plains.

Screams of fear and confusion accompanied by echoes of powerful footsteps lay before them in the center of the eighteenth floor.

Bell's party threw themselves toward the giant, screaming a battle cry with all of their might.

CHAPTER 6 **PRAISE TO THE HEROES**

The ceiling had lost its white light, casting a dark blue curtain over the entirety of the eighteenth floor.

The adventurers gathering in the central square of Rivira could see everything from the top of the island in the middle of the lake.

"Just what is that…?"

A darkly hulking figure was running around the middle of the floor, chasing something. While they couldn't see what, they could hear bloodcurdling screams from their position next to the cliff beside the central square all too clearly.

An Irregular of this magnitude had never been encountered on this floor. The adventurers of Rivira were known for their ability to protect themselves, but none of them knew how to react to this. They all just stood there, watching.

"—Boris! Boris, are you here?!"

"A-Andromeda?! Where the heck you come from, thin air?! Right out of the sky…?"

"That doesn't matter right now! Boris, tell the adventurers to gather their weapons, we are going to slay that thing!"

Asfi's voice was fraught with desperation as she pleaded with the strongest man in Rivira, the owner of Rivira's Exchange. The beast of a man wore an eye patch over his left eye. He was not, however, thrilled about this proposal and took a step toward the girl.

"S-slay?! Don't be an idiot, Andromeda. And who said our weapons stock needs to be wasted to take that thing down?! It'd be better to get our asses out of here!"

"Escape is not an option! The southern cliff face has collapsed, making it impossible for anyone to leave this floor!"

The large man didn't take well to backtalk. However, his good eye happened to catch a cloud of dirt rising from the south. His neck slowly turned, jaw dropping lower and lower as he started to comprehend the situation.

"We buy ourselves some time, then make like inmates and burrow our way out..."

"A pitiful attempt at humor. How much time do you think it would take to remove enough stone to make the passage usable? Half a day? A full day? It would be interesting to see if any adventurers could buy enough of this time you mentioned for you to clear a path or if everyone would be wiped out first."

"...I-it's just a Goliath. There's no need for everyone to rush out there..."

"Does that look like *just a Goliath* to you?"

Asfi looked out over the cliff toward the black shadow rampaging under the cover of night. They could feel the impact of its mighty fists every time the Goliath swatted the ground from this distance.

"This is just my intuition, but I believe that the Goliath and our exit being cut off are linked. No one will be able to escape as long as that thing draws breath. It would be pointless to hope for reinforcements."

"...Damn it all to hell."

The man's muscular shoulders dropped the moment that Asfi finished her explanation.

The Goliath took another swing off in the distance, accompanied by even more screams of pain and another tremor.

"All right, maggots! You heard her, we're ending that monster here and now! I will personally see to it that anyone who chickens out will never set foot in this town again!"

All of the adventurers in the square couldn't move for a moment after Boris gave the order. Then, as if someone flipped a switch, every single one of them sprang into action. Equipping themselves with their best weapons, they exited the town and rushed toward the plain.

Asfi watched as the stragglers completed their preparations and set out as Rivira fell silent. Placing her hand on the railing above the cliff, she watched their advance.

"I suppose I should get moving…!"

Taking one last look at the giant, she planted her right foot on top of the railing and jumped off.

The great plain had turned into a hellish battlefield.

The Goliath had targeted Mord's group of adventurers. The ones who were unable to get out of the way fast enough were thrown sky-ward with each swing of its monolith-like fists. Even if they managed to dodge the blow, the impact on the ground was powerful enough to throw their bodies into the air like tissue paper.

"UWWAAAHHHH!!" Everyone could hear the screams of their allies, but none of them were able to think about anything but themselves. Self-preservation instincts had taken over as all of them desperately tried to put some distance between themselves and the black giant.

Their desperation had turned to madness, unfortunate allies flying through the air while their own fear made them scatter like flies in a futile attempt to escape.

"…oooo."

The Goliath followed each of its targets with a piercing gaze.

Physically, its body shape wasn't all that much different from an orc. Short but thick legs supported an upper body that made up about 60 percent of its total height. It slouched forward, long hair flowing halfway down its back.

The Goliath's eyes kept jumping from small shadow to small shadow as they ran in circles beneath it. So it stopped watching. Instead, it focused its two blood-colored orbs on the shadows far-thest away and leaned toward the ground.

A second later, the giant set off an explosion from its mouth.

"———AAAAAOOOOO!!"

A roar and a sonic boom erupted from between its jaws.

The blast made impact at the feet of the adventurer farthest away from the Goliath. The man was caught so off guard that he couldn't even scream as he was launched into the air along with large grassy chunks of the Dungeon floor. Mord and the rest of the adventurers watched him hit the ground like a puppet whose strings had been cut. Their eyes grew large as every hair on their bodies stood on end.

"H-howl…?!"

This was no ordinary howl used to inspire fear and intimidate. This was a magical attack that turned the Goliath's throat into a cannon. Its sheer power and range made the hellhounds' fire breath look childish by comparison.

Mord's group was trapped in a nightmare. If they were too close, they would be physically crushed. But they would be shot down one by one if they tried to run away. Each one of the adventurers turned pale as a ghost.

"OOOOOOOOOOOOOOOOOOOOOOOOOOOOOOOOO!!"

The Goliath leaned back and roared toward the ceiling. The sound carried to the far corners of the floor—and monsters responded.

"WHA?!"

From the forest, from the plain, from the wetlands.

Every single one of the monsters that was lurking on the eighteenth floor started to make their way toward the Goliath. The adventurers broke out in a cold sweat as they saw various types of monsters emerge and surround them.

Another wave of monsters arrived, cutting off any possible escape routes while growling and cackling at their prey.

"*Hyeeeeee—!*"

All of the adventurers had no choice but to draw their weapons, but now the Goliath was moving again. It released howl after howl, blasting adventurers and monsters alike into the air as it closed in on one particular target.

The giant's shadow overtook him. The werewolf adventurer could feel both of the monster's bloodred eyes lock onto his back.

He watched the shadow of a giant fist rise—monster or adventurer, whatever that wrecking ball–size appendage hit would die instantly. The Goliath roared once again as it brought the fist crashing down.

"—!"

However, another adventurer arrived on the scene as if riding a gust of wind.

Lyu's cape fluttered as she made her move. Taking advantage of the Goliath's blind spot, she jumped up its leg from the side with amazing speed—and buried her wooden sword directly into its left knee with a powerful strike. Waves of pain coursed through the beast's leg as all the adventurers heard a loud snap. Without one of its legs for support, the Goliath's fist missed the werewolf adventurer by a considerable margin.

Ouka and Mikoto arrived on the scene, trying to keep fear from appearing on their faces as they passed through the panicking adventurers toward the giant.

"HAAAAAAAAAAA!!"

"YAAHHHHHHHHH!!"

Ax and katana hit the same knee that Lyu had just attacked, but what happened next left the two of them speechless.

Sharp pain traveled through both of their wrists. Ouka's battle-ax shattered on impact as Mikoto's katana blade broke in two.

The beast's iron hide was stronger than both of their weapons combined. They didn't even leave a scratch.

"Retreat at once!"

Lyu's sharp order reached their ears in time to snap them out of their shocked daze.

Ouka and Mikoto stared into the palms of their now-empty hands before looking straight up—and into the bloodred pupils of the Goliath's eyes. They were very angry eyes. The giant twisted its waist as it swung its massive right arm behind its back.

"GEH, EHHHHHHHHHHHHHH?!"

"~~~~~~~~~~~~~~~~~~~~~~~?!"

Its arm whipped through the air as it swept forward. The Goliath's fist traveled halfway around its body before finally striking the ground. While Ouka and Mikoto managed to dodge it at the last moment, the impact threw them into the air as they were blown backward by the wind in the giant's fist's wake.

But the Goliath wasn't going to leave it at that. It took another step forward and opened its jaws.

"Blasphemous Burn!"

The monster's head was caught in a huge explosion just before it released a howl.

Another roar from the giant was muffled as its face emerged from a cloud of ash and sparks, its mouth still spewing smoke. Its eyes quickly found the cause of the explosion, Welf and his anti-magic Magic.

A howl required magic power; that's what triggered it. The red-haired man stood in the plain not too far away, his eyes focused on the beast's burned mouth...When suddenly—

Welf's eyes widened as he saw what the beast had in store for him. The Goliath was already in position for another howl, and the young man could see the magic energy gathering deep inside its throat.

"Ha!!"

"GUH?!"

The howl aimed at Welf had missed. "Uwoo?!" he yelled as the ground behind him exploded. It was thanks to Lyu that he was still alive.

She had scampered up the giant's seven-meder-tall body and hit it in the back of the head to change the trajectory of the howl. She used her momentum to spin and land a kick directly to the giant's cheek before retreating to the ground.

"Strong...as well as fast. This is no ordinary Goliath."

Lyu whispered to herself, her eyebrows sinking under her hood as the Goliath recovered in no time at all.

The Goliath that appeared on the seventeenth floor was about Level 4. The Goliath she was facing now was completely different from the ones that she and her former allies had slain countless times before. Its Defense was strong enough to make even her hands go numb after impact, its ability to use a howl, but most of all it had reflexes that did not match its massive size.

—This enemy had the potential to be Level 5.

That was Lyu's conclusion. A feeling of dread and despair started to well up within her as she tried to come up with a plan of attack all by herself.

Retreat was pointless. The moment anyone showed their back to it or lost the will to fight, they became a target. Lyu's years of experience and combat instincts told her as much.

With the weapon created from a holy tree in her homeland, the wooden sword Alvs Lumina, in her hand, the beautiful elvish warrior decided to use a distraction tactic to engage the beast, and repeatedly attacked its legs.

"*Urrgh—OOOOOOOOOOOOOOOOOOUUUGGH!!*"

Lyu's Level 4 attacks were powerful enough to inflict pain on the beast. She was even fast enough to avoid its gaze, nothing more than a small shadow running around the Goliath.

The Goliath roared angrily, swinging its arms around as if trying to swat a particularly annoying fly.

About 100 meders south of where Lyu was fighting against the Goliath, Mord and the other adventurers were engaged in a widespread brawl with large swarms of monsters.

"Scott, Guile, where are you?! Save me, save me, please?!"

Mord was beginning to panic, trapped in the midst of monster roars and adventurers' screams. He called out to his two closest friends, but there was no response.

Mad beetles, bugbears, gun liberla, Minotaurs…middle-level monsters of all types assailed him with various combinations of claws and horns. He had somehow managed to dodge every blow and even counterattack with his broken longsword up to this point, but the attacks kept coming from all angles.

His mind was at its limit. Forward-backward-left-right, there was something trying to kill him no matter where he looked.

"GAARRRRRRRRRR!!"

"Ugho?!"

A bugbear's swat had caught him in the shoulder. The monster's claws ripped the armor from his body and knocked the sword out of his hands as he collapsed to the ground.

Flat on his back, he rolled to protect his injured shoulder and looked up in time to see three bugbears converge over him.

Mord's consciousness started to contort out of terror. Each of the monster's three boulder-like bodies was just a few celch away.

He caught a glimpse of their hungry mouths opening, sharp fangs glinting in the dim light as all of them went in to take a bite at once.

"S-STOOOOOOOPP!!"

However, a yell reached his ears before the monsters' teeth sank in. Something flashed in front of his eyes.

"...Wha?"

A small human had just used Mord's greatsword to decapitate one of the bugbears—a boy with white hair.

The boy placed himself between Mord and the remaining two monsters. Wasting no time or momentum, he thrust the sword's long, thick blade deep into the closest beast's chest. The weapon pierced the magic stone inside the monster and it collapsed into a pile of ash.

The remaining bugbear took a swing at the boy's head, but he easily dodged it and spun into a counterattack.

"...Why, you of all people..."

The boy was already on to his next target. Mord watched the back of his white head disappear into the chaos as words spilled out of his mouth.

Gashi! Someone grabbed ahold of the back of his collar.

"You're in Mr. Bell's way—let's fix that."

"Geh! Owowowow!! Who are—OUCH! DAMMIT! MY ASS!!"

Mord's view suddenly changed as he was pulled along the ground on his back.

A prum girl, Lilly, carried her large backpack over her shoulders while dragging him with one hand—exactly the same way she would carry the corpse of a monster—over the ground without much concern for his well-being. However, the ground was not smooth due to small crystals that came up naturally from the Dungeon soil. The man yelped in pain every time he hit one.

There was no panic in Lilly's movements. Part of being a supporter was being able to accurately assess the movements of monsters and adventurers to stay clear of battle while fulfilling her duties. She weaved in and out of the brawl, dragging Mord closely behind her until they were finally out of danger.

"Please find somewhere to hide if you are unable to fight. Don't waste the life that Mr. Bell saved."

Lilly let go of Mord's collar as soon as they were in a monster-free area of the plain.

The wide-eyed man quickly sat up and asked her a question.

"H-hey?! Why is he…helping us?"

Even now, Mord could see Bell taking on monster after monster to save the adventurers who not too long ago were cheering at his pain. Bolts of scarlet lightning erupted from the boy's outstretched arm, slaying monsters in their tracks no matter the distance.

Lilly turned to him as he watched the battle from afar and said:

"Be grateful that Mr. Bell isn't the type of person to hold a grudge."

Lilly squinted her eyes and stuck her tongue out with a "Bleh!" before turning her back on him and rushing back into the fray.

Tup, tup, tup. Lilly's footsteps got quieter, leaving Mord alone with his thoughts.

The man looked dejected and whispered to himself:

"What the hell was that…"

The only answers he received were the fierce sounds of battle.

"Chigusa, are you sure it's okay for us to leave?"

"Y-yes…First, if we don't gather enough weapons…"

They were on the west side of the plain, moving away from the battle.

Hestia and Chigusa ran toward the lake as fast as they could, a pouch and a backpack filled with items shaking as they went.

"I've never experienced it myself but…weapons and shields break all the time when fighting floor bosses. So if we can't get enough spares, Captain Ouka and the others…"

Chigusa's long bangs covered her eyes as she spoke between

breaths. Hestia hit her fist to her palm as if to say *I got it* and nodded back to her. Of course, fighting a monster of that caliber for a long period of time would require a large stock of weaponry.

Chigusa and Hestia were on their way to the town of Rivira. They were hoping to persuade the adventurers there to provide weapons and items for the fight. Chigusa was only Level 1 and Hestia was far below that—the two of them would only be a liability on the front lines. So they entrusted Lilly with the support of Bell and the others and decided that this was the best way to help them.

"Wah...?! Ch-Chigusa?!"

"...!"

A bugbear spotted the girls just as the tree bridge to the island in the middle of the lake came into view. It charged straight at them. They had managed to evade any encounters with monsters up until now, but there was no way to avoid this one.

Chigusa bit her lip as she jumped in front of Hestia to protect her. The monster's forepaws slammed into the ground with each step, the vibrations in her boots getting stronger and stronger with each passing second. When suddenly—an arrow pierced the monster's head through its eyes.

"Whoa!"

An elvish archer was the one who brought the bugbear to a screeching halt. He was not alone—the adventurers of Rivira had arrived.

They ran around Hestia and Chigusa toward the floor boss on the other side of the plain.

"Chigusa, reinforcements!"

"The town's adventurers...!"

The two of them were filled with hope and admiration, blushing as more and more adventurers came into view.

The ones who had already passed them were yelling out signals to one another and pointing in different directions. They split into three groups: one hung back to eliminate the monsters blocking the path to the battlefield; one broke off to assist Bell in the brawl; and the rest made a bead for the floor boss.

All of them had weapons drawn and ready, yelling at the top of their lungs as they charged forward.

"You're always so reliable in a pinch!"

The first person out of Rivira's reinforcements to reach the floor boss was none other than Asfi.

She had weaved her way through the surprised yelps of other adventurers all the way to the feet of the Goliath. Reaching into her belt holster, she withdrew two small bottles and hurled them at the beast.

The giant was still trying to follow Lyu's quick movements when both of the bottles hit it square in the face, exploding on contact.

"OOOOOOOOOOOOOOOOOOOO?!"

"Oh come on, at least singe a little…!"

Most monsters in the middle levels would have been incinerated by just one of those Burst Oil grenades—as an item maker, these were her specialty. However, they left no mark on the Goliath's thick skin.

The giant counterattacked with a howl, but Asfi was able to dodge it easily and meet up with Lyu.

"Lyon! I believe you figured it out already, but our reinforcements are preparing to launch a large magic assault. Please keep the Goliath entertained until they're ready!"

"Understood. You and I shall take turns drawing its attention."

"Eh? No, wai—"

"All right, you maggots! Andromeda is going to be the decoy, so get those spells going!"

"—Boris?! You're going to regret this!"

Being given the most dangerous role in their operation, Asfi silently cried to herself as she and Lyu raced out in opposite directions to surround the giant. It was up to them to buy enough time for the others to prepare, with speed as their only advantage.

"We've got more than enough weapons, dammit! If anything breaks, come get a new one!"

A small group had gathered on a hill a little ways from the Goliath. The inhabitants of Rivira had established makeshift bases next to the crushed Central Tree and a short distance from the rock slide that covered the southern tunnel. Swords, spears, and shields were lined up on the outside of the bases with more spares on the inside. Dwarves and animal people with muscular builds took broadswords, greatswords, and thick shields without hesitation as they headed for battle. Hestia and Chigusa arrived at the supply base just behind them.

"W-we have a shot!"

"A-amazing..."

Hestia and Chigusa watched as hundreds of adventurers from many different *Familias* worked together to trap the giant monster.

"Surround it—! Surround it—!!"

The adventurers moved to set up a perimeter around the Goliath. Even though none of them knew one another very well, much less fought side by side, they stayed close together while maintaining enough space not to bump into anyone.

Elves and other magic users gathered together in small groups and started reciting their spells to cast Magic. Magic circles of various sizes, shapes, and colors appeared at the feet of a select few. These mages had acquired the Advanced Ability "Conjure," which increased the power and range of all magic. It was proof of their prowess as magic users.

However, their magic required a very long spell to cast. Each magic user was reciting their spells as quickly as possible.

Their clear and rhythmical voices were quite pleasing to the ear. Unfortunately, they were completely defenseless in the middle of casting. Therefore, groups of dwarves wielding thick shields that stood as high as they were tall stepped forward to protect them.

"—AAOO!"

The Goliath had noticed their presence and launched a howl at the closest group, but the wall of dwarves held strong against the attack. Not even the slightest bit of energy made it past their shields to the magic casters.

When compared to a direct hit from the giant's fist, a howl wasn't all that powerful. As long as the monster didn't get close enough to land a punch or a kick, the dwarves' shields were more than a match for the Goliath's ranged attack.

Knowing this, the lines of Level 3 adventurers left the attacking duties to Lyu and Asfi to keep the walls protecting the mages intact.

"We need a front line! Get in there! Cut that thing down and claim your glory!"

Fearless groups of attackers came out from behind the walls and charged toward the beast. Whipping themselves into a rage, the attackers broke off into parties of four to five adventurers as they closed the distance.

The first ones to arrive waited for Lyu or Asfi to distract it long enough for a window of opportunity to attack one of the beast's two legs. The Goliath looked down in surprise as greatswords, hammers, and axes slammed into its lower body before looking up as a shadow flashed in front of its face. Asfi threw another one of her Burst Oil grenades into its eyes, momentarily blinding the massive creature. It cried out in anger and frustration as six groups of attackers continued their assault on its knees and feet.

"Bell, you all right?!"

"Welf!"

Rivira's enforcements had rescued Mord's group from the monster brawl, allowing Bell to join the adventurers at the forward base. He had never seen so many magic users casting at the same time and was a bit overwhelmed by their intensity as Welf came running up to him.

"What about Mikoto and Ouka?!"

"They're fine; joined up with the guys fighting the normal monsters."

The Goliath might be taking center stage, but many smaller battles were taking place around the forward base. Considering that the tunnel to the seventeenth floor and the path to the lower levels under the Central Tree was cut off, no new monsters would be appearing on the eighteenth floor. At the same time, there was a considerably large amount of monsters on this floor already. Bell scanned the battle and quickly found Mikoto and Ouka fighting alongside lower-level magic users and adventurers to protect their stronghold.

"So, what now? Want to join me in the monster cull?"

"I..."

Bell paused for a moment, when another voice came from a little ways behind him.

"Yo! Rabbit boy! Get over here for a piece of the action! Or are you too scared?!"

A group of attackers was getting ready for another run and their leader called out half jokingly to Bell.

They had heard the rumors and invited him to join them in the adventurer style, a challenge.

"...Show 'em how it's done. I wanna brag that I've got a contract with the guy who took down this floor boss, got that?"

"—Count on it!"

Bell smiled as Welf gave his shoulder a small shove. The boy nodded as they wished each other luck and went their separate ways.

Bell raced off to join the group of attackers, caught up with them, and joined their formation. A large man with an eye patch gave him an affirmative jerk of his chin as if welcoming him as soon as Bell arrived.

"Little Rookie! Are you goin' in with those weapons?!"

"A greatsword, please, the best one you've got!"

"I hear ya. Take this one!"

One of the attackers in the group took a spare greatsword off his back and handed it to Bell. The boy thanked him. Bell held the greatsword in his right hand, resting the back of the blade on his shoulder as the group of attackers, four in all, left the forward base and charged toward the giant.

However, it saw the group coming and ran to meet them.

"""OH, SHIT!"""

"Huh?"

The "brave" attackers immediately changed course, leaving Bell behind. Still a relative newbie, Bell didn't recognize the danger in time to get out of the Goliath's path like they did.

Bell wondered if maybe he was falling into a trap as he charged toward the Goliath, alone. The giant's damaged, bloodshot eyes managed to lock onto the single figure charging toward it.

Zing! The monster's ferocious aura hit him hard. Bell looked around, searching for an escape route, when suddenly—the image of locks of golden hair passed through the back of his mind.

"—"

The girl who'd slain a floor boss just like this one, on her own. An image of the knight who was far more powerful than him.

Bell's ruby-red eyes flashed with intensity as he looked up. Gripping the greatsword in his right hand with all of his might, the boy kicked off the ground and charged headlong toward his target.

"OOOOOOOOOOOOOOOOOOOOOOOOOOOOOOOOOO OOO!!"

"—!"

He pointed the sword at the giant's leg and sped up.

One path, straightforward to the target—*Don't run, fight!* He reached his top speed. He managed to pass under the beast's oncoming fist by the slimmest of margins, the ground behind him erupting in a cloud of dirt and crystals.

Legs a blur beneath him, he stayed on course. He was now inside the Goliath's defenses, but the threatening presence of its massive fist just behind him kept his senses on high alert as he closed in on his target, the beast's left leg. Grabbing the hilt of the greatsword with both hands, he swung—and hit.

"Gah!!"

A dull impact. The creature's hide was too strong to pierce; however, the impact did inflict some damage.

Bell's strike caused the floor boss's leg to quiver. The damage inflicted by the hit-and-run raids of the attackers had been immense.

Bell took a page out of their book and escaped between the legs of the giant and out behind it, amid cheers from the people who'd witnessed his deed.

"Mr. Cranell, that was reckless."

"L-Lyu..."

"No amount of life will save you if you try that again."

Lyu caught up with him, running side by side as she scolded him.

Bell could feel her sky-blue glare coming from underneath the hood. His shoulders sank like those of a child being put in timeout.

"I will give a signal; follow my lead to attack. You should be able to keep up."

"…! Yes!"

Lyu looked forward before speaking. Bell nodded enthusiastically and moved behind her.

The two advanced like master and apprentice as they continued their assault on the floor boss.

The attackers tenaciously targeted the floor boss's legs in an effort to bring it to ground, or at the very least restrict its mobility. Although they were unable to injure the Goliath enough to keep it in one spot due to its extremely thick hide, their attacks made the beast's movements clumsy and awkward.

The mages finished their spells just as a group of attackers celebrated another successful run.

"Front lines, get back! Big stuff's comin' in!"

Lyu, Bell, and the other attackers immediately withdrew. They had drawn the Goliath into the middle of a small network of magic users protected by walls. The beast's bloodred eyes opened wide once it realized what was about to happen.

Every single magic caster grinned, knowing there was no escape for their target now, and thrust their staffs upward.

New colors flashed throughout the battlefield. Magic circles shone brightly as wave after wave of magic hit the beast all at once.

"_____?!"

Magic of every element continued to pound the monster. It was assailed by burgeoning balls of flame, followed by thunderbolts in the shape of spears, all while being caught between massive tornadoes and skewered by a rain of long, thick ice shards. A group of attackers equipped with magic swords added yet another round of flames to the assemblage of smoke and explosions that had completely engulfed the Goliath's body.

At long last, the magic barrage came to a stop. Everyone's ears were ringing as the echoes of the last explosion died out. Every set of eyes was trained on the ball of smoke in the middle of the battlefield…A massive arm emerged as the smoke started to clear, but there was no hand attached. Next, a heavily damaged head and shoulders were revealed as they slumped forward. The Goliath's skin was torn to shreds, exposing raw muscle and spewing blood from every angle.

White smoke billowed out of its mouth as the beast tried to draw breath, showing just how much damage it had absorbed.

The adventurer ranks yelled out in celebration.

"Let's finish it off, maggots!! ATTAAAAACK!!"

All of the attackers moved in at once. They came in from every angle, all of them looking to be the one who delivered the final blow.

This time, their target was the Goliath's head.

"…?"

"Lyu?"

Bell had the same triumphant smile on his face as the other attackers, until he noticed that Lyu's shoulders were shaking.

Her eyes were very serious, narrowed beneath her hood, until they suddenly snapped open.

"—FUOOOO."

The other adventurers noticed it at about the same time, too.

The Goliath should have been too badly injured to move, and yet it raised its head. The injuries that it had sustained were gone.

Red specks of light emerged from its body, more specifically from its wounds. The adventurers watched in horror as the Goliath's skin regenerated right before their eyes. The red specks were multiplying while all the damage was being erased. Soon, all that was left on its body were scars.

The Goliath stood up with renewed vigor.

"Self-regeneration?!"

Screamed Asfi in disbelief. The Goliath recovered from its injuries at an astounding pace and locked its eyes on the attackers who had charged in close—then the stunned and horrified mages—before raising its arms above its shoulders and bringing its hands together above its head.

Then it brought both massive fists straight down into the ground.

"_____"

The great plain split.

The ferocious explosion sent a destructive shock wave through the ground. The attackers were instantly swallowed up by an ever-expanding tsunami of debris. It was no time at all before the adventurer walls were overwhelmed and the mages overtaken.

Everything was launched into the air.

"Huh…?!"

Bell had retreated alongside Lyu, but he couldn't believe what he was seeing.

Their defensive web was destroyed in an instant.

The attackers got the worst of it and most were on the ground, writhing in pain. But it wasn't just them—the magic users hadn't fared well, either. There were too many adventurers shaking on their hands and knees for Bell to count.

Smoke wafted up from the cracks in the ground, shrouding a battlefield that looked like a scene from hell.

"It turned magic energy into healing power…?!"

The remaining crystals on the ceiling cast blue light over the battlefield. However, the Goliath glowed red. Its body was surrounded by thousands and thousands of red specks, the by-product of burned magical energy.

The same energy it used for a howl had been used to accelerate its natural healing ability.

Asfi gawked at the living nightmare, a monster with the ability to regenerate—a power only attributed to floor bosses.

The remaining adventurers still able to stand looked at the Goliath. It was covered in so many red specks that it appeared to be burning in the darkness.

To Bell, it looked as if Sodom had emerged from the fires of hell to punish evil in this world.

"——AAAH!"

The Goliath's assault began without warning. It shot a howl at anything that moved, putting even more adventurers out of commission. They were blown backward, crushed under its impact, and were fading in and out of consciousness.

"Oh no…Boris, reestablish formations, now!"

"How the hell am I supposed to do that?!"

Confusion and fear had completely overtaken the adventurers, who weren't used to working in larger numbers. Some were retreating to regroup; others were healing the wounded. A few magic users had begun casting another spell. There was no unity, only panic.

Seeing their teamwork completely fall apart, the Goliath seized the opportunity to use its trump card.

"OOOOOOOOOOOOOOOOOOOOOOOOOOOOOO!!"

"That bastard. More monsters…?!"

Every remaining monster on the eighteenth floor responded to the Goliath's second summoning call with a howl of their own. Not wasting any time, a fresh wave of monsters appeared on the great plain.

The surviving adventurers suddenly had a lot more on their plate than they could handle.

"…Mr. Cranell, stay here. Join their ranks and repel the monsters."

"L-Lyu! What about you?!"

"I will join Andromeda and keep the Goliath at bay."

Bell looked at her with a mixture of surprise and concern as the elf took a few steps toward the giant.

"Our forces will be overwhelmed if that monster is allowed to roam free. We will buy as much time as possible for another volley of magic attacks…May fortune smile upon you."

She cut the conversation short, as if to say there was no time. Bell watched her cape flutter as she sped off toward the giant, then looked around.

Broken and shattered weapons littered the ground. Fallen attackers and wall members were trying to climb to their feet while other adventurers fought desperately to protect them. Their screams echoed throughout the battlefield.

They were locked in a losing battle. Even if they somehow managed to mount another assault, there was no guarantee they could take down the Goliath.

Bell's throat shook as he tried to steady himself. His gaze drifted down to his right hand.

—That's the only chance.

Argonaut. A Skill bestowed on Bell with the power to turn the tides of any situation. He decided to use it.

Unfortunately, Argonaut was a double-edge sword that required enormous amounts of physical endurance and mental power. More than likely Bell would become nothing more than a lump on the battlefield after he launched the attack. He had one shot.

If it doesn't work…If I can't fight…—Bell began charging as many thoughts ran through his mind.

"Faster, faster…!"

Launching the attack at anything less than full power would be a waste. He had to put everything he had into one blast.

Gritting his teeth as screams of pain echoed around him, small sparkles of white light began to gather around his right wrist.

"This is horrible…!"

Lilly was on her way to the supply base when she saw what had happened to the defensive network. Her jaw dropped as she surveyed the landscape.

The Goliath looked unharmed while adventurers' motionless bodies were sprawled out in all directions. What was worse, groups of monsters were moving in from every angle to put the nail in the proverbial coffin. Lilly kicked off the ground as fast as she could and raced up the hill toward the base.

"Are there still weapons and items here?!"

"Supporter?!"

"Gather everything we have! Lilly will deliver them to the front!"

Lilly's arrival got Hestia's attention, as well as the few people left at the base. Like Lilly, they were people who would only get in the way should they join the fight, so they protected their position and took care of as many injured adventurers as they could.

All of them were stunned, looking out at the battlefield with blank expressions.

"You'll deliver them? Are you sure you can do that?!"

"No one else can move! Lilly has a much better chance than someone scared stiff!"

It went without saying that the adventurers unable to fight, as well as the ones protecting the base, couldn't leave. On top of that, even the adventurers who had received treatment wouldn't be able to accomplish anything right away should they return to battle. Lilly practically threw her large backpack into the center of the base as she and Hestia ran around looking for items and weapons to fill it with.

"What about Miss Chigusa?"

"She ran off as soon as she saw the explosion. Probably found her way to Ouka and Mikoto by now."

Most likely, she couldn't bear to just stand on the sidelines. Lilly could definitely relate to the human girl as an image of what most likely transpired flashed through her head.

Even though she would be done for if targeted by a monster, Lilly's devotion to Bell and Welf gave her the courage to fulfill her duties as a supporter in the face of danger.

Ignoring Hestia's looks of concern, Lilly filled her backpack to the top with anything that could be useful.

"Eh…?"

"Supporter?"

Lilly's hand had found a large weapon when fumbling through an old cargo box. She suddenly came to a stop.

Her eyes caught a glimpse of something very interesting. Hestia drifted to her side out of curiosity.

"Is that a drop item…?"

The exposed black surface of the item shimmered in the dim light. It was roughly the shape of a sword but wrapped in cloth rather than a sheath. It could very well be a big black bone. A very poorly made hilt was attached to the bottom part of the "blade." The cloth appeared to have writing on it, most likely the owner's name. However, the fabric was so dirty and ruffled that it was impossible to read.

There was a good chance that this was a spare weapon owned by someone who often visited Rivira. Many adventurers used the town as a place to store their backup weapons rather than carry them to the nineteenth floor and beyond because they took up too much space. The weapon must've been withdrawn from storage because of the emergency situation.

"Hardly any effort went into this at all…No, wait…"

Lilly gulped as she looked down at the item that could very well have been a natural weapon found within the Dungeon. The girl leaned in close to assess its density, cutting edge, and overall destructive power.

This was once a piece of a large monster, a claw or a fang that became a drop item.

What's more, that monster was from the lower levels.

Lilly immediately dropped the weapon in her other hand and snatched up the black item before jamming it into her backpack.

"Oi, hey! Supporter?!"

The backpack was bursting at the seams, but Lilly was able to carry it easily because of her own Skill, Alter Assist. She didn't respond to Hestia's call as she left the base as fast as her legs could carry her.

If I can get this to Mr. Bell…!

—If this weapon were combined with his white light, then perhaps… maybe…

Lilly's backpack shook from side to side, the weapon's black tip sticking out of the top as she raced off to find Bell.

"!"

The Goliath's finger passed just by Lyu's body.

She fought to control the adrenaline rush caused by the enemy's attack missing her by a hair and rushed forward to strike its exposed legs. The giant's earsplitting roars filled her ears while she stayed put after her first strike and landed two more before escaping.

"Lyon, that will get you killed!"

"Everyone is fighting with their lives on the line. I should do no less."

Lyu responded with unwavering resolve to Asfi's voice calling out to her from a distance.

She fought against the giant logically, adjusting her position and attack angles as necessary. The Goliath was unable to ignore Lyu's sharp and precise strikes. Her cape was in shambles due to her constant, almost reckless assault.

"Andromeda, shall we attack its core?"

"Impossible. Its hide is too thick. None of our weapons is powerful enough to break the magic stone from the outside."

Asfi dodged another howl with a flying leap and landed next to Lyu in midstride. Both of them took advantage of this reprieve to take a swig of potion while on the run.

"What about Magic?"

"...My spell takes an absurdly long time and is rather dull. There is no possibility it will have any effect on that Goliath with its regenerative capabilities. Don't hold your breath."

Asfi's white cloak fluttered as she wiped her mouth with her arm, a look of hopelessness on her face. "Understood," Lyu calmly responded to this information.

"That being the case, we need another volley from the mages."

"It will just heal again after taking a direct hit."

"If so, we hit it again and again until it can't heal anymore."

"Are you insane...?!"

Asfi reached for her belt as Lyu picked up speed, leaving her behind. She changed her own path and withdrew more Burst Oil grenades, hitting the Goliath in the face on her way past.

The two women attacked the giant again and again despite knowing the outcome. The Goliath loomed over them, still surrounded by the burning glow of the red specks of light. Their situation had become even direr than before.

"The magic users…!"

—Meanwhile, a short distance away from their battle with the Goliath…

Ouka had made his way into the middle of what was left of the defensive net and rushed to the aid of an injured mage.

Those who had weathered the initial shock wave well enough to continue casting were being targeted by the Goliath with howls before they could finish. Unable to move or protect themselves while reciting their spells, each was caught up in an explosion one by one. Still others were attacked by random monsters in the area. There was no way to mount an assault.

Their magic attacks were vitally important to the success or failure of the battle against the floor boss. Without them, the Goliath's physical attacks and defense would overwhelm the other adventurers.

No walls were forming to protect them. The magic users were completely exposed.

Ouka watched Lyu's and Asfi's maneuvers in despair, knowing that they were done for at this rate.

"Ouka!"

"Chigusa?!"

He turned to face the girl who called out to him and answered her.

At first he was shocked that she would come this far into a dangerous area by herself. Then he saw her backpack—filled to the brim with items and equipped with a shield. He breathed a sigh of relief.

He ran to her at full speed, almost jumping to close the distance.

"Chigusa, the shield!"

His words didn't register with Chigusa right away as Ouka stopped just out of arm's reach. Then they clicked. Her normally hidden but beautiful eyes emerged from under her bangs. They were filled with fear.

She violently shook her head from side to side.

"Chigusa!!"

"No, you'll die…! If you join a wall against that thing…you'll… you'll die, Ouka!"

Tears flowed down her cheeks as she practically screamed at him.

The large man fought back tears of his own. Steadying himself, he looked down at the crying girl with as much sincerity as he could muster.

"Chigusa, please, don't rob me of my honor!"

"…?!"

"I don't want to be known as someone who only talked while others died in vain. I don't want to be the one who ran away. I'm a proud member of *Takemikazuchi Familia*!"

Chigusa's head was still, her eyes frozen in place as more tears emerged.

Her face contorted, then she nodded. Slipping her arms out of the straps of the backpack, she set it down and handed Ouka the shield.

He said a quick thank-you as he equipped it, and then ran out into the field without looking back.

Chigusa stood there sobbing, watching Ouka recede farther and farther away.

The white sparkles of light stopped circling Bell's arm.

"Full power…!"

Three minutes. That's how long it currently took Bell to fully charge Argonaut.

The lights shimmering, making pinging sounds like chimes in the summer breeze, Bell held his right arm straight out to his side and kicked off the ground into a full sprint.

He cut through the great plain like an arrow toward the raging Goliath. He wanted to make sure that he hit the beast with everything he had, meaning he needed to reach point-blank range.

"Mr. Cranell?!"

Lyu was first to notice him, followed closely by Asfi, and the rest of the adventurers engaged in battle with monsters soon followed suit. So did the bloodred eyes of the giant that towered over him.

Bell's body was already pulsing with so much energy that the pressure of the Goliath eyes had no effect on him as he barreled forward.

"It can't be—Lyon, get out of there!"

Asfi knew that Bell had vaporized an infant dragon with an attack described to be exactly like this. She gave the order to withdraw as soon as she saw the lights around his right arm. Lyu hesitated for only a moment before vacating the boy's line of fire.

Then, Bell came to a stop less than a stone's throw away from the giant.

The Goliath stared him down and opened its jaws.

"————OOO!!"

An extremely powerful howl laced with magical energy.

At the same time, Bell set his feet and flung his arm forward.

A roar just as loud as the beast's erupted from his mouth:

"FIREBOLT!!"

His feet plunged into the dirt beneath the grass.

The sheer power of the electric inferno blasting out of his arm forced his body backward.

His Firebolts intercepted the incoming howl, breaking it to pieces in midair.

"————"

The white sparkles shimmered marvelously as they were drawn up and into the burning lightning bolts. A deafening blast drowned out all other noise. The lightning bolts hit the Goliath in the mouth—and kept on going.

The Firebolt Magic vanished in an instant, leaving only a small sliver of the right side of the giant's head still attached to its body. The beast didn't even have time to roar in fear. Only a small piece of its right eye sat on a broken cheekbone as the floor boss staggered backward. Bell's magic blast traveled all the way to the opposite wall, exploding on impact off in the distance.

He'd missed his target.

Bell had been aiming for the Goliath's chest, but he was unable to control the blast at full power and had hit it in the head by accident.

Bell stood there with his arm still out, eyes wide as he watched the Goliath closely. Everyone around him gawked in awe at the attack that had so easily pierced the hide that they couldn't crack.

No living thing could survive without its head.

We won—came the hopeful voices of many adventurers. However.

A geyser of red specks shot out from the beast's neck.

"?!"

The geyser grew into a volcano in the middle of the darkness. The adventurers watched in horror as the Goliath's face began to regenerate. Despair took hold of their hearts as they watched a new bloodred eye wiggle freely without a socket.

The Goliath was still alive even after losing its head. It had withstood a fully charged, Argonaut-supported Firebolt using its otherworldly life force and recovery ability to survive.

Bell's ace in the hole had failed.

The newly reformed left eye joined its partner in finding the white-haired boy standing in the middle of the grass. The two red orbs glared down at him with intense hatred.

"—Bell, run away!!"

Gone was Lyu's calm demeanor. The Goliath unleashed yet another howl right on top of the boy as she screamed out to him.

The giant's healing process was not yet complete—bits and pieces of muscle and fangs rained down on Bell. Argonaut had completely drained his Strength and Agility; he couldn't get out of the way and took a direct hit.

Bell's feet left the ground as his body was cut and sliced in midair along with the dirt. The next thing the boy's eyes saw was the Goliath's mountainous frame coming right for him.

The beast went after him, roaring at the top of its lungs. Lyu and Asfi could not reach him in time. The Goliath already had its massive arm cocked behind its back.

Unavoidable, instant death was on its way.

Time seemed to freeze for Bell as he waited for the giant's fist to come down.

Then, *he* arrived.

"—"

A large man wielding a shield jumped in front of Bell.

Ouka arrived in time to place himself between Bell and the

Goliath at the last possible second. He braced his body against his shield to protect the boy from a direct hit. Bell saw the Goliath's fingers momentarily bend inward as the fist swallowed Ouka and the shield whole in slow motion.

Blood shot out of the man's mouth. Ouka's body hit Bell's with bone-shattering force. The shock of the impact traveled through the shield, through Ouka, and straight into him. The two of them were launched into the air, their eyes open to the brink.

"OOOOOOOOOOOOOOOOOOOOOOOOOOOOOOOOOOOOOOO OOO!!"

More splatters of blood. A broken *Familia* emblem.

Their bodies spun through the air as the Goliath roared triumphantly behind them.

"Bell—"

A shocked Hestia watched the scene unfold from the supply base.

She immediately came out from behind the protective barrier and rushed down the hill.

"Mr. Bell—"

Lilly watched his limp body fly through the air, the weapon she was too late to give him still in her backpack. She immediately changed course and rushed toward the battlefield.

"Bell..."

Welf's voice shook as the name of his friend came out of his mouth.

The sounds of battle around him seemed distant as a certain set of words popped into his head.

"*Stop compromising allies for your pride.*"

The words of a certain goddess cut into his mind like a sharp thorn through skin. They pierced his very soul.

Remorse and guilt flooded through him as his face morphed into something like that of a scolded child. He stood in place for only a moment before turning around to face the forest behind him.

"Damn it all!!"

Throwing his broadsword into the dirt, Welf took off into the eastern forest as fast as he could go.

"Ouka…!"

"Captain Ouka!"

Chigusa, her cheeks glistening with tears, and a mournful Mikoto arrived at the spot where their leader had slid to a stop. They embraced his broken and bloodied body. Ouka's eyelids hung loosely over his closed eyes as the two girls worked together to move him out of danger.

"No—?!"

At the same time, Lyu rushed to Bell's side and quickly scooped him into her arms. She carried him to a safe place like a merciful wind guiding a boat out of a storm.

"Mr. Cranell, Mr. Cranell! Answer me!"

Lyu set him down on the grass between the remains of the Central Tree and the supply base on the southern side of the eighteenth floor. The boy didn't respond as he lay silently on his back.

"Why now of all times…!"

The elf threw her hood back as she rummaged through the item pouch attached to her waist. Her eyes filled with regret.

There were no high potions left. To say the boy was critically injured would be an understatement. A normal potion would have almost no effect. Most of Bell's light armor, including his breastplate, was shattered. His inner shirt and skin were torn to shreds by the shards of the beast's fangs still sticking out of his body. A quick glance was all that Lyu needed to tell that his ribs were broken in several places.

Her eyes quivered as she looked at all of the boy's wounds, each leaking fresh blood.

"Bell!"

"Goddess Hestia…"

Hestia was the first to arrive on the scene because the supply base was so close.

The color drained from the goddess's face the moment she saw Bell's horrific condition, and she plunged her hand into her own item pouch. But just like Lyu, the pupils of her eyes shrank when she realized she didn't have any high potions, either. She had used her entire stock while assisting adventurers injured during the battle.

"Hood—no, elf-lady. How is he?!"

"Breathing, but his wounds are deep. I fear the bones in his arms and legs might also be…"

Hestia and Lyu kneeled on either side of the boy, who had taken a direct hit from a Level 5 howl.

The sounds of combat still sounded off in the distance, but a voice cut through the din.

"Lyon, get back here at once!"

It was Asfi's scream. She was engaging the Goliath alone. Her eyes shot open as the beast prepared to fire another howl. She wrapped herself in her white cloak just before impact.

The shock-absorbent fabric of her own design withstood the blast, but the young woman's thin body went flying.

"…Elf-lady, please go. Buy us as much time as you can."

Hestia's expression stiffened as Lyu watched Asfi climb back to her feet.

"Bell *will* wake up. And once he does, he *will* kill that monster."

"But, Goddess Hestia…"

"You saw, didn't you?! Bell can do it. Bell can finish that thing!"

Lyu was captivated by the absoluteness in Hestia's eyes. "Understood," she said with a curt nod.

Regaining her composure, the side of the elf's face disappeared behind her hood as she raced back to the battlefield.

"…Open your eyes, Bell!"

With Lyu gone, Hestia was alone with him. She held the boy's right hand and called out to him.

Bell's eyes were hidden behind his white bangs, his mouth partially open. But he didn't move.

"You can hear them, can't you?! Everyone's fighting against that scary monster!"

Lyu's and Asfi's shrill voices, the yells of other adventurers, the roars of the monsters, the Goliath's howls—the noises came at them from every angle.

Hestia squeezed both of her hands around Bell's limp fingers. A tragic chorus of weapon clashes and courageous battle cries filled the air.

"You can do it; you're the only one who can! You're the only one who can save them, Bell…!"

Her beloved family member was badly injured, yet she urged him to battle as her eyes welled up with tears.

Her voice became more and more desperate as she begged to see his ruby-red eyes open once again.

She took in a deep breath and yelled from the bottom of her lungs with all the power she could muster:

"Get up, Bell!!"

Her voice reached him.

The voice of the goddess whom he loved and respected more than anyone else reached Bell's consciousness in the deepest, darkest corner of his mind. He couldn't feel his body, and yet there was a powerful warmth surrounding a right hand that didn't exist.

Bell could feel his "teeth" grinding in response to the goddess's repeated, tearful cries. They carved their way through the darkness, drawing him out.

His soul ignited. Hestia's flame, one more time.

His body came back into existence, twitching. He could see the light at the end of the darkness. All that was left was to stand.

Out of the darkness, to the other side of the light. To the place where the goddess's voice was calling him.

His body still would not move on command, so Bell focused on the warmth enveloping his right hand. Despite his best efforts, it would not move or even quiver in the direction of the light.

Dammit! the boy screamed at his body, fully knowing that it was at its physical limit—and then.

"If...if you have what it takes to be called a hero—"

"____"

Another voice cut through the darkness.

"Hermes?!"

A twinge of surprise in the goddess's voice appeared along with the voice of another god.

Bell knew that voice, those words, that echo—he remembered them.

"It's not someone able to draw a sword, or someone willing to raise a shield, or someone who heals others."

It was a voice he'd heard long ago.

Back when he was very young. Words that shaped who he would become.

Words from a divine messenger, a voice from his past—his grandfather's.

"Only someone who's willing to risk it all can be called a hero."

The voice of the god became his grandfather's.

"Protect your allies. Rescue the ladies. Put yourself on the line."

A new light rose through the darkness, taking the form of his grandfather, the past.

"It's okay to break, to lose heart, to cry out in pain. The one to claim victory in the end always emerges from the defeated."

He remembered. He remembered it all.

He remembered the words that those smiling lips said next.

"Follow through on your dream, shout it out for everyone to hear. The one who does—"

Yes, that's the one who—

"—the one who does becomes a glorious hero."

"!!"

He awakened.

"Bell…"

Hestia could barely speak as the boy sat up on his own.

The god standing over the boy's injured body, watching over him, was Hermes.

The image of Bell's trembling body was reflected in the deity's orange gaze as the boy climbed to his feet.

Rise, fight, go to a sword so as not to disgrace his memory.

But most of all, to save the people who meant the most to him.

To go to the limits—beyond the limits, to put everything on the line.

"Mr. Bell!"

Lilly's small figure appeared behind them. She used every muscle in her tiny frame to take a large weapon out of her backpack and throw it in his direction.

The large black sword carved arcs through the air as it whisked toward them. Bell's arm sprang to life as he snatched the weapon out of the air with one hand.

Gripping the blade's thick hilt with both hands, he swung the blade forward as he set his feet into a powerful stance.

His ruby-red eyes flicked forward and focused on the form of the terrifying giant off in the distance.

Let the aspirations burn.

Let the dreams roar.

If there was one advantage that Bell Cranell had over anyone else, it would be this one irreplaceable memory from his youth—that's because it was all he had.

"!"

He started to charge Argonaut. At the same time, the characters engraved into his back began to glow red.

Limit Release.

A temporary state in which surrounding conditions combined with emotion to overload the Falna contained within a deity's Blessing. Skill power increased exponentially during a Limit Release.

A stone that would send ripples through a battlefield; a sword aimed for the giant's throat.

White sparkles swirled around Bell's body as he charged for the attack before they climbed high into the air.

Ping, ping, ping, the sound of chimes. *Gong, gong*—they turned into the sound of church bells.

In a clearing on the edge of the forest, southeast of where the battle against the rampaging Goliath was taking place...

Mord's group of adventurers had peeled away from the main forces. They were on the brink of losing their will to fight.

"I can't take this anymore! We can't win!"

"We gotta get out of here! Maybe if we found a hiding place in the forest...!"

A violent beast that no one could stop was on the loose. No matter how many monsters they slew, another one appeared to take its place.

The situation was hopeless, just as dark as the false night that covered the floor. One person after another raised their voices in despair and threatened to leave on their own.

"No turning tail, ya cowards!!"

It was Mord who stopped them.

"The hell are you saying, Mord?! We don't stand a chance against that monstrosity! What's the point in staying?!"

"*We fight!* Are ya seriously considering running away when all those guys and ladies need our help?!"

Mord yelled as loud as he could and pointed toward Lyu and Asfi's desperate struggle to keep the Goliath contained. The others just looked at him, unable to understand why he was so passionate.

"So yer just goin' to bow out, not doing jack shit?! How the fuck are ya okay with that?!"

Mord's passion had turned to anger, his eyes alight with a flame burning within him.

He broke off eye contact with those closest to him and looked around. The adventurers strong enough to form a wall were badly injured. The magic users were holding their own arms in pain. The man unleashed a verbal torrent upon them as they looked back at him with stunned eyes.

"Hey, all ya filthy elves, are y'all just talk?! And you archaic dwarves there—those muscles just for show?!"

Wave after wave of insults came out of his mouth. He waved his sword around, taking even more shots at their pride before the adventurers started to climb to their feet. All of the commotion caught the attention of the mad beetle, and it charged. Mord quickly dispatched it before continuing his tirade yet again—then the sound of a bell echoed through the air.

"_____"

The unmistakable clang of church bells rang down from far above their heads.

Time stood still for all of them. There wasn't a single adventurer whose eyes remained small as the grand echoes filled their ears and reached their hearts.

The group looked to the south only to see a single adventurer, a boy holding an absolutely massive black sword and illuminated by swirling white lights. The boy's white hair reflected in their eyes.

No words were necessary.

His light cut through the darkness, lifting their spirits with hope.

"—Let's goooooooooooooooo!! All of you bastardssssssssssssssssss!! Cut them down, CUT THEM DOWNNNNNNNNNNNNNNNN!!"

Every single adventurer charged forward at Mord's command.

The Goliath had realized the threat and summoned more monsters to its cause. However, Mord wasn't going to let the monsters reach Bell, even at the cost of his own life. Ranks of adventurers and monsters collided.

"OOOOOOOOOOOOOOOOOOOOOOOOOOOOOOOOOOOOOO OOO!!"

The Goliath charged forward at the sound of the bells spreading across the floor.

Its roar was a much higher pitch than before, summoning all monsters still alive in an instant. Its red glare now a few shades lighter, the beast set its sights solely on the boy standing in the southern plain.

"The Goliath…!"

"Has it recognized Mr. Cranell as its enemy?"

The area around the boy had become a widespread brawl between Mord's adventurers and the surviving monsters. The giant was heading right for it. Asfi watched in shock as the Goliath completely ignored her and Lyu's attacks. Meanwhile, the elf was in hot pursuit, doing her best to avoid the small quakes the monster was making as it ran. Her eyes locked onto her target.

"We protect. The Goliath will not touch him!"

Lyu yelled out to her companion with no waver in her voice.

The Goliath paid her no attention as it quickly galloped along on its short, stubby legs. Fighting her way through the blasts of wind whenever its feet hit the ground, Lyu lined herself up beside it and hit one of its knees with all of her strength.

The beast quickly lost its balance—a low center of gravity and high speed were not a good combination. The wide-eyed Goliath fell forward and hit the great plain with a thunderous bang.

The ground cracked on impact, sending a thick cloud of dirt into the air. The Goliath's face morphed into an expression of disbelief as all of its limbs were on the ground for the first time.

"Did that actually happen…?!"

Shaking off a sense of awe at what she'd just seen, Asfi moved in to start her own attack. The floor boss was trying to raise itself off the ground. However, the two women showed their opponent no mercy.

"GUH—OOOOOOoooooOOOOOOOOOooooooOOOOOOO OOO?!"

Face, hands, shoulders, thighs, and back—Lyu's wooden sword and Asfi's daggers struck every possible target with blinding speed. The Goliath's rage increased as it roared out in pain. Forgetting its original target for the moment, the Goliath swung all of its limbs around as if trying to swat the world's strongest mosquitoes out of the sky. It even used howls in an attempt to keep them at bay.

Seeing the giant thrash around in desperation, Lyu started to cast a spell.

"—*Distant sky above the forest. Limitless stars set into an eternal night.*"

She continued her assault on the Goliath as the spell came from her lips. A bewildered Asfi watched as the elf continued to attack the beast even faster than she could while focusing on her Magic.

"*Listen to my feeble voice and grant the protection of starlight. Bestow the light of mercy upon those who have abandoned you.*"

Simultaneous high-speed combat and Magic: "Concurrent Casting."

It would not be an overstatement to say that magic required a tremendous amount of concentration and verbal enunciation to trigger. High output—a magic's power was rated by the length of the spell. The longer the spell, the more powerful the magic. Therefore, all magic users needed to stand in one place and focus all of their attention into reciting their spell.

However, Lyu was reciting a spell and attacking at the same time. The slightest slip of the tongue could result in Ignis Fatuus, and yet here she was attacking, moving, dodging, and casting at a blistering pace. Even to a top-class adventurer such as Asfi, it was extremely impressive.

The amount of mental stamina and courage required to pull this off was enormous, not to mention knowledge of close-quarters combat and rhetorical expertise.

Executing a combat style that even the Kenki wouldn't dare

attempt, Lyu kept up a strong physical assault while continuing to cast her magic.

"Synchronized battle and casting…!"

—Mikoto noticed what Lyu was doing and was just as fascinated as Asfi.

She had left the care of the critically injured Ouka to Chigusa and returned to the battlefield, only to be baffled by what she saw. The way that the elf dodged the Goliath's massive fists thrashing about while still attacking with unrelenting force was nothing short of gale winds in a hurricane. At the same time, the beauty and grace of her lithe form shook Mikoto to her very core.

"What power…!"

Mikoto could see that the elvish warrior was far beyond her own strength. At first it made her realize her own weakness, but then showed her a level of power that she could attain. At last, she swore that one day she would reach the same plateau and stand next to the elf as equals.

She shook her head and took a look around—the adventurers around her were engaged in a spirited fight with the remaining monsters. Seeing their bravery and courage, Mikoto ran off to join the fight against the Goliath and assist Lyu.

If her own Magic could help them, could buy more time for Bell… She found a low spot in the plains and began to cast a spell.

"Fear, strong and winding—"

She focused all of her mental energy into this one attack.

There was no point saving any to continue the fight. She poured everything she had into her spell, enunciation strong and steady.

"I call upon the god, the destroyer of any and all, for guidance from the heavens. Grant this trivial body divine power beyond power."

Mikoto's and Lyu's incantations reverberated through the air.

Meanwhile, the Goliath managed to get its knees under its body and started to right itself.

"You couldn't stay down for just a little longer?!"

Whether it finally gained control of its anger or it remembered what Bell was doing, the giant continued its advance across the great plain. Asfi quipped at the beast in frustration because Lyu's magic was not yet ready.

"I didn't want to use this in front of so many people, but…!"

A tone of resignation in her voice, she reluctantly leaned down and stroked the sides of her sandals.

"—Talaria."

The golden wing decorations that were wrapped around the sides of each sandal flinched before coming to life.

Two wings from each sandal, four in all, spread out as Asfi took flight.

"?!"

The Goliath tilted its head in disbelief as the girl flew in front of its face. Even Lyu and the other adventurers were momentarily stunned by the girl zipping through the air.

Winged sandals, Talaria. A high-level magic item reserved for Perseus herself.

Long ago, the young queen of an island nation had such a yearning to travel the skies that she used Enigma to create an item that made her dream come true. With these two sandals firmly strapped to her feet, Asfi alone was able to take to the air.

An item that leveled the playing field against airborne monsters. Her white cloak fluttered behind her as she looped around the Goliath like a bird, faster and faster as she closed in on the giant's face.

Holding her dagger upside down in her left hand, she made her move.

"_____?!"

The Goliath roared in pain as the dagger tore through one of its red eyes.

"—*Come, wind of winds, wandering traveler of the ages. Across the skies, through the fields, faster than any, farther than all. Light of stardust, tear my enemies asunder!*"

The Goliath cupped its injured eye with one hand and looked up at Lyu as the elf finished her spell.

Lyu's thin eyebrows curved downward at the motionless beast before she unleashed her magic.

"Luminous Wind!!"

Hundreds of small orbs surrounded by swirling green wind

appeared around her. Thrusting her outstretched arms forward, the stardust slammed into the beast in a torrent of magical energy and piercing wind. Each hit carved away a piece of the Goliath's hide, causing countless bursts of blood every second.

It was a powerful type of magic, very fitting for an elf, and it was driving the Goliath backward—until.

"AAAAAAAAAA ————!!"

"?!"

The Goliath stopped its retreat and pressed forward into the stardust onslaught.

Fresh waves of red specks launched from the monster's body, encasing it in a pulsing spiral of light. Its wounds healed just as fast as the remaining stardust orbs could open new ones, while the monster advanced on Lyu and Asfi's position right in front of it.

"Descend from the heavens, seize the earth——shinbu tousei!!"

The Goliath's arm was extended, on a direct course for Asfi, while its shoulder was coming down on Lyu. That was the instant that Mikoto's magic was complete.

"Futsu no Mitama!"

A sword composed of violet light appeared directly over the Goliath's head and descended.

At the same time, several lights similar to magic circles appeared on the ground, surrounding the giant.

The sword of light skewered the giant's body, triggering a cage of gravity around the beast.

"————?!"

A force field descended from the hilt of the sword ten meders in the air to create a dome. The leading edge of the field put a barrier between the two women and the Goliath just before the monster's attacks could connect. Trapped inside the dome, the floor boss's outstretched right arm fell to the ground, followed closely by its knees. The Goliath groaned in pain as the ground beneath it collapsed under the pressure of Mikoto's magic.

This was her trump card. Takemikazuchi had all but forbidden her to use this magic inside the closed spaces of the Dungeon. Her magic had the power to crush things in a certain area by dramatically increasing the effect of gravity. The Goliath was being pushed lower and lower by the violet dome that was holding it prisoner.

She had been reluctant to use it until now because she might have caught the attackers and magic users under the dome by accident. Lyu and Asfi were clearly impressed as they watched the giant squirm.

"Guh, aaaahhh…!"

Mikoto's face distorted in pain, grabbing her outstretched right arm with her left hand.

Crick, crick, crick—the dome started to give way as the giant that had been literally brought to its knees was slowly climbing back to its feet.

The Goliath's body rose higher and higher, fighting against the gravity with all of its might. Mikoto focused all of her mental energy in a futile attempt to push the monster back down.

She wasn't strong enough. The Goliath's status was far beyond hers. She didn't stand a chance.

The Goliath rose higher and higher, the force field warping to the giant's will. All the while, Bell was still charging up for his attack.

Welf was running.

He made his way through a forest inundated with silence, using the light of the crystals to find his way through the dense foliage. The only sounds that could be heard were his heavy breathing and quick footsteps as the young man arrived in a part of the forest he recognized.

"Damn it, Bell, that big guy…DAHH!!"

He couldn't get the image out of his mind of the Goliath punching Ouka and Bell. That large man couldn't have wanted to take that hit, but he still protected Bell. All Welf could do was just stand and watch.

It was funny, in a way. The thought of himself just standing there as everything happened. A whirlpool of regret raged within him.

"Lady Hephaistos, I…"

The weapon wrapped in white cloth he'd received from Hestia, sent to him by his own goddess. It also happened to be a weapon that Welf forged himself.

He had made it immediately after joining *Hephaistos Familia*, at her command. It was his first work as a member of the group.

His skills proven, he had given the weapon to Hephaistos because the very sight of it filled him with self-loathing. He swore to never make another one.

She had said that was okay, for now. But she did leave him with the words, "You will regret not using this power once you have attained something important."

"Stop compromising allies for your pride."

Everything the crimson-haired, crimson-eyed goddess had told him replayed over and over in his head.

His self-centered arrogance had led him to swear not to become a magic swordsmith. Even more, his ego refused to let him use one.

If he'd been able to let go of his vanity, things might have turned out differently.

"I…!"

Welf hated magic swords.

They gave anyone the power to take down the strongest of enemies with a flick of the wrist. They were nothing more than a magical weapon that indulged its user. They destroyed his family, other smiths, and users by rotting them from the inside.

But above all else, magic swords would inevitably break and leave their user behind.

Welf loathed magic swords.

"…!"

Suddenly, a hill of trees he'd seen before came into view. He was sure that the weapon had fallen among them and was sitting somewhere in the tall grass.

Sleeping, never used by anyone, the hilt untouched and pure.

Not broken, simply at rest.

"Hey, where are you?! Say something!!"

He yelled down the hill as he made his way farther and farther into the woods.

It was much darker now than he remembered because of the subtle glow of the blue crystals far above his head. It was as if a dark blanket had been cast over the forest.

"Ironic isn't it? I know, I KNOW!! I threw you away and now I'm asking you for help!"

Welf knew there was no chance of a response, but he kept screaming at the top of his lungs anyway.

His head was on a swivel as he crisscrossed his way through the dense forest.

"But there's someone who needs my help! Please——let me break you!!"

A soft red glow appeared out of nowhere as if to answer his call.

Welf saw it immediately and sprinted to its side. It was sticking out of a pile of moss, hilt high in the air.

The white cloth was starting to unravel, exposing the top part of the blade and guard-less handle attached to it. The blade of the weapon pulsed and flickered like a flaming red jewel at his feet. Welf swiftly grabbed the hilt and pulled it into the air.

Resting the weapon on his right shoulder, he raced back up the hill.

"...!"

Welf grimaced at this new weight on his shoulders.

The strength of a magic sword—it would shatter as soon as it was used too many times. That was the price for a weapon that wielded the same power as magic. That was its unavoidable fate.

It could never become the trusted partner of its user, never experience the good times or the bad. It could never be counted on to be there until the end, always breaking first.

Welf hated magic swords. They would abandon their user without fail.

Magic swords could never fulfill their duty as a weapon. That was their destiny, and he hated it.

—That was it, pointless and painful sympathy.

While corrupting users and smiths alike, each individual sword could never fill the role of a dependable partner in battle. Therefore, they were left to sleep with no chance of meeting a user who would honestly consider it a valuable partner.

As someone who could forge magic swords, Welf felt sorry for them——felt their pain.

"!"

He emerged from the forest. He could see the Goliath trapped under a cracking, violet dome off in the distance. Monsters and adventurers were engaged in an all-out brawl directly in front of him. Bell stood not too far behind their battle, a large black sword in his hands.

The sound of church bells flooding his ears, Welf immediately understood what was going on. Swearing he wouldn't let Bell take another hit like that, he charged away from the forest and toward the chaos in front of him.

A swarm of monsters cut him off in no time. The red-haired man moved the cloth-covered weapon into position.

"All of you! If you don't have a death wish, get out of the waaayyyy!!"

Welf swung the blade sideways in front of his chest—a wildfire stampeded forward.

The wide-eyed adventurers managed to get out of its path at the last moment, armor singed as every single monster was reduced to ash on contact. The great plain turned into a smoldering mess in its wake.

The adventurers stared in disbelief as the last bit of white cloth burned away, revealing the rest of the blade.

There were no decorations to be seen, just a long crimson blade and a handle. The absolutely stunning weapon looked as though it were carved directly out of solid rock, simple and beautiful.

Crack! A small line grew down the middle of the blade just below Welf's hand. Welf glared down at the magic sword that started to fall apart after just one use before he took off yet again.

"It's breaking...?!"

Mikoto yelled out a warning to the others as the giant slammed both of its fists into the outer barrier created by her gravity magic.

"OOOOOOOOOOOOOOOOOOOO!" it roared as the field shattered around it, releasing the Goliath from its cage. Lyu and Asfi once again prepared for battle—when Welf ran out in front of them.

The young man stood in front of the Goliath, his right hand gripping the hilt of the sword he was holding behind his back.

A strange calm filled the air as man and beast locked eyes. Then suddenly, heroically—

One swing.

And just for this one attack, Welf yelled the name of his magic sword at the top of his lungs.

"Burning Moon, Kadukiiiiiiiiiiiiiiiiiiiiiiiiiiiiiiiiiiiiiiiiiiiiiii!!!"

The blaze instantly cast bright shadows over everything and everyone.

A crimson pyre sprang to life. Flames erupted from the blade of the magic sword; the Goliath was engulfed in a scorching inferno.

The Goliath's howls of pain were drowned out by the roaring fire as its body was overrun by the flames.

"_____AAAAaaaaa?!"

The giant's body burned as if trapped in the fires of hell.

Its self-regeneration couldn't keep up. The fire burned away any progress it made. The moment one of the red specks healed a piece of its hide, the flames burned it away. The Goliath only had enough magic energy to maintain a physical form, and it was running out of energy fast.

For the first time during this long fight, permanent damage had been seared into the floor boss's skin.

"My word, a Crozzo Magic Sword…!"

"It's stronger—stronger than the original magic?!"

Asfi and Lyu watched the firestorm intensify right in front of their eyes. This was not the power of some conjured magic. They were witnessing a power strong enough to incinerate an elves' forest in the blink of an eye.

As the legend said, Crozzo's Magic Swords were strong enough to "set fire to the ocean." Every ounce of that strength had just been unleashed.

"____"

The sword released one final torrent of flames before a small network of cracks appeared on the blade.

The cracks started to multiply, cutting deeper and deeper until finally the blade shattered right in front of Welf.

"—Sorry."

His shoulders drooped as he whispered under his breath while he watched the thousands of shards fall to the ground, clinking as they hit.

—*Three minutes.*

Bell stood silently when he realized how much time had passed.

He had been patiently waiting, his ruby-red gaze trained straight forward.

And right in the middle of his field of vision stood the black giant, Goliath. At this moment, most of its body was hidden by massive flames and billowing smoke. However, its red glow was by far the brightest source of light in the darkness that covered the eighteenth floor.

Bell aimed the massive black sword in his hands toward the beast that had repelled so many other adventurers' attacks with ease.

His Skill required a mental image of a hero to trigger. The image in his mind: the Great Hero David.

A hero who had defended his homeland by standing up to and defeating an enormous enemy in combat.

David's heroic deeds etched into his mind's eye, Bell slowly but surely started to lean forward.

"—Everyone, open a pathhhhhhhhhhhhhhhh!!"

He sprang forward.

Hestia's order came from behind as he closed the distance, slicing through the great plain.

He was on a straight path toward the glowing red monster. Even more church bells rang out as his black sword was bathed in his own

© Suzuhito Yasuda

white light. Even the blood flowing out of his wounds seemed to propel him forward. His friends had given him this window of opportunity to attack—it would be the last, and he had to make it count.

The adventurers still in the field heard Hestia's order and immediately made way.

Welf, Mikoto, Lyu, and Asfi—

Everyone caught a glimpse of his face as Bell sped by.

Their eyes were filled with belief, hope, and the urge to support him—*Go!*

Bell picked up even more speed. No one could look away.

"OOOOOOOOOOOOOOOOOOOOOOOOOOOOOOOOOOO OOOOOOOOOOOOOOOOOOOOOOOOOOOOOOOOOOOOO OOO?!"

The red eyes of the burning Goliath caught a glimpse of Bell's advance.

It bellowed with a mixture of anger and fear as it pulled one of its massive, burning arms behind its back.

The giant was ready to punch. That attack had already destroyed so much, injured so many adventurers, including Bell. He knew the risk, but he didn't slow down.

—As Hestia had said before, Bell possessed a "heroic strike."

Her words etched deeply into his soul, Bell pulled the large black sword in an arc over his right shoulder.

Less and less distance.

The Goliath's body loomed over him, a presence that could crush him at any moment.

At the same time, power flowed into his grip, adrenaline coursing through his veins.

Focusing every ounce of his being into the blade of the sword, Bell jumped into the air and took a swing.

"YAAAHHHHHHHHHHHHHHHHHHHHHHHHHHHHHHHH-HHHHHH!!"

Explosion on impact.

"_____"

Welf and everyone else was forced to shield their eyes from the intense white light.

Bell's war cry had drowned out the Goliath's roar until the explosion erased all other sounds.

No one could hear a sound for several seconds. However, once their ears did recover…utter silence. The battle had been decided.

A few adventurers worked up the courage to lower their hands and arms for a better look. They saw a giant with no torso and no right arm lying in the middle of the circle of ash.

The legs and left arm made no sound, a bizarre statue in the aftermath.

And just in front of it, standing how he landed after the follow-through of his attack, was Bell. The black sword was broken, white smoke emerging from what was left of the weapon.

No one said a word, only tried to remember every single detail of this spectacle.

"…He…cut it down."

Time flowed once again as those words fell out of Welf's awestruck mouth.

Bell lost his balance and his knee hit the ground. Using the broken sword as a cane, the boy watched as the Goliath's legs and left arm disintegrated into ash in front of him.

The monster's magic stone had been destroyed along with its upper body. Its remains slowly started to fall apart and disappear.

SHHHH. A light breeze started carrying a portion of the large amount of ash into the "sky," revealing a drop item—Goliath's Hide.

"UUWWWAHHHHHHHHHHHHHHHAAAAAAAAAY-YYYYYYYYYYYYYYYAAAAAAAAAAAAHHHHHHHHHHHHA AAAAAAAAAAAAAAAAAAAAAOOOOOOOOOOOOOOOOOOO OOOOOOO!!"

Cheers rang out a moment later.

The adventurers surrounding the battlefield raised their fists triumphantly, embraced their allies, and shed tears of happiness as they yelled as loud as they could. Flashes of silver light filled the area. They were waving their broken swords, spears, axes, and shields as their song of victory echoed throughout the eighteenth floor.

The great plain shook with their waves of sound that were too distorted to form words.

Everything that had just transpired in the Dungeon felt like a lie in this moment of jubilation. The walls and ceiling were silent; there was no threat of any new monsters appearing. The residents of Rivira celebrated alongside Mord's adventurers, their faces red with excitement and joy.

"Bell!"

"Mr. Bell!"

Hestia was the first to run to his side, wiping away tears as she went. It didn't take long for Lilly, Welf, Lyu, and Mikoto to reach him as well. Even some of the other adventurers gathered around.

What remained of the crystal flower in the middle of the ceiling shined a blue spotlight down upon him.

Bell and his allies were surrounded by continuous congratulatory cheers as the entire eighteenth floor seemed to embrace them.

"Ahhh…ahhh, glorious!"

Hermes was alone after Hestia left the southern supply base.

His orange eyes sparkled as he watched Bell at the center of the children's celebration.

The deity laughed as if he'd been intoxicated by the excitement that was swirling around him.

"These eyes have seen it! I, Hermes, have seen it all! Your grandson, your parting gift to this world!"

Hermes's fervor grew more and more as he called out to someone, somewhere.

He thought back to the boy's grandfather's words.

"The boy has a backbone. The boy has patience.—However, he severely lacks character."

Bell's grandfather had told him that the boy didn't have what it would take.

"Have you gone blind, saying things like that?!"

Would you still make that claim if you saw this?! The deity laughed to himself as he gestured toward the boy in the distance.

Hermes threw his head back toward the sky, mouth wide open, laughing in a way that could be called crazy.

"Rejoice, Great Lord Zeus! Your grandson is the real deal! The last hero your *Familia* left behind!"

Hermes's enthusiasm had yet to subside as he continued.

"Well, I'm no Oracle but…Ahhhh! I can't keep this to myself!"

Hermes looked out over the great plain filled with adventurers, as if he were watching a play, and yelled out.

"It's coming, it's coming! A new era is coming! Could be ten years from now, five years, one year, or even tomorrow! But something will happen in Orario to usher in the new era!"

It was his divine intuition.

It had been a thorn in his side for some time.

"Seriously, has there ever been a better group of heroes alive at the same time since the prehistoric days?!"

"The Brave" Finn Deimne.

"Nine Hell" Riveria Ljos Alf.

Oujya "Warlord" Ottar.

Kenki "Sword Princess" Aiz Wallenstein.

It was hard to find a better collection of valiant individuals throughout all of history.

Each of them had a level of character and strength that would measure up well with the greatest heroes of all time, and they were all here at once.

"No, definitely not! With so many worthy children so close together, there's no way something huge couldn't happen!"

Add the Little Rookie into the equation, his untapped potential on top of all of the others' proven strength and power, and Hermes's intuition became firm conviction.

"And I'll see it, I'll see it all! These eyes will watch all of them as they carve their names into history, until the day they die!"

Their humanity, their praise, their joy.

Hermes's vision of the future came together in his head as he watched the adventurers gathering around the white-haired boy.

The deity's eyes opened even wider.

"The story they will create, bound by the love of their gods. The *Familia Myth*!"

It would become the ultimate show.

The most charming of charms.

The pastime to end all pastimes.

"Aaaahhh—"

It was so exciting.

"Coming down to this world was the best decision I've ever made!"

The children were still dancing, fist-pumping and yelling with glee. He opened both of his arms toward them and sang a song to praise the heroes.

EPILOGUE

THE ONE WHO TARGETS THE RABBIT

The master's gaze
particular with a
"Bell Cranell.
my own."
The deity's
the room il
color of su

【BELL ◆ CRANELL】

BELONGS TO: *HESTIA FAMILIA*
RACE: HUMAN
JOB: ADVENTURER
DUNGEON RANGE: EIGHTEENTH FLOOR
WEAPON: HESTIA KNIFE
CURRENT WORTH: 28,000 VALS

《SALAMANDER WOOL》
- FABRIC ENCHANTED WITH FAIRY MAGIC,
  HIGH RESISTANCE TO THE ELEMENT OF FIRE
- CAN BE WORN AS AN INNER SHIRT,
  JACKET, ROBE, ETC.
- 87,000 VALS EACH WITH A COUPON

STATUS

Lv. 2

STRENGTH: F 365   DEFENSE: G 271   UTILITY: F 349
AGILITY: E 469   MAGIC: G 270

《MAGIC》

【FIREBOLT】　　　　　• SWIFT STRIKE MAGIC

《SKILL》　　　　　　　• RAPID GROWTH
　　　　　　　　　　　• CONTINUED DESIRE
　　　　　　　　　　　　RESULTS IN CONTINUED
【REALIS PHRASE】　　　GROWTH
　　　　　　　　　　　• STRONGER DESIRE
　　　　　　　　　　　　RESULTS IN STRONGER
　　　　　　　　　　　　GROWTH

【HEROIC DESIRE,　】　• CHARGES AUTOMATICALLY
　ARGONAUT　　　　　　WITH ACTIVE ACTION

《USHIWAKAMARU》

• FORGED BY WELF, FIRST OF ITS KIND
• SHORT, CRIMSON BLADE. NICKNAME: "MINOTAN"
• CREATED FROM THE MINOTAUR HORN DROP ITEM.
  STRONG WEAPON WITH SLIGHT FIRE ELEMENT.
• SURPRISINGLY DESTRUCTIVE DESPITE SMALL SIZE,
  CURRENTLY MORE POWERFUL THAN THE HESTIA KNIFE.
• BELL HAD A DREAM WHERE HE WAS ALMOST KILLED BY
  A RAGING MINOTAUR WHEN HE FELL ASLEEP WITH THIS
  WEAPON UNDER HIS PILLOW.
• IT SEEMS TO HAVE BEEN FORGED WITH BELL IN MIND.

Afterword

"Pure Dungeon Fantasy"—I forget where, but I have a feeling I've seen my books advertised with this catchphrase. But to be honest, I don't think that all that much has transpired inside the Dungeon itself. Adventurers venture into the Dungeon to gain experience points by slaying monsters and repeating the process. That's about it.

So, I wanted to go all out inside the Dungeon before the story transitions back to the surface. That idea is what led me to write Volume 5.

When most people hear the word "dungeon," images of a dark labyrinth with some kind of valuable treasure hidden in its deepest room and guarded by a strong monster probably come to mind. Therefore, I felt there had to be a large monster at the end. Something big enough and powerful enough to push these adventurers to the brink of despair—a dragon would've worked well, too. This may just be my opinion, but whether the heroes fight or flee, I feel it's an important part of the fantasy genre. I was finally able to make this a reality in Volume 5. I get the feeling that some people out there are saying, "Shouldn't that have been in Volume 1?" But I'm not listening.

Whether the monster stares down at you while breathing fire, physically attacks you with its arms and legs, or has a piercing gaze that turns everything to stone, it needs to be far stronger than any of the heroes alone. However, I believe that the heroes of the fantasy stories are at their absolute coolest when they overcome injuries and setbacks to band together and defeat a powerful foe.

No matter how old I get, I will never forget how excited I felt as a kid when heroes moved into action.

Nothing would make me happier than if you experience the same kind of rush while reading this book.

And now, please allow me to express my gratitude.

First, to my supervisor Mr. Kotaki, thank you for all of your helpful advice. Next, I need to thank Mr. Suzuhito Yasuda for all of the beautiful illustrations. Both of you helped to make this book what it is today. Also, I would like to acknowledge all of the hardworking employees of GA Bunko. This series would never have been possible without your help. I am extremely grateful.

And above all, I would like to thank you, the reader. I will do my best to keep writing stories that are worthy of being described as "interesting." I would be honored to see you again in the next installment.

Until then,

Fujino Omori